ARRANGED MARRIAGE

ALSO BY CHITRA BANERJEE DIVAKARUNI:

Dark Like the River (1987)

The Reason for Nasturtiums (1990)

Black Candle (1991)

Anchor Books
DOUBLEDAY
New York   London   Toronto
Sydney   Auckland

Stories by
Chitra Banerjee Divakaruni

ARRANGED
MARRIAGE

AN ANCHOR BOOK
PUBLISHED BY DOUBLEDAY
a division of Bantam Doubleday Dell Publishing Group, Inc.
1540 Broadway, New York, New York 10036

ANCHOR BOOKS, DOUBLEDAY, and the portrayal of an anchor
are trademarks of Doubleday, a division of Bantam Doubleday Dell
Publishing Group, Inc.

"The Bats" has appeared previously in *Zyzzyva* (Spring 1993).
"Clothes" has appeared previously in the anthology
Home to Stay (Greenfield Review Press, 1990).

Book design by Jennifer Ann Daddio

Library of Congress Cataloging-in-Publication Data

Divakaruni, Chitra Banerjee, 1956–
Arranged marriage: stories / by Chitra Banerjee Divakaruni. —
1st Anchor Books ed.
p.   cm.
1. East Indian Americans—Social life and customs—Fiction.
2. Women immigrants—United States—Social life and customs—
Fiction.   3. India—Social life and customs—Fiction.   I. Title.
PS3554.I86A89   1995
813'.54—dc20   94-37210
CIP

ISBN 0-385-47558-6

First Anchor Books Edition: August 1995

3   5   7   9   10   8   6   4   2

To

my mother, Tatini, with gratitude
my husband, Murthy, with love
my sons, Anand and Abhay, with hope

CONTENTS

THE BATS

THAT YEAR MOTHER CRIED A LOT, NIGHTS. OR MAYBE she had always cried, and that was the first year I was old enough to notice. I would wake up in the hot Calcutta dark and the sound of her weeping would be all around me, pressing in, wave upon wave, until I could no longer tell where it was coming from. The first few times it happened, I would sit up in the narrow child's bed that she had recently taken to sharing with me and whisper her name. But that would make her pull me close and hold me tight against her shaking body, where the damp smell of talcum powder and sari starch would choke me until I couldn't bear it any longer and would start to struggle away. Which only made her cry more. So after some time I learned to lie rigid and unmoving under the bedsheet, plugging my fingers into my ears to block out her sobs. And if I closed my eyes very tight and held them that way long enough, little dots of light would appear against my eyelids and I could almost pretend I was among the stars.

One morning when she was getting me ready for school, braiding my hair into the slick, tight pigtail that I disliked because it always hung stiffly down my back, I noticed something funny about her face. Not the dark circles under her eyes. Those were always there. It was high up on her cheek, a yellow blotch with its edges turning purple. It looked like my knee did after I bumped into the chipped mahogany dresser next to our bed last month.

"What's that, Ma? Does it hurt?" I reached up, wanting to touch it, but she jerked away.

"Nothing. It's nothing. Now hurry up or you'll miss the bus. And don't make so much noise, or you'll wake your father."

Father always slept late in the mornings. Because he worked so hard at the Rashbihari Printing Press where he was a foreman, earning food and rent money for us, Mother had explained. Since she usually put me to bed before he came home, I didn't see him much. I heard him, though, shouts that shook the walls of my bedroom like they were paper, the sounds of falling dishes. Things fell a lot when Father was around, maybe because he was so large. His hands were especially big, with blackened, split nails and veins that stood up under the skin like blue snakes. I remembered their chemical smell and the hard feel of his fingers from when I was little and he used to pick me up suddenly and throw me all the way up to the ceiling, up and down, up and down, while Mother pulled at his arms, begging him to stop, and I screamed and screamed with terror until I had no breath left.

The Bats

A couple of days later Mother had another mark on her face, even bigger and reddish-blue. It was on the side of her forehead and made her face look lopsided. This time when I asked her about it she didn't say anything, just turned the other way and stared at a spot on the wall where the plaster had cracked and started peeling in the shape of a drooping mouth. Then she asked me how I would like to visit my grandpa for a few days.

"Grandpa!" I knew about grandpas. Most of my friends in the third grade had them. They gave them presents on birthdays and took them to the big zoo in Alipore during vacations. "I didn't know I had a grandpa!"

I was so excited I forgot to keep my voice down and Mother quickly put a hand over my mouth.

"Shhh. It's a secret, just for you and me. Why don't we pack quickly, and I'll tell you more about him once we're on the train."

"A train!" This was surely a magic day, I thought, as I tried to picture what traveling on a train would be like.

We packed fast, stuffing a few saris and dresses into two bags Mother brought out from under the bed. They were made from the same rough, nubby jute as the shopping bag that Father used to bring home fresh fish from the bazaar, but from their stiffness I could tell they were new. I wondered when Mother bought them and how she'd paid for them, and then I wondered how she would buy our tickets. She never had much money, and whenever she asked for any, Father flew into one of his rages. But maybe she'd been saving up for this trip for a long time. As we packed, Mother kept stopping as though she was listening

3

for something, but all I heard was Father's snores. We tip-toed around and spoke in whispers. It was so exciting that I didn't mind not having breakfast, or even having to leave all my toys behind.

I was entranced by the steamy smell of the train, the shriek of its whistle—loud without being scary—that an-nounced when a tunnel was coming up, its comforting, joggly rhythm that soothed me into a half sleep. I was lucky enough to get a window seat, and from it I watched as the narrow, smoke-streaked apartment buildings of Calcutta, with crum-pled washing hanging from identical boxlike balconies, gave way to little brick houses with yellow squash vines growing in the yard. Later there were fields and fields of green so bright that when I closed my eyes the color pulsed inside my lids, and ponds with clusters of tiny purple flowers floating on them. Mother, who had grown up in the country, told me they were water hyacinths, and as she watched them catch the sunlight, it seemed to me that the line of her mouth wavered and turned soft.

After a while she pulled me close and cupped my chin in her hand. From her face I could see she had something im-portant to say, so I didn't squirm away as I usually would have. "My uncle—your grandpa—that we're going to see," she said, "lives way away in a village full of bamboo forests and big rivers with silver fish. His house is in the middle of a meadow where buffaloes and goats roam all day, and there's a well to drink water from."

"A real well!" I clapped my hands in delight. I'd only seen wells in picture books.

"Yes, with a little bucket on a rope, and if you like you

can fill the bucket and carry it in." Then she added, a bit hesitantly, "We might be staying with him for a while."

Staying with a grandpa-uncle who had a well and buffaloes and goats and bamboo forests sounded lovely, and I told Mother so, with my best smile.

"Will you miss your father?" There was a strange look in her eyes.

"No," I said in a definite tone. Already, as I turned my head to look at a pair of long-tailed birds with red breasts, his loud-voiced presence was fading from my mind.

When the train finally dropped us off on a dusty little platform with a yellow signboard that spelled out *Gopalpur* in big black letters, not a soul was in sight. The afternoon sun burned right into my skull, and my stomach felt like it had been empty for years.

"Where's Grandpa-uncle? Why isn't he here?"

Mother didn't answer for a moment. Then she said, "He doesn't know we're coming." She put on a bright expression, but I could see a small muscle jumping in her cheek. "Now, don't you worry. You just take the little bag and I'll take the big one, and in no time at all we'll be at his house."

But the sun had dipped behind the jagged leaves of the coconut palms on the horizon before we reached Grandpa-uncle's home. Mother lost her way a couple of times—because they had put in new roads, she said. The roads looked pretty old to me, with deep buffalo-cart ruts running along them, but I didn't say anything. And when she asked me if I was hungry, I said no.

Finally, there it was, a tiny house, almost a play house, with mud walls and straw on the roof like in my storybook pictures. Mother knocked on the door, and after a while an old man came out. He must have been the oldest man in the whole world. All his hair was white, and he had a long white beard as well. He squinted at us in surprise, but when she told him who we were, he took us in and gave us some puffed rice and sweet creamy milk. From his own cow, he told me, as he watched me gulp it down. Then he ruffled my hair and sent me to the backyard to play with the chickens. I had never seen real live chickens up close before and immediately loved how they squacked and flapped their wings and how fast they could run when chased.

I was having a wonderful time with them when Mother came out. The first thing I noticed was that she was crying. I had never seen her cry in the daytime before, and it frightened me, because somehow I'd always believed that daytime was a safe time into which dark night things couldn't intrude. Now I stood watching her, hating the way her lips twisted and her nostrils flared, hating the thin red lines that wavered across the whites of her eyes. My mouth went dry and I felt like I was going to throw up. Then I saw she was smiling through the tears.

"Uncle says we can stay here as long as we want, that I never have to go back to . . ."

"To what, Ma?"

But she only wiped at her eyes and told me to come in and see where I was going to sleep.

The Bats

Grandpa-uncle soon became my best friend. All day I would follow him around as he went about his job, which was taking care of the *zamindar*'s orchards. He taught me the names of all the trees—mango, lichee, *kul*—and let me taste the first ripe fruits. He pointed out hares and squirrels and *girgitis* that hid in the grass, their shiny greenish bodies pulsing in the sun. On his off-days he took me fishing and taught me how to hold the rod right and how to tell when there was a nibble, and although all I caught were scraggly little things that we threw back in the pond, he always encouraged me and said I was learning a lot. He himself was a good fisherman, patient and cheerful, with a stillness about him that drew the fish to his hook. He was considerate as well, and whenever he brought home a catch for Mother to cook, he always cleaned and cut it up first, because the sight of blood made her feel sick.

All of this was so exciting that I didn't spend much time with Mother, though I did notice she was kind of quiet. Then one night I woke up to her crying, just like before. I lay there listening to those racking, muffled sobs that seemed to go on forever. It was like sliding into a dark, bottomless hole. I gripped my bedsheet, twisting it around my knuckles as though it could save me. A part of me wanted to go and put my arms around her, but the other part was afraid of what she might tell me, what she might want. So I just lay there, my shoulders and jaws and fists tight and aching, trying to believe that her crying was one of the night sounds coming in through the open window, like the cries of the *jhi-jhi* bugs and the yellow-beaked *kokil,* and after a time I was too tired to stay awake because all day I had been helping Grandpa-uncle with the bats.

The bats were a real problem. They had descended, all of a sudden, on the mango orchard, and within a day they had bitten into and ruined hundreds of mangoes. Grandpa-uncle tried everything—sticks and drums and magic powder from the wisewoman in the next village—but nothing worked. Finally he had to use poison. I never really saw how he did it because he made me stay away, but the next morning there were bat carcasses all over the orchard. We couldn't leave them to rot, of course, so Grandpa-uncle went around with a big jute sack and picked them up. I went along and pointed them out to him with a stick. He said I was a good helper, that without me he never would have managed to spot them all with his failing eyes.

You would have thought that after the first week the bats would have figured it out and found another place to live. But no. Every morning there were just as many dead bodies. I asked Grandpa-uncle about this. He shook his head and said he didn't understand either.

"I guess they just don't realize what's happening. They don't realize that by flying somewhere else they'll be safe. Or maybe they do, but there's something that keeps pulling them back here." I wanted to ask him what that something was, but just then I found a real whopper lying under the hibiscus bush, all purply-black and crinkled up, the biggest I had ever seen, and forgot about my question.

Maybe the bats did catch on, because a few days later we found only about ten bodies, and only three the next day. Grandpa-uncle was even more pleased than I was. I knew how much he hated the job because of how he grimaced each time he bent over to pick up a carcass and how there was a white, pinched look about his mouth by the time the sack was full. He said we would celebrate by going fishing at Kalodighi, the big lake which was all the way at the other end of the village.

We started early the next day, while the tall grasses next to the meadow path were still bent over and sparkly with dew. Grandpa-uncle carried the poles, the little tin bucket filled with worms he had collected at dawn, and a knife to gut the fish we caught. I held tight to the knotted cloth in which Mother had packed *chapatis* and potato curry for our lunch, and some *sandesh* made with new jaggery as a special dessert treat. From time to time I gave little skips of excitement, because though I'd heard a lot about Kalodighi, where the water was so deep that it looked black, and where the best and biggest fish were to be found, Grandpa-uncle hadn't taken me there yet. Maybe, I thought, today I would finally catch such a big fish that Grandpa-uncle and Mother would be really proud of me.

When I saw the waters of Kalodighi stretching all the way to the horizon, shiny and black just like Grandpa-uncle said it would be, I knew it had to be the largest lake in the entire world. Near the shore there were little ripples, but in the middle of the lake the water lay quiet and powerful, deep beyond imagining.

"Kind of like there's a mystery hiding in there," I whispered hesitantly to Grandpa-uncle, afraid he wouldn't understand, but he nodded and whispered back that he knew exactly what I meant. We sat in silence under the broad reddish-green leaves of a plantain tree and watched the water for a while. Dragonflies flitted from lotus leaf to lotus leaf, the scent of *champa* blossoms lay lightly on the air, I leaned my head against Grandpa-uncle's shirt with its pungent tobacco smell, and my whole chest ached with the wish that I could spend the rest of my life just like this.

But soon it was time for lunch. We ate the soft *chapatis* and the spicy *alu* curry that I loved even though it made my eyes water, and the sweet balls of *sandesh* melted on my tongue, just as I knew they would. We cupped the cool lake water in our hands and drank, and it was even sweeter than the *sandesh*.

"Next week I'm going to start teaching you to swim," said Grandpa-uncle as he set up his fishing rod. He laughed at the excitement flooding my face. I'd asked and asked him for swimming lessons, but before today he'd always said no. "I figured I'd better do it before I get too old," he added in explanation.

I knew he was joking because he could never get too old, and I told him so, but he only smiled and rubbed at his chest the way he often did and told me to mind my rod.

The rest of the afternoon we fished—or rather we sat waiting with our poles for the sleeping fish to wake and bite, and though I was unlucky as always, when the sun hung above the lake as red as the marriage *bindi* on Mother's forehead, Grandpa-uncle caught a great *rui* fish that sent up sprays of rainbow water as it leaped and thrashed at the end of his line. When he cut its stomach open, there was a silver ring inside. Grandpa-uncle didn't say anything, but I could tell that even he was excited. As he washed it in the lake, the thick band with words carved on it in a language that neither of us could read glinted in the dark water.

"This must be the magic ring of the sorcerer of Kalodighi, the one that grants all wishes," he said, holding it out to me. "See the ancient spell carved onto it? One day when the sorcerer lay sleeping in his silken pleasure boat, his hand trailing in the cool water, a *rui* fish came up and bit off his ring finger. . . ."

"Grandpa-uncle!" I protested, looking at him sharply to see if he had a twinkle in his eye like when he told me tales of witches and water fairies.

"Everyone knows the story," he said, slipping the ring into the pocket of his *kurta* and nodding at me seriously. "If you don't believe me, ask your mother when we get home."

But when we reached home that evening, I had no chance to ask Mother anything. She was waiting for us on the porch, holding on to an envelope, which surprised me because we never got any letters.

"It's from him," she said in answer to the question in our eyes. "He wants us to come back. He promises it won't happen again."

The tin bucket fell from Grandpa-uncle's hand and clattered noisily over the steps. He sat down heavily, leaning against the mud wall. "How did he know where you were?"

Mother looked away. She was gripping the envelope so tightly that the tips of her fingernails were white. "I wrote to him." And then, defensively, "I couldn't stand it, the stares and whispers of the women, down in the marketplace. The loneliness of being without him."

Grandpa-uncle looked up and saw me watching, and fished around in his *kurta* pocket for a coin. He asked me if I would go get him some tobacco from Kesto's shop. I ran all the way there and back, but by that time they had finished discussing the matter, and Mother told me that I should go to bed early as we would be leaving next morning.

"But I can't leave now! Grandpa-uncle is going to teach me to swim!"

She had a vague smile on her face and I could tell she wasn't really listening. I had to say it a couple more times, and then she replied that I could join a swimming class once we were back in Calcutta.

"I don't want a swimming class! I want Grandpa-uncle!" I kicked at our bags which she had packed even before Grandpa-uncle and I had returned from the lake. I tried to find words for all the things boiling up inside me. But all I could shout was "I hate you! I hate you!"

Grandpa-uncle took me outside and told me that I mustn't talk to Mother that way, that she had many troubles and that I must be an especially good daughter to her and help take care of her. He held me on his lap and stroked my hair as he talked, as though I were a baby, and I didn't protest like I normally would have. Then, until dinnertime, he pointed out the different stars and told me their stories. He showed me the black warrior with his sword, the seven wise men who can tell when the end of the world will be, and the Dhruva star named for the little boy who went into the forest and met God.

12

The Bats

Late in the night a sound woke me. At first I thought it was Mother, crying again, but then I realized it was coming from the alcove where Grandpa-uncle slept ever since he gave us his bedroom. I tiptoed over and he was lying with his *kurta* unbuttoned, rubbing at his chest, breathing heavily, trying to be silent.

"Where does it hurt, Grandpa-uncle?"

He pointed to his chest and I rubbed it for a while, feeling the crisp white curly hairs under my palm. Then he said he felt much better and made me go back to bed so that Mother wouldn't wake up.

"Don't tell her anything," he whispered when I was at the door. "She'll just worry."

The next morning he looked as good as ever, so that I wondered if I had dreamed it all. He carried our bags to the station and blessed us when we touched his feet, and just before we left he slipped something wrapped in a piece of cloth into my palm.

"Don't open it till you're on the train," he said in my ear. Then, straightening up, "the next time you're here we'll go swimming together."

"That's right," Mother said, smiling at me, "and you'll be able to show Uncle how well you learned to swim."

Her eyes were all shiny and lit up, so I nodded and tried to smile back although my lips felt stiff and dry, their edges ready to crack, like leather *chappals* left too long in the sun.

Now the train was moving. Grandpa-uncle waved at us from the platform and I waved back, craning my neck through the window so I could see him as long as possible, even though Mother warned me I would get coal dust in my eyes.

"I don't know why you're carrying on like this," she said a bit irritably when I finally sat down. "We'll come to see him —all three of us—next *puja* vacation."

I wanted to tell her how, as the train picked up speed, Grandpa-uncle had become smaller and smaller until he was no bigger than a matchstick doll. And then he had disappeared. But Mother was frowning, biting at her lower lip and rummaging through her purse for something, so I didn't say it. Instead, I looked up at the sky. It was full of monsoon clouds, black and crinkly like bats' wings. That was when I knew she had deceived me, that nothing was going to happen the way she said it would.

I turned to face her, the anger thick and hot as melted metal filling my arms and legs, rising from my stomach into my throat so I could spit it out at her. I gathered my breath for it. But when I saw her eyes, wide like a little girl's as she reread the letter, I realized she hadn't been lying on purpose. She just didn't *know* the way I did.

The compartment seemed to turn end over end in slow motion, so that I had to lean back into the hard wooden bench. Everything I stared at—bunks, suitcases, windows, sky —appeared to be upside down. Would they ever right themselves again?

"I told you all that coal dust would make you sick," Mother said, an edge of satisfaction beneath the concern in her voice. "Here, you'd better take some *amchur*."

I silently put a pinch of the sour grains under my tongue. When Mother was busy with the letter once more, I went back to the window and leaned my forehead against its rusty bars. And as I waited for the velvet-green fields of young rice

14

to turn back into city walls crusted with soot and graffiti and spat-out wads of betel leaf, I held the packet Grandpa-uncle had given me tight in my fist. I didn't need to open it. I knew already what was inside.

I kept it for a long time, the silver ring from our fish, secreted in the bottom of an underwear drawer, or in the pocket of a dusty suitcase. I changed its hiding place often so that Mother would not find it and ask questions. Not that she would have —she had more serious things to worry about. From time to time, when things got bad, I would shut myself in my room, take out the ring, and hold it in my hand until the cool metal grew blood-warm. I would run my finger over the runes, wishing I could speak the spell to take me back to that day at the lake with Grandpa-uncle. Sometimes I pressed it to my lips and whispered words I had memorized from books about magic that I borrowed from the library. But none of them ever worked, so perhaps it was not a magic ring at all. Still, I took it wherever Mother and I moved, even when we had to travel real light, real quick. I never knew what Father would do to the things we left behind. One time he burned them. One time he threw them all in the rubbish heap. When we returned he bought us everything new, shiny-bright, as though the past were only a word, with no real meaning to it.

Then once we had to leave in the middle of the night, too suddenly to take anything with us. Mother stumbled behind me down the lightless passage—we hadn't dared to switch on the light—holding the wadded end of her sari to her face, the blood seeping through its white like a dark, crumpled flower. I pulled at her hand to hurry her along, my own shoulder still throbbing from when Father had flung me against the wall as I tried to stop him. When we came back a few weeks later (this time even before our bruises had faded all the way) I looked for the ring everywhere. But it was gone.

CLOTHES

THE WATER OF THE WOMEN'S LAKE LAPS AGAINST MY breasts, cool, calming. I can feel it beginning to wash the hot nervousness away from my body. The little waves tickle my armpits, make my sari float up around me, wet and yellow, like a sunflower after rain. I close my eyes and smell the sweet brown odor of the *ritha* pulp my friends Deepali and Radha are working into my hair so it will glisten with little lights this evening. They scrub with more vigor than usual and wash it out more carefully, because today is a special day. It is the day of my bride-viewing.

"Ei, Sumita! Mita! Are you deaf?" Radha says. "This is the third time I've asked you the same question."

"Look at her, already dreaming about her husband, and she hasn't even seen him yet!" Deepali jokes. Then she adds, the envy in her voice only half hidden, "Who cares about friends from a little Indian village when you're about to go live in America?"

I want to deny it, to say that I will always love them and all the things we did together through my growing-up years— visiting the *charak* fair where we always ate too many sweets, raiding the neighbor's guava tree summer afternoons while the grown-ups slept, telling fairy tales while we braided each other's hair in elaborate patterns we'd invented. *And she married the handsome prince who took her to his kingdom beyond the seven seas.* But already the activities of our girlhood seem to be far in my past, the colors leached out of them, like old sepia photographs.

His name is Somesh Sen, the man who is coming to our house with his parents today and who will be my husband "if I'm lucky enough to be chosen," as my aunt says. He is coming all the way from California. Father showed it to me yesterday, on the metal globe that sits on his desk, a chunky pink wedge on the side of a multicolored slab marked *Untd. Sts. of America.* I touched it and felt the excitement leap all the way up my arm like an electric shock. Then it died away, leaving only a beaten-metal coldness against my fingertips.

For the first time it occurred to me that if things worked out the way everyone was hoping, I'd be going halfway around the world to live with a man I hadn't even met. Would I ever see my parents again? *Don't send me so far away*, I wanted to cry, but of course I didn't. It would be ungrateful. Father had worked so hard to find this match for me. Besides, wasn't it every woman's destiny, as Mother was always telling me, to leave the known for the unknown? She had done it, and her mother before her. *A married woman belongs to her husband, her in-laws.* Hot seeds of tears pricked my eyelids at the unfairness of it.

"Mita Moni, little jewel," Father said, calling me by my childhood name. He put out his hand as though he wanted to touch my face, then let it fall to his side. "He's a good man. Comes from a fine family. He will be kind to you." He was silent for a while. Finally he said, "Come, let me show you the special sari I bought in Calcutta for you to wear at the bride-viewing."

"Are you nervous?" Radha asks as she wraps my hair in a soft cotton towel. Her parents are also trying to arrange a marriage for her. So far three families have come to see her, but no one has chosen her because her skin-color is considered too dark. "Isn't it terrible, not knowing what's going to happen?"

I nod because I don't want to disagree, don't want to make her feel bad by saying that sometimes it's worse when you know what's coming, like I do. I knew it as soon as Father unlocked his mahogany *almirah* and took out the sari.

It was the most expensive sari I had ever seen, and surely the most beautiful. Its body was a pale pink, like the dawn sky over the women's lake. The color of transition. Embroidered all over it were tiny stars made out of real gold *zari* thread.

"Here, hold it," said Father.

The sari was unexpectedly heavy in my hands, silk-slippery, a sari to walk carefully in. A sari that could change one's life. I stood there holding it, wanting to weep. I knew that when I wore it, it would hang in perfect pleats to my feet and shimmer in the light of the evening lamps. It would dazzle Somesh and his parents and they would choose me to be his bride.

When the plane takes off, I try to stay calm, to take deep, slow breaths like Father does when he practices yoga. But my hands clench themselves on to the folds of my sari and when I force them open, after the *fasten seat belt* and *no smoking* signs have blinked off, I see they have left damp blotches on the delicate crushed fabric.

We had some arguments about this sari. I wanted a blue one for the journey, because blue is the color of possibility, the color of the sky through which I would be traveling. But Mother said there must be red in it because red is the color of luck for married women. Finally, Father found one to satisfy us both: midnight-blue with a thin red border the same color as the marriage mark I'm wearing on my forehead.

It is hard for me to think of myself as a married woman. I whisper my new name to myself, Mrs. Sumita Sen, but the syllables rustle uneasily in my mouth like a stiff satin that's never been worn.

Somesh had to leave for America just a week after the wedding. He had to get back to the store, he explained to me. He had promised his partner. The store. It seems more real to me than Somesh—perhaps because I know more about it. It was what we had mostly talked about the night after the wedding, the first night we were together alone. It stayed open

Clothes

twenty-four hours, yes, all night, every night, not like the Indian stores which closed at dinnertime and sometimes in the hottest part of the afternoon. That's why his partner needed him back.

The store was called *7-Eleven*. I thought it a strange name, exotic, risky. All the stores I knew were piously named after gods and goddesses—*Ganesh Sweet House, Lakshmi Vastralaya for Fine Saris*—to bring the owners luck.

The store sold all kinds of amazing things—apple juice in cardboard cartons that never leaked; American bread that came in cellophane packages, already cut up; canisters of potato chips, each large grainy flake curved exactly like the next. The large refrigerator with see-through glass doors held beer and wine, which Somesh said were the most popular items.

"That's where the money comes from, especially in the neighborhood where our store is," said Somesh, smiling at the shocked look on my face. (The only places I knew of that sold alcohol were the village toddy shops, "dark, stinking dens of vice," Father called them.) "A lot of Americans drink, you know. It's a part of their culture, not considered immoral, like it is here. And really, there's nothing wrong with it." He touched my lips lightly with his finger. "When you come to California, I'll get you some sweet white wine and you'll see how good it makes you feel. . . ." Now his fingers were stroking my cheeks, my throat, moving downward. I closed my eyes and tried not to jerk away because after all it was my wifely duty.

"It helps if you can think about something else," my friend Madhavi had said when she warned me about what most husbands demanded on the very first night. Two years married, she already had one child and was pregnant with a second one.

I tried to think of the women's lake, the dark cloudy green of the *shapla* leaves that float on the water, but his lips were hot against my skin, his fingers fumbling with buttons, pulling at the cotton night-sari I wore. I couldn't breathe.

"Bite hard on your tongue," Madhavi had advised. "The pain will keep your mind off what's going on down there."

But when I bit down, it hurt so much that I cried out. I couldn't help it although I was ashamed. Somesh lifted his head. I don't know what he saw on my face, but he stopped right away. "Shhh," he said, although I had made myself silent already. "It's OK, we'll wait until you feel like it." I tried to apologize but he smiled it away and started telling me some more about the store.

And that's how it was the rest of the week until he left. We would lie side by side on the big white bridal pillow I had embroidered with a pair of doves for married harmony, and Somesh would describe how the store's front windows were decorated with a flashing neon Dewar's sign and a lighted Budweiser waterfall *this big.* I would watch his hands moving excitedly through the dim air of the bedroom and think that Father had been right, he was a good man, my husband, a kind, patient man. And so handsome, too, I would add, stealing a quick look at the strong curve of his jaw, feeling luckier than I had any right to be.

The night before he left, Somesh confessed that the store wasn't making much money yet. "I'm not worried, I'm sure it soon will," he added, his fingers pleating the edge of my sari. "But I just don't want to give you the wrong impression, don't want you to be disappointed."

In the half dark I could see he had turned toward me. His face, with two vertical lines between the brows, looked young, apprehensive, in need of protection. I'd never seen that on a man's face before. Something rose in me like a wave.

"It's all right," I said, as though to a child, and pulled his head down to my breast. His hair smelled faintly of the American cigarettes he smoked. "I won't be disappointed. I'll help you." And a sudden happiness filled me.

That night I dreamed I was at the store. Soft American music floated in the background as I moved between shelves stocked high with brightly colored cans and elegant-necked bottles, turning their labels carefully to the front, polishing them until they shone.

Now, sitting inside this metal shell that is hurtling through emptiness, I try to remember other things about my husband: how gentle his hands had been, and his lips, surprisingly soft, like a woman's. How I've longed for them through those drawn-out nights while I waited for my visa to arrive. He will be standing at the customs gate, and when I reach him, he will lower his face to mine. We will kiss in front of everyone, not caring, like Americans, then pull back, look each other in the eye, and smile.

But suddenly, as I am thinking this, I realize I cannot recall Somesh's face. I try and try until my head hurts, but I can only visualize the black air swirling outside the plane, too thin for breathing. My own breath grows ragged with panic as I think of it and my mouth fills with sour fluid the way it does just before I throw up.

I grope for something to hold on to, something beautiful and talismanic from my old life. And then I remember. Somewhere down under me, low in the belly of the plane, inside my new brown case which is stacked in the dark with a hundred others, are my saris. Thick Kanjeepuram silks in solid purples and golden yellows, the thin hand-woven cottons of the Bengal countryside, green as a young banana plant, gray as the women's lake on a monsoon morning. Already I can feel my shoulders loosening up, my breath steadying. My wedding Benarasi, flame-orange, with a wide *palloo* of gold-embroidered dancing peacocks. Fold upon fold of Dhakais so fine they can be pulled through a ring. Into each fold my mother has tucked a small sachet of sandalwood powder to protect the saris from the unknown insects of America. Little silk sachets, made from *her* old saris—I can smell their calm fragrance as I watch the American air hostess wheeling the dinner cart toward my seat. It is the smell of my mother's hands.

I know then that everything will be all right. And when the air hostess bends her curly golden head to ask me what I would like to eat, I understand every word in spite of her strange accent and answer her without stumbling even once over the unfamiliar English phrases.

Late at night I stand in front of our bedroom mirror trying on the clothes Somesh has bought for me and smuggled in past his parents. I model each one for him, walking back and forth, clasping my hands behind my head, lips pouted, left hip thrust out just like the models on TV, while he whispers applause. I'm breathless with suppressed laughter (Father and Mother

24

Sen must not hear us) and my cheeks are hot with the delicious excitement of conspiracy. We've stuffed a towel at the
bottom of the door so no light will shine through.

I'm wearing a pair of jeans now, marveling at the curves
of my hips and thighs, which have always been hidden under
the flowing lines of my saris. I love the color, the same pale
blue as the *nayantara* flowers that grow in my parents' garden.
The solid comforting weight. The jeans come with a close-
fitting T-shirt which outlines my breasts.

I scold Somesh to hide my embarrassed pleasure. He
shouldn't have been so extravagant. We can't afford it. He just
smiles.

The T-shirt is sunrise-orange—the color, I decide, of
joy, of my new American life. Across its middle, in large black
letters, is written *Great America*. I was sure the letters referred to the country, but Somesh told me it is the name of an
amusement park, a place where people go to have fun. I think
it a wonderful concept, novel. Above the letters is the picture
of a train. Only it's not a train, Somesh tells me, it's a roller
coaster. He tries to explain how it moves, the insane speed,
the dizzy ground falling away, then gives up. "I'll take you
there, Mita sweetheart," he says, "as soon as we move into our
own place."

That's our dream (mine more than his, I suspect)—moving out of this two-room apartment where it seems to me if we
all breathed in at once, there would be no air left. Where I
must cover my head with the edge of my Japan nylon sari (my
expensive Indian ones are to be saved for special occasions—
trips to the temple, Bengali New Year) and serve tea to the old
women that come to visit Mother Sen, where like a good

Indian wife I must never address my husband by his name.
Where even in our bed we kiss guiltily, uneasily, listening for
the giveaway creak of springs. Sometimes I laugh to myself,
thinking how ironic it is that after all my fears about America,
my life has turned out to be no different from Deepali's or
Radha's. But at other times I feel caught in a world where
everything is frozen in place, like a scene inside a glass paper-
weight. It is a world so small that if I were to stretch out my
arms, I would touch its cold unyielding edges. I stand inside
this glass world, watching helplessly as America rushes by,
wanting to scream. Then I'm ashamed. Mita, I tell myself,
you're growing westernized. Back home you'd never have felt
this way.

We must be patient. I know that. Tactful, loving children. That is the Indian way. "I'm their life," Somesh tells me
as we lie beside each other, lazy from lovemaking. He's not
boasting, merely stating a fact. "They've always been there
when I needed them. I could never abandon them at some old
people's home." For a moment I feel rage. You're constantly
thinking of them, I want to scream. But what about me? Then
I remember my own parents, Mother's hands cool on my
sweat-drenched body through nights of fever, Father teaching
me to read, his finger moving along the crisp black angles of
the alphabet, transforming them magically into things I knew,
water, dog, mango tree. I beat back my unreasonable desire
and nod agreement.

Somesh has bought me a cream blouse with a long
brown skirt. They match beautifully, like the inside and outside of an almond. "For when you begin working," he says.

Clothes

But first he wants me to start college. Get a degree, perhaps in teaching. I picture myself in front of a classroom of girls with blond pigtails and blue uniforms, like a scene out of an English movie I saw long ago in Calcutta. They raise their hands respectfully when I ask a question. "Do you really think I can?" I ask. "Of course," he replies.

I am gratified he has such confidence in me. But I have another plan, a secret that I will divulge to him once we move. What I really want is to work in the store. I want to stand behind the counter in the cream-and-brown skirt set (color of earth, color of seeds) and ring up purchases. The register drawer will glide open. Confident, I will count out green dollars and silver quarters. Gleaming copper pennies. I will dust the jars of gilt-wrapped chocolates on the counter. Will straighten, on the far wall, posters of smiling young men raising their beer mugs to toast scantily clad redheads with huge spiky eyelashes. (I have never visited the store—my in-laws don't consider it proper for a wife—but of course I know exactly what it looks like.) I will charm the customers with my smile, so that they will return again and again just to hear me telling them to have a nice day.

Meanwhile, I will the store to make money for us. Quickly. Because when we move, we'll be paying for two households. But so far it hasn't worked. They're running at a loss, Somesh tells me. They had to let the hired help go. This means most nights Somesh has to take the graveyard shift (that horrible word, like a cold hand up my spine) because his partner refuses to.

"The bastard!" Somesh spat out once. "Just because he

put in more money he thinks he can order me around. I'll show him!" I was frightened by the vicious twist of his mouth. Somehow I'd never imagined that he could be angry.

Often Somesh leaves as soon as he has dinner and doesn't get back till after I've made morning tea for Father and Mother Sen. I lie mostly awake those nights, picturing masked intruders crouching in the shadowed back of the store, like I've seen on the police shows that Father Sen sometimes watches. But Somesh insists there's nothing to worry about, they have bars on the windows and a burglar alarm. "And remember," he says, "the extra cash will help us move out that much quicker."

I'm wearing a nightie now, my very first one. It's black and lacy, with a bit of a shine to it, and it glides over my hips to stop outrageously at mid-thigh. My mouth is an O of surprise in the mirror, my legs long and pale and sleek from the hair remover I asked Somesh to buy me last week. The legs of a movie star. Somesh laughs at the look on my face, then says, "You're beautiful." His voice starts a flutter low in my belly.

"Do you really think so," I ask, mostly because I want to hear him say it again. No one has called me beautiful before. My father would have thought it inappropriate, my mother that it would make me vain.

Somesh draws me close. "Very beautiful," he whispers. "The most beautiful woman in the whole world." His eyes are not joking as they usually are. I want to turn off the light, but "Please," he says, "I want to keep seeing your face." His fingers are taking the pins from my hair, undoing my braids. The escaped strands fall on his face like dark rain. We have already decided where we will hide my new American clothes—the jeans and T-shirt camouflaged on a hanger among Somesh's pants, the skirt set and nightie at the bottom of my suitcase, a sandalwood sachet tucked between them, waiting.

I stand in the middle of our empty bedroom, my hair still wet from the purification bath, my back to the stripped bed I can't bear to look at. I hold in my hands the plain white sari I'm supposed to wear. I must hurry. Any minute now there'll be a knock at the door. They are afraid to leave me alone too long, afraid I might do something to myself.

The sari, a thick voile that will bunch around the waist when worn, is borrowed. White. Widow's color, color of endings. I try to tuck it into the top of the petticoat, but my fingers are numb, disobedient. It spills through them and there are waves and waves of white around my feet. I kick out in sudden rage, but the sari is too soft, it gives too easily. I grab up an edge, clamp down with my teeth and pull, feeling a fierce, bitter satisfaction when I hear it rip.

There's a cut, still stinging, on the side of my right arm, halfway to the elbow. It is from the bangle-breaking ceremony. Old Mrs. Ghosh performed the ritual, since she's a widow, too. She took my hands in hers and brought them down hard on the bedpost, so that the glass bangles I was wearing shattered and multicolored shards flew out in every direction. Some landed on the body that was on the bed, covered with a sheet. I can't call it Somesh. He was gone already. She took an edge of the sheet and rubbed the red marriage mark off my forehead. She was crying. All the women in the room were crying except me. I watched them as though from the far end of a tunnel. Their flared nostrils, their red-veined eyes, the runnels of tears, salt-corrosive, down their cheeks.

It happened last night. He was at the store. "It isn't too bad," he would tell me on the days when he was in a good mood. "Not too many customers. I can put up my feet and watch MTV all night. I can sing along with Michael Jackson as loud as I want." He had a good voice, Somesh. Sometimes he would sing softly at night, lying in bed, holding me. Hindi songs of love, *Mere Sapnon Ki Rani,* queen of my dreams. (He would not sing American songs at home out of respect for his parents, who thought they were decadent.) I would feel his warm breath on my hair as I fell asleep.

Someone came into the store last night. He took all the money, even the little rolls of pennies I had helped Somesh make up. Before he left he emptied the bullets from his gun into my husband's chest.

"Only thing is," Somesh would say about the night shifts, "I really miss you. I sit there and think of you asleep in bed. Do you know that when you sleep you make your hands into fists, like a baby? When we move out, will you come along some nights to keep me company?"

My in-laws are good people, kind. They made sure the body was covered before they let me into the room. When someone asked if my hair should be cut off, as they sometimes do with widows back home, they said no. They said I could stay at the apartment with Mrs. Ghosh if I didn't want to go to the crematorium. They asked Dr. Das to give me something to calm me down when I couldn't stop shivering. They didn't say, even once, as people would surely have in the village, that it was my bad luck that brought death to their son so soon after his marriage.

They will probably go back to India now. There's nothing here for them anymore. They will want me to go with them. You're like our daughter, they will say. Your home is with us, for as long as you want. For the rest of your life. *The rest of my life.* I can't think about that yet. It makes me dizzy. Fragments are flying about my head, multicolored and piercing sharp like bits of bangle glass.

I want you to go to college. Choose a career. I stand in front of a classroom of smiling children who love me in my cream-and-brown American dress. A faceless parade straggles across my eyelids: all those customers at the store that I will never meet. The lace nightie, fragrant with sandalwood, waiting in its blackness inside my suitcase. The savings book where we have $3605.33. *Four thousand and we can move out, maybe next month.* The name of the panty hose I'd asked him to buy me for my birthday: sheer golden-beige. His lips, unexpectedly soft, woman-smooth. Elegant-necked wine bottles swept off shelves, shattering on the floor.

I know Somesh would not have tried to stop the gunman. I can picture his silhouette against the lighted Dewar's sign, hands raised. He is trying to find the right expression to put on his face, calm, reassuring, reasonable. *OK, take the money. No, I won't call the police.* His hands tremble just a little. His eyes darken with disbelief as his fingers touch his chest and come away wet.

I yanked away the cover. I had to see. *Great America, a place where people go to have fun.* My breath roller-coasting through my body, my unlived life gathering itself into a scream. I'd expected blood, a lot of blood, the deep red-black of it crusting his chest. But they must have cleaned him up at the hospital. He was dressed in his silk wedding *kurta*. Against its warm ivory his face appeared remote, stern. The musky aroma of his aftershave lotion that someone must have sprinkled on the body. It didn't quite hide that other smell, thin, sour, metallic. The smell of death. The floor shifted under me, tilting like a wave.

I'm lying on the floor now, on the spilled white sari. I feel sleepy. Or perhaps it is some other feeling I don't have a word for. The sari is seductive-soft, drawing me into its folds.

Sometimes, bathing at the lake, I would move away from my friends, their endless chatter. I'd swim toward the middle of the water with a lazy backstroke, gazing at the sky, its enormous blueness drawing me up until I felt weightless and dizzy. Once in a while there would be a plane, a small silver needle drawn through the clouds, in and out, until it disappeared. Sometimes the thought came to me, as I floated in the middle of the lake with the sun beating down on my closed eyelids, that it would be so easy to let go, to drop into the dim brown world of mud, of water weeds fine as hair.

Once I almost did it. I curled my body inward, tight as a fist, and felt it start to sink. The sun grew pale and shapeless; the water, suddenly cold, licked at the insides of my ears in welcome. But in the end I couldn't.

They are knocking on the door now, calling my name. I push myself off the floor, my body almost too heavy to lift up, as when one climbs out after a long swim. I'm surprised at how vividly it comes to me, this memory I haven't called up in years: the desperate flailing of arms and legs as I fought my way upward; the press of the water on me, heavy as terror; the wild animal trapped inside my chest, clawing at my lungs. The day returning to me as searing air, the way I drew it in, in, in, as though I would never have enough of it.

That's when I know I cannot go back. I don't know yet how I'll manage, here in this new, dangerous land. I only know I must. Because all over India, at this very moment, widows in white saris are bowing their veiled heads, serving tea to in-laws. Doves with cut-off wings.

I am standing in front of the mirror now, gathering up the sari. I tuck in the ripped end so it lies next to my skin, my secret. I make myself think of the store, although it hurts. Inside the refrigerated unit, blue milk cartons neatly lined up by Somesh's hands. The exotic smell of Hills Brothers coffee brewed black and strong, the glisten of sugar-glazed donuts nestled in tissue. The neon Budweiser emblem winking on and off like a risky invitation.

I straighten my shoulders and stand taller, take a deep breath. Air fills me—the same air that traveled through Somesh's lungs a little while ago. The thought is like an unexpected, intimate gift. I tilt my chin, readying myself for the arguments of the coming weeks, the remonstrations. In the mirror a woman holds my gaze, her eyes apprehensive yet steady. She wears a blouse and skirt the color of almonds.

SILVER
PAVEMENTS,
GOLDEN ROOFS

I'VE LOOKED FORWARD TO THIS DAY FOR SO LONG THAT when I finally board the plane I can hardly breathe. In my hurry I bump into the air hostess who is at the door welcoming us, her brilliant pink smile an exact match for her brilliant pink nails.

"Sorry," I say, "so very very sorry," like the nuns had taught me to in those old, high-ceilinged classrooms cooled by the breeze from the convent *neem* trees. And I am. She is so blond, so American.

"No problem," she replies, her smile as golden as the wavy hair that falls in perfect curls to her shoulder. I have never heard the expression before. *No problem,* I whisper to myself as I make my way down the aisle, in love with the exotic syllables. *No problem.* I finger my long hair, imprisoned in the customary tight braid that reaches below my waist. It feels coarse and oily. As soon as I get to Chicago, I promise myself, I will have it cut and styled.

The air inside the plane smells different from the air I've known all my life in Calcutta, moist and weighted with the smell of mango blossoms and bus fumes and human sweat. This air is dry and cool and leaves a slight metallic aftertaste on my lips. I lick at them, wanting to capture that taste, make it part of me forever.

The little tray of food is so pretty, so sanitary. The knife and fork sealed in their own plastic packet, the monogrammed paper napkin. I want to save even the shiny tinfoil that covers the steaming dish. I feel sadness for my friends—Prema, Vaswati, Sabitri—who will never see any of this. I picture them standing outside Ramu's *pakora* stall, munching on the spicy batter-dipped onion rings that our parents have expressly forbidden us to eat, looking up for a moment, eyes squinched against the sun, at the tiny silver plane. I pick up the candy in its crackly pink wrap from the dessert dish. *Almond Roca,* I read, and run my fingers over its nubby surface. I slip it into my purse, then take it out, laughing at my silliness. I am going to the land of Almond Rocas, I remind myself. The American chocolate melts in my mouth, just as sweet as I thought it would be.

But then the worries come.

I hardly know Aunt Pratima, my mother's younger sister with whom I am to stay while I attend college. And her husband, whom I am to call Bikram-uncle—I don't know him at all. They left India a week after their wedding (I was eight then) and have not been back since. Aunt is not much of a letter writer; every year at Bijoya she sends us a card stating how much she misses us, and that's all. In response to my letter asking for permission to stay with her, she wrote back only, *yes of course, but we live very simply.*

I wasn't quite sure what to make of it. All the women I know—my mother, her friends, my other aunts—are avid talkers, filling up lazy heat-hazed afternoons with long, gossipy tales while they drink tea and chew on betel leaves and laugh loud enough to scare away the *ghu-ghu* birds sleeping under the eaves. I couldn't ask my mother—she'd been against my coming to America and would surely use that letter to strengthen her arsenal. So I told myself that was how Americans (Aunt Pratima had lived there long enough to qualify as one) expressed themselves. Economically. And that second part, about living simply—she was just being modest. We all knew that Bikram-uncle owned his own auto business.

Now I look down on the dazzle-bright clouds packed tight as snow cones, deceptively solid. (But I know they are only mist and gauze, unable to save us should an engine fail and the plane plummet downward.) I pull my blue silk sari, which I bought specially for this trip, close around me. The air feels suddenly stale, heavy with other people's exhalations. I think, *What if Uncle and Aunt don't like me? What if I don't like them?* I remember the only picture I've seen of them, the faded sepia marriage photo where they gazed into the camera, stoic and unsmiling, their heavy garlands pulling at their necks. (Why had they never sent any other pictures?) What if they hadn't really wanted me to come and were only being polite? (Americans, I'd heard, liked their privacy. They liked their lives to be smooth and uninterrupted by the claims of relatives.) What if they're not even at the airport? What if they're there but I don't recognize them? I imagine myself stranded, my suitcases strewn around me, the only one left in a large, echoing building after all the happily reunited families have gone home. Maybe I should have listened to Mother after all, I say to myself. Should have let her arrange that marriage for me with Aunt Sarita's neighbor's nephew. Saying it makes the fear something I can see and breathe, like the gray fog that hangs above the smoking section of the aircraft, where someone has placed me by mistake.

Later, of course, I will laugh at my foolishness. Aunt and Uncle are there, just as Aunt had promised, and I pick them out right away (how can I not?) from among the swirl of smart business suits and shiny leather briefcases, the elegant skirts that swing above stiletto-thin high heels.

Bikram-uncle is a short, stocky man dressed in greasy mechanic's overalls that surprise me. He has a belligerent mustache and very dark skin and a scar that runs up the side of his neck. (Had it been hidden in the wedding photo under the garlands?) I am struck at once by how ugly he is—the garlands had hidden that as well—how unlike Aunt, who stoops a bit to match her husband's height, her fine, nervous hands worrying the edge of her shawl as she scans the travelers emerging from Immigration.

I touch their feet like a good Indian girl should, though I am somewhat embarrassed. Everyone in the airport is watching us, I'm sure of it. Aunt is embarrassed too, and shifts her weight from leg to leg. Then she kisses me on both cheeks, but a little hesitantly—I get the feeling she hasn't done something like this in a long time.

"O Jayanti!" she says. "I am having no idea you are growing so beautiful. And so fair-skinned. And you such a thin thin girl with scabby knees when I left India. It is making me very happy." Her voice is soft and uncertain, as though she rarely speaks above a whisper, but her eyes are warm, flecked with bits of light.

I don't know what Uncle thinks. This makes me smile too widely and speak too fast and thank them too effusively for taking me in. I start to take out letters and packets from my carry-on bag.

"This is from Mother," I tell Aunt. "This fat one wrapped in twine is from Grandfather. And here's a jar of the lemon-mango pickle you used to like so much—Great-aunt Rama made it herself when she heard—"

Bikram-uncle interrupts. Unlike Aunt, who speaks refined Bengali, he uses a staccato American English. His accent jars my ears. I have trouble understanding it.

"Can we get going? I got to be back at work. You women can chat all day once you get home."

His voice isn't unkind. Still I feel reprimanded, as though I am a little girl again, and spitefully I wonder how a marriage could ever have been arranged between a man like Bikram-uncle and my aunt, who comes from an old and wealthy landowning family.

The overalls are part of the problem. They make him seem so—I hesitate to use the word, but only briefly—*low-class*. Why, even Mr. Bhalani, who owned the Lakshmi Motor Works near the Mint, always wore a starched white linen suit and a diamond on his little finger. Now as I stare from the back of the car at the fold of neck that overlaps the grimy collar of Uncle's overalls, I feel that something is very wrong.

But only for a moment. Outside, America is whizzing by the fogged-up car window, blurry silhouettes of brick and stone and tall black glass that glint in the sun, making me dizzy. I wipe the moisture from the pane with the edge of my sari.

"What's this?" I ask. "And this?"

"The central post office," Aunt replies, laughing a little at my excitement. "The Sears Tower." But a lot of the time she says, "I am not knowing this one." Uncle busies himself with swerving in and out of traffic, humming along with the song on the radio.

The apartment is another disappointment, not at all what an American home should be like. I've seen the pictures in *Good Housekeeping* and *Sunset* at the USIS library, and once our neighbor Aditi brought over the photos her *chachaji* had sent from Akron, Ohio. I remember clearly the neat red brick house with matching flowery drapes, the huge, perfectly mowed lawn green like it had been painted, the shiny concrete driveway on which sat two shiny motorcars. And Akron isn't even as big as Chicago. And Aditi's *chachaji* only works in an office, selling insurance.

This apartment smells of stale curry. It is crowded with faded, overstuffed sofas and rickety end tables that look like they've come from a larger place. A wadded newspaper is wedged under one of the legs of the dining table. Uncle and

Aunt are watching me, his eyes defiant, hers anxious. I shift
my gaze to the dingy walls hung with prints of landscapes,
cattle standing under droopy weeping willows looking vaguely
bored, (surely they are not Aunt's choice?) and try to keep my
face polite. My monogrammed leather cases are an embarrassment in this household. I push them under the bed in the
tiny room I am to occupy—it is the same size as my bathroom
at home. I remember that cool green mosaic floor, the claw-
footed marble bathtub from colonial days, the large window
that looks out on my mother's crimson and gold dahlias, and
want to cry. But I tell Aunt that I will be very comfortable
here, and I thank her for the rose she has put in a jelly jar and
placed on the windowsill.

Aunt cooks happily all afternoon. Whenever I offer help she
says, "No no, you just sit and rest your feet and tell me what-
all's going on at home."

Dinner turns out to be an elaborate affair—a spicy al-
mond-chicken curry arranged over hot rice, a spinach-lentil
dal, a yogurt cucumber *raita*, fried potato *pakoras*, crisp
golden *papads*, and sweet white *kheer*—which has taken
hours to prepare—for dessert. I have a guilty feeling that Aunt
and Uncle don't usually eat this way, and as we sit down I
glance at Uncle for confirmation. But he has already started
on the food. He eats quickly and with concentration, without
raising his head. When he wants more he points silently, and
Aunt hurries to serve him. He has taken a shower and put on
the muslin *kurta-pajama* I brought him as a gift from India.
With his hair brushed back wetly and *chappals* on his feet, he

41

could be any Indian man sitting down to his dinner after a hard day's work. As I watch Aunt ladle more *dal* onto his plate, I have a strange sense of disorientation, and for a moment I wonder whether I've left Calcutta at all.

"I think he is liking you," whispers Aunt Pratima when we are alone in the kitchen. She stops spooning dessert into bowls to touch me lightly on the wrist, her face bright. "See how he is wearing the clothes you brought for him? Most nights he does not even change out of his overalls, let alone take a shower."

I am dubious. Uncle's attitude toward me, as far as I can tell, is one of testy tolerance. But I give Aunt a hug and hope, for her sake, that she is right. And as I help her pour tea into chipped cups of fine bone china that look like they might have once been part of her dowry, I make a special effort. I offer Uncle my most charming smile.

"I can't believe I'm finally here in the U.S.," I tell him. "I've heard so much about Chicago—Lake Michigan, which is surely big as an ocean, the Egyptian museum with mummies three thousand years old, and is it true that the big downtown stores have real silver mannequins in their windows?"

Uncle grunts noncommittally, regarding the teacups with disfavor. He stomps into the kitchen where I hear him rummage in the refrigerator.

"I can't wait to see it all!" I call after him. "I'm so glad I have the summer, though of course I'm looking forward to starting at the university in September!"

"You will do well, I know." Aunt nods encouragingly. "You are such a smart girl to be getting into this university where people from all over the world are trying to become students. Soon you will have many many American friends, and—"

"Don't be too sure of that," Bikram-uncle breaks in, startling me. His voice is harsh, raspy. He stands in the kitchen doorway, drinking from a can which glints in his fist. "Things here aren't as perfect as people at home like to think. We all thought we'd become millionaires. But it's not so easy."

"Please," Aunt says, but he seems not to hear her. He tips his head back to swallow, and the scar on his neck glistens pinkly like a live thing. *Budweiser*, I read as he sets the can down, and am shocked to realize he's drinking beer. At home in Calcutta none of the family touches alcohol, not even cousin Ramesh, who attends St. Xavier's College and sports a navy-blue blazer and a British accent. Mother has always told me what a disgusting habit it is, and she's right. I remember Grandfather's village at harvesttime, the farmhands lying in ditches, drunk on palm-toddy, flies buzzing around their faces. I try not to let my distaste show on my face.

Now Uncle's tone is dark and raw. The bitterness in it coats my mouth like the *karela* juice Mother used to give me to cool my liver.

"The Americans hate us. They're always putting us down because we're dark-skinned foreigners, *kala admi*. Blaming us for the damn economy, for taking away their jobs. You'll see it for yourself soon enough."

What has made him detest this country so much?

I look beyond Uncle's head at the window. All I can see is a dark rectangle. But I know the sky outside is filled with

43

strange and beautiful stars, and I am suddenly angry with him for trying to ruin it all for me. I take a deep breath. I tell myself, I'll wait to make up my own mind.

At night I lie in my lumpy bed under a coarse green blanket. I try to sleep, but the night noises that still seem unfamiliar after a week—the desperate *whee-whee* of a siren, the wind sighing as it coils about the house—keep me awake. Small sounds filter, too, through the walls from Aunt's bedroom. And though they are quite innocent—the bedsprings creaking as someone turns over in sleep, footsteps and then the hum of the exhaust as the bathroom light is switched on—each time I stiffen with embarrassment. I cannot stop thinking of Uncle and Aunt. I would rather think only of Aunt, but like the shawls of the bride and groom at an Indian wedding ceremony, their lives are inextricably knotted together. I try to imagine her arriving in this country, speaking only a little English, red-veiled, wearing the heavy, elaborate jewelry I've seen in the wedding photo. (What happened to it all? Now Aunt only wears a thin gold chain and the tiniest of pearls in her ears.) Her shock at discovering that her husband was not the owner of an automobile empire (as the matchmaker had assured her family) but only a mechanic who had a dingy garage in an undesirable part of town.

I haven't seen Uncle's shop yet. Of course I haven't seen anything else either, but as soon as the weather—which has been a bone-chilling gray—improves, I plan to. I've already called the people at Midwest Bus Tours, which picks up passengers from their homes for an extra five dollars. But I have a feeling I'll never get to see the shop, and so—again spitefully —I make it, in my head, a cheerless place that smells of sweat and grease, where the hiss of hydraulics and the clanging of tools mix with the curses of mechanics who are all as surly as Bikram-uncle.

But soon, with the self-absorption of the young, I move on the wings of imagination to more exciting matters. In my Modern Novel class at the university, I sit dressed in a plaid skirt and a matching sweater. My legs, elegant in knee-high boots like the ones I have seen on one of the afternoon TV shows that Aunt likes, are casually crossed. My bobbed hair swings around my face as I spiritedly argue against the handsome professor's interpretation of Dreiser's philosophy. I discourse brilliantly on the character of Sister Carrie until he is convinced, and later we go out for dinner to a quiet little French restaurant. Candlelight shines on the professor's reddish hair, on his gold spectacle frames. On the rims of our wineglasses. Chopin plays in the background as he confesses his admiration, his love for me. He slips onto my finger a ring with stones that sparkle like his eyes and tells me of the trips we will go on around the world, the books we will coauthor when I am his wife. (No arranged marriage like Aunt's for me!) After dinner he takes me to his apartment overlooking the lake, where fairy lights twinkle and shiver on the water. He pulls me down, respectfully but ardently, on the couch. His lips are hot against my throat, his . . .

But here my imagination, conditioned by a lifetime of maternal censorship, shuts itself down.

After lunch the next day I walk out onto the narrow balcony. It is still cold, but the sun is finally out. The sky stretches over me, a sheet of polished metal. The skyscrapers of downtown Chicago float glimmering in the distance, enchanted towers out of an old storybook. The air is so new and crisp that it makes me suddenly happy, full of hope.

As a child in India, sometimes I used to sing a song. *Will I marry a prince from a far-off magic land, where the pavements are silver and the roofs all gold?* My girlfriends and I would play skipping games to its rhythm, laughing carelessly, thoughtlessly. And now here I am. *America*, I think, and the word opens inside me like a folded paper flower placed in water, filling me until there is no room to breathe.

The apartment with its faded cushions and its crookedly hung pictures seems newly oppressive when I go back inside. Aunt is in the kitchen—where I have noticed she spends most of her time—chopping vegetables.

"Can we go for a walk?" I ask. "Please?"

Aunt looks doubtful. "It is being very cold outside," she tells me.

"Oh no," I assure her. "I was just out on the balcony and it's lovely, it really is."

"Your uncle does not like me to go out. He is telling me it is dangerous."

"How can it be dangerous?" I say. It's just a ploy of his to keep her shut up in the house and under his control. He would like to do the same with me, only I won't let him. I pull her by the hand to the window. "Look," I say. The streets are clean and empty and very wide. A gleaming blue car speeds by. A bus belches to a stop and two laughing girls get down.

I can feel Aunt weakening. But she says, "Better to wait. This weekend he is taking us to the mall. So many big big shops there, you'll like it. He says he will buy pizza for dinner. Do you know pizza? Is it coming to India yet?"

I want to tell her that the walls are closing in on me. My brain is dying. Soon I will turn into one of those mournful-eyed cows in the painting behind the sofa.

"Just a short walk for some exercise," I say. "We'll be back long before Uncle. He need not even know."

Maybe Aunt Pratima hears the longing in my voice. Maybe it makes her feel guilty. She lifts her thin face. When she smiles, she seems not that much older than me.

"In the village before marriage I was always walking everywhere—it was so nice, the fresh air, the sky, the ponds with lotus flowers, the dogs and goats and chickens all around. Of course, here we cannot be expecting such country things. . . ."

I wait.

"No harm in it, I am thinking," she finally says. "As long as we are staying close to the house. As long as we are coming back in time to fix a nice dinner for your uncle."

"Just a half-hour walk," I assure her. "We'll be back in plenty of time."

As we walk down the dim corridor that smells, just like the apartment, of stale curry (do the neighbors mind?), she adds, a bit apologetically, "Please do not be saying anything to Uncle. It will make him angry." She shakes her head. "He worries too much since . . ."

47

I want to ask her since what, but I sense she doesn't want to talk about it. I give her a bright smile.

"I won't say a word to Uncle. It'll be our secret."

In coats and saris we walk down the street. A few pedestrians stare at us silently as they sidle past. I miss the bustle of the Calcutta streets a little, the hawkers with their bright wares, the honking buses loaded with people, the rickshaw-wallahs calling out *make way*, but I say, "It's so neat and quiet, isn't it?"

"Every Wednesday the cleaning truck is coming with big brushes to sweep the streets," Aunt tells me proudly.

The sun has ducked behind a cloud, and it is colder than I had thought. When I look up the April light is a muted glare that hurts my eyes.

"It is probably snowing later today," Aunt says.

"That's wonderful! You know, I've only seen snow in movies! It always looked so pretty and delicate. I didn't think I'd get to see any this late in the year. . . ."

Aunt pulls her shapeless coat tighter around her. "It is not that great," she says. Her tone is regretful, as though she is sorry to disillusion me. "It melts inside the collar of your jacket and drips down your back. Cars are skidding when it turns to ice. And see how it looks like afterward. . . ." She kicks at the brown slush on the side of the road with a force that surprises me.

I like my aunt though, the endearing way in which her eyes widen like a little girl's when she asks a question, the small frown line between her eyebrows when she listens, the sudden, liquid shift of her features when she smiles. I remember that she'd been considered a beauty back home, someone who deserved the good luck of having a marriage arranged with a man who lived in America.

As we walk, the brisk, invigorating air seems to loosen something inside of Aunt. She talks and talks. She asks about the design on my sari, deep rose-embroidered peacocks dancing against a cream background. Is this being the latest fashion in India? (She uses the word *desh*, country, to refer to India, as though it were the only one in the world.) "I am always loving Calcutta, visiting your mother in that beautiful old house with marble fountains and lions." She wants to know what movies are showing at the Roxy. Do children still fly the moon-shaped kites at the Maidan and do the street vendors still sell puffed rice spiced with green chilies? How about Victoria Memorial with the black angel on top of the white marble dome, is it still the same? Is it true that New Market with all those charming little clothing stores has burnt down? Have I been on the new subway she has read about in *India Abroad*? The words pour from her in a rush. "Imagine all those tunnels under the city, you could be getting lost in there and nobody will be finding you if you do not want them to." I hear the hunger in her voice. And so I hold back my own eagerness to learn about America and answer her the best I can.

The street has narrowed now and the apartment buildings look run-down, even to me, with peeling walls and patchy yellow spots on lawns where the snow has melted. There are chain-link fences and garbage on the pavement. Broken-down cars, their rusted hoods gaping, sit in several front yards. The sweet stench of rot rises from the drains. I am disconcerted. I thought I had left all such smells behind in Calcutta.

"Shouldn't we be going back, Aunt?" I ask, suddenly nervous.

Aunt Pratima looks around blindly.

"Yes yes, my goodness, is it that late already? Look at that black sky. It is so nice to be talking to someone about home that I am forgetting the time completely."

We start back, lifting up our saris to walk faster, our steps echoing along the empty sidewalk, and when we go back a bit Aunt stops and looks up and down the street without recognition, her head pivoting loosely like a lost animal's.

Then we see the boys. Four of them, playing in the middle of the street with cans and sticks. They hadn't been there before, or maybe it is a different street we are on now. The boys look up and I see that their sallow faces are grime-streaked. Their blond hair hangs limply over their foreheads, and their eyes are pale and slippery, like pebbles left under-water for a long time. They may be anywhere from eight to fourteen—I can't tell their ages as I would with boys back home. They scare me on this deserted street although surely there's no reason for fear. They're just boys after all, with thin wrists that stick out from the sleeves of too-small jackets, standing under a tree on which the first leaves of spring are opening a pale and delicate green. I glance at Aunt Pratima for reassurance, but the skin on her face stretches tightly across her sharp, fragile cheekbones.

The boys bend their heads together, consulting, then the tallest one takes a step toward us and says, "Nigger." He says it softly, his upper lip curling away from his teeth. The word arcs through the empty street like a rock, an impossible word which belongs to another place and time. In the mouth of a red-faced gin-and-tonic drinking British official, perhaps, in his colonial bungalow, or a sneering overseer out of *Uncle Tom's Cabin* as he plies his whip in the cotton fields. But here is this boy, younger than my cousin Anup, saying it as easily as one might say *thank you* or *please*. Or *no problem.*

Now the others take up the word, chanting it in high singsong voices that have not broken yet, *nigger, nigger,* until I want to scream, or weep. Or laugh, because can't they *see* that I'm not black at all but an Indian girl of good family? When our chauffeur Gurbans Singh drives me down the Calcutta streets in our silver-colored Fiat, people stop to whisper, *Isn't that Jayanti Ganguli, daughter of the Bhavanipur Gangulis?*

I don't see which boy first picks up the fistful of slush, but now they're all throwing it at us. It splatters on our coats and runs down our saris, leaving long streaks. I take a step toward the boys. I'm not sure what I'll do when I get to them —shake them? explain the mistake they've made? smash their faces into the pavement? but Aunt holds tight to my arm.

"No, Jayanti, no."

I try to pull free but she is surprisingly strong, or perhaps I'm not trying hard enough. Perhaps I'm secretly thankful that she's begging me—*Let's go home, Jayanti*—so that I don't have to confront those boys with more hate in their eyes than boys should ever have. There is slush on Aunt's face; her trembling lips are ash-colored. She's sobbing, and when I put out my hand to comfort her I realize that I too am sobbing.

Half running, tripping on the wet saris which slap at our

legs, we retreat down the street. The voices follow us for a long time. *Nigger, nigger.* Slush-voices, trickling into us even when we've finally found the right road back to our building, which had been only one street away all the time. Even when in the creaking elevator we tidy each other as best we can, wiping at faces, brushing off coats, holding each other's shivering hands, looking away from each other's eyes.

The light has burned out in the passage outside the door. Aunt Pratima fumbles in her purse for the key, saying, "It was here, I am keeping it right here, where can it *go*?"

In their thin Indian shoes, my feet are colder than I have ever imagined possible. My teeth chatter as I say, "It's all right, calm down, Auntie, we'll find it."

But Aunt's voice quavers higher and higher, a bucking, runaway voice. She turns her purse upside down and shakes it, coins and wrappers and pens and safety pins tumbling out and skittering to the edges of the passage. Then she gets down on all fours on the mangy brown carpet to grope through them.

That is when Bikram-uncle opens the door. He is still wearing his grease-stained overalls. "What the hell is going on?" he says, looking down at Aunt. Standing across from him, I look down too, and see what he must be seeing, the parting in Aunt Pratima's tightly pulled-back hair, the stretched line of the scalp pointing grayly at her lowered forehead like an accusation.

"Where the hell have you been?" Bikram-uncle asks, more loudly this time. "Get in here right now."

I kneel and help Aunt gather up some of her things, leaving the rest behind.

Inside, Bikram-uncle yells, "Haven't I *told* you not to

walk around this trashy neighborhood? Haven't I *told* you it wasn't safe? Don't you remember what happened to my shop last year, how they smashed everything? And still you had to go out, had to give them the chance to do *this* to you." He draws in a ragged breath, like a sob. "My God, look at you."

I try not to stare at Aunt's mud-splotched cheek, her ruined coat, her red-rimmed, pleading glance. But I can't drag my eyes away. Once when I was little, I'd looked down into an old well behind Grandfather's house and seen my face, pale and distorted, reflected in the brackish water. I have that same dizzying sensation now. *Is this what my life too will be like?*

"It was my fault," I say. "Aunt didn't want to go."

But no one hears me.

Aunt takes a hesitant, sideways step toward Uncle. It is a small movement, something an injured animal might make toward its keeper. "They were only children," she says in a wondering tone.

"Bastards," cries Uncle, his voice choking, his accent suddenly thick and Indian. "Bloody bastards. I want to kill them, all of them." His entire face wavers, as though it will collapse in on itself. He raises his arm.

"No," I shout. I run toward them. But my body moves slowly, as though underwater. Perhaps it cannot believe that he will really do it.

When the back of his hand catches Aunt Pratima across the mouth, I flinch as if his knuckles had made that thwacking bone sound against my own flesh. My mouth fills with an ominous salt taste.

Will I marry a prince from a far-off magic land?

I put out my hand to shield Aunt, but Uncle is quicker. He has her already tight in his grasp. I look about wildly for something—perhaps a chair to bring crashing down on his head. Then I hear him.

"Pratima," he cries in a broken voice, "Pratima, Pratima." He touches her face, his fingers groping uncertainly like a blind man's, his whole body shaking.

"Hush, Ram," says my aunt. "Hush." She strokes his hair as though he were a child, and perhaps he is.

"Pratima, how could I. . . ."

"Shhh, I am understanding."

"Something exploded in my head . . . it was like that time at the shop . . . remember . . . how the fire they started took everything. . . ."

"Don't be thinking of it now, Ram," says Aunt Pratima. She pulls his head down to her breast and lays her cheek on his hair. Her fingers caress the scar on his neck. Her face is calm, almost happy. She—they—have forgotten me.

I feel like an intruder, a fool. How little I've understood. As I turn to tiptoe away to my room, I hear my uncle say, "I tried so hard, Pratima. I wanted to give you so many things— but even your jewelry is gone." Grief scrapes at his voice. "This damn country, like a *dain,* a witch—it pretends to give and then snatches everything back."

And Aunt's voice, pure and musical with the lilt of a smile in it, "O Ram, I am having all I need."

54

Now it is night but no one has thought to turn on the family-room lights. Bikram-uncle sits in front of the TV, his feet up on the rickety coffee table. He is finishing his third beer. The can gleams faintly as it catches the uneven blue flickers from the tube. I feel I should say something to him, but he is not looking at me, and I don't know what to say. Aunt Pratima is in the kitchen preparing dinner as though this were an evening like all others. I should go and help her. But I remain in my chair in the corner of the room. I am not sure how to face her either, how to start talking about what has happened. (In my head I am trying to make sense of it still.) Am I to ignore it all (*can* I?)—the hate-suffused faces of the boys, the swelling spreading its dark blotch across Aunt's jaw, the memory of Uncle's head pressed trembling to her breast? *Home,* I whisper desperately, *homehomehome,* and suddenly, intensely, I want my room in Calcutta, where things were so much simpler. I want the high mahogany bed in which I've slept as long as I can remember, the comforting smell of sun-dried cotton sheets to pull around my head. I want my childhood again. But I am too far away for the spell to work, for the words to take me back, even in my head.

Then out of the corner of my eye I catch a white movement. It is snowing. I step outside onto the balcony, drawing my breath in at the silver marvel of it, the fat flakes cool and wet against my face as in a half-forgotten movie. It is cold, so cold that I can feel the insides of my nostrils stiffening. The air—there is no smell to it at all—carves a freezing path all the way into my chest. But I don't go back inside. The snow has covered the dirty cement pavements, the sad warped shingles of the rooftops, has softened, forgivingly, the rough noisy edges of things. I hold out my hands to it, palms down, shivering a little.

The snow falls on them, chill, stinging all the way to the bone. But after a while the excruciating pain fades. I am thinking of hands. The pink-tipped blond hand of the air hostess as she offers me a warm towelette that smells like unknown flowers. The boy's grimy one pushing back his limp hair, then tightening into a fist to throw a lump of slush. Uncle's with its black nails, its oddly defenseless scraped knuckles, arcing through the air to knock Aunt's head sideways. And Aunt's hand, stroking that angry pink scar. Threading her long elegant fingers (the fingers, still, of a Bengali aristocrat's daughter) through his graying hair to pull him to her. All these American hands that I know will keep coming back in my dreams.

Will I marry a prince from a far-off magic land
Where the pavements are silver and the roofs all
gold?

When I finally look down, I notice that the snow has covered my own hands so they are no longer brown but white, white, white. And now it makes sense that the beauty and the pain should be part of each other. I continue holding them out in front of me, gazing at them, until they're completely covered. Until they do not hurt at all.

THE WORD LOVE

You practice them out loud for days in front of the bathroom mirror, the words with which you'll tell your mother you're living with a man. Sometimes they are words of confession and repentance. Sometimes they are angry, defiant. Sometimes they melt into a single, sighing sound. *Love*. You let the water run so he won't hear you and ask what those foreign phrases you keep saying mean. You don't want to have to explain, don't want another argument like last time.

"Why are you doing this to yourself?" he'd asked, throwing his books down on the table when he returned from class to find you curled into a corner of the sagging sofa you'd bought together at a Berkeley garage sale. You'd washed your face but he knew right away that you'd been crying. Around you, wads of paper crumpled tight as stones. (This was when you thought writing would be the best way.) "I hate seeing you like this." Then he added, his tone darkening, "You're acting like I was some kind of a criminal."

You'd watched the upside-down titles of his books splaying across the table. *Control Systems Engineering. Boiler Operations Guide. Handbook of Shock and Vibration.* Cryptic as tarot cards, they seemed to be telling you something. If only you could decipher it.

"It isn't you," you'd said, gathering up the books guiltily, smoothing their covers. Holding them tight against you. "I'd have the same problem no matter who it was."

You tried to tell him about your mother, how she'd seen her husband's face for the first time at her wedding. How, when he died (you were two years old then), she had taken off her jewelry and put on widow's white and dedicated the rest of her life to the business of bringing you up. *We only have each other*, she often told you.

"So?"

"She lives in a different world. Can't you see that? She's never traveled more than a hundred miles from the village where she was born; she's never touched cigarettes or alcohol; even though she lives in Calcutta, she's never watched a movie."

"Are you serious!"

"I love her, Rex." *I will not feel apologetic*, you told yourself. You wanted him to know that when you conjured up her face, the stern angles of it softening into a rare smile, the silver at her temples catching the afternoon sun in the backyard under the pomegranate tree, love made you breathless, as though someone had punched a hole through your chest. But he interrupted.

The Word Love

"So don't tell her," he said, "that you're living in sin. With a foreigner, no less. Someone whose favorite food is sacred cow steak and Budweiser. Who pops a pill now and then when he gets depressed. The shock'll probably do her in."

You hate it when he talks like that, biting off the ends of words and spitting them out. You try to tell yourself that he wants to hurt you only because *he's* hurting, because he's jealous of how much she means to you. You try to remember the special times. The morning he showed up outside your Shakespeare class with violets the color of his eyes. The evening when the two of you drove up to Grizzly Peak and watched the sunset spreading red over the Bay while he told you of his childhood, years of being shunted between his divorced parents till he was old enough to move out. How you had held him. The night in his apartment (has it only been three months?) when he took your hands in his warm strong ones, asking you to move in with him, please, because he really needed you. You try to shut out the whispery voice that lives behind the ache in your eyes, the one that started when you said yes and he kissed you, hard.

Mistake, says the voice, whispering in your mother's tones.

Sometimes the voice sounds different, not hers. It is a rushed intake of air, as just before someone asks a question that might change your life. You don't want to hear the question, which might be *how did you get yourself into this mess,* or perhaps *why,* so you leap in with that magic word. *Love,* you tell yourself, *lovelovelove.* But you know, deep down, that words solve nothing.

And so you no longer try to explain to him why you *must* tell your mother. You just stand in the bathroom in front of the crooked mirror with tarnished edges and practice the words. You try not to notice that the eyes in the mirror are so like her eyes, that same vertical line between the brows. The line of your jaw slants up at the same angle as hers when she would lean forward to kiss you goodbye at the door. Outside a wino shouts something. Crash of broken glass and, later, police sirens. But you're hearing the street vendor call out *momphali, momphali, fresh and hot,* and she's smiling, handing you a coin, saying, *yes, baby, you can have some.* The salty crunch of roasted peanuts fills your mouth, the bathroom water runs and runs, endless as sorrow, the week blurs past, and suddenly it's Saturday morning, the time of her weekly call.

She tells you how Aunt Arati's arthritis isn't getting any better in spite of the turmeric poultices. It's so cold this year in Calcutta, the *shiuli* flowers have all died. You listen, holding on to the rounded *o*'s, the long liquid *e*'s, the *s*'s that brush against your face soft as night kisses. She's trying to arrange a marriage for cousin Leela who's going to graduate from college next year, remember? She misses you. Do you like your new apartment? How long before you finish the Ph.D. and come home for good? Her voice is small and far, tinny with static. "You're so quiet. . . . Are you OK, *shona*? Is something bothering you?" You want to tell her, but your heart flings itself around in your chest like a netted bird, and the words that you practiced so long are gone.

"I'm fine, Ma," you say. "Everything's all right."

The Word Love

The first thing you did when you moved into his apartment was to put up the batik hanging, deep red flowers winding around a black circle. The late summer sun shone through the open window. Smell of California honeysuckle in the air, a radio next door playing Mozart. He walked in, narrowing his eyes, pausing to watch. You waited, pin in hand, the nubs of the fabric pulsing under your palm, erratic as a heart. "Not bad," he nodded finally, and you let out your breath in a relieved shiver of a laugh.

"My mother gave it to me," you said. "A going-away-to-college gift, a talisman. . . ." You started to tell him how she had bought it at the Maidan fair on a day as beautiful as this one, the buds just coming out on the mango trees, the red-breasted bulbuls returning north. But he held up his hand, *later*. Swung you off the rickety chair and carried you to the bed. Lay on top, pinning you down. His eyes were sapphire stones. His hair caught the light, glinting like warm sandstone. Surge of electric (love or fear?) up your spine, making you shiver, making you forget what you wanted to say.

At night after lovemaking, you lie listening to his sleeping breath. His arm falls across you, warm, *protective*, you say to yourself. Outside, wind rattles the panes. A dry wind. (There hasn't been rain for a long time.) *I am cherished.*

But then the memories come.

Once when you were in college you had gone to see a popular Hindi movie with your girlfriends. Secretly, because

Mother said movies were frivolous, decadent. But there were no secrets in Calcutta. When you came home from classes the next day, a suitcase full of your clothes was on the doorstep. A note on it, in your mother's hand. *Better no daughter than a disobedient one, a shame to the family.* Even now you remember how you felt, the dizzy fear that shriveled the edges of the day, the desperate knocking on the door that left your knuckles raw. You'd sat on the doorstep all afternoon, and passersby had glanced at you curiously. By evening it was cold. The numbness crept up your feet and covered you. When she'd finally opened the door after midnight, for a moment you couldn't stand. She had pulled you up, and you had fallen into her arms, both of you crying. Later she had soaked your feet in hot water with boric soda. You still remember the softness of the towels with which she wiped them.

Why do you always focus on the sad things, you wonder. Is it some flaw in yourself, some cross-connection in the thin silver filaments of your brain? So many good things happened, too. Her sitting in the front row at your high school graduation, face bright as a dahlia above the white of her sari. The two of you going for a bath in the Ganga, the brown tug of the water on your clothes, the warm sleepy sun as you sat on the bank eating curried potatoes wrapped in hot *puris*. And further back, her teaching you to write, the soft curve of her hand over yours, helping you hold the chalk, the smell of her newly washed hair curling about your face.

But these memories are wary, fugitive. You have to coax them out of their dark recesses. They dissipate, foglike, even as you are looking at them. And suddenly his arm feels terribly heavy. You are suffocating beneath its weight, its muscular, hairy maleness. You slip out and step into the shower. The wind snatches at the straggly nasturtiums you planted on the little strip of balcony. *What will you remember of him when it is all over?* whispers the papery voice inside your skull. Light from the bathroom slashes the floor while against the dark wall the hanging glows fire-red.

The first month you moved in with him, your head pounded with fear and guilt every time the phone rang. You'd rush across the room to pick it up while he watched you from his tilted-back chair, raising an eyebrow. (You'd made him promise never to pick up the phone.) At night you slept next to the bedside extension. You picked it up on the very first ring, struggling up out of layers of sleep heavy as water to whisper a breathless hello, the next word held in readiness, *mother*. But it was never her. Sometimes it was a friend of yours from the graduate program. Mostly it was for him. Women. Ex-girlfriends, he would explain with a guileless smile, stressing the *ex*. Then he would turn toward the window, his voice dropping into a low murmur while you pretended sleep and hated yourself for being jealous.

She always called on Saturday morning, Saturday night back home. The last thing before she went to bed. You picture her sitting on the large mahogany bed where you, too, had slept when you were little. Or when you were sick or scared. Outside, crickets are chanting. The night watchman makes his rounds, calling out the hour. The old *ayah* (she has been there from before you were born) stands behind her, combing out her long hair which lifts a little in the breeze from the fan, the silver in it glimmering like a smile. It is the most beautiful hair in the world.

And so you grew less careful. Sometimes you'd call out from the shower for him to answer the phone. And he would tease you (*you sure now?*) before picking it up. At night after the last kiss your body would slide off his damp, glistening one —and you didn't care which side of the bed it was as long as you had him to hold on to. *Or was it that you wanted her, somehow, to find out?* the voice asks. But you are learning to not pay attention to the voice, to fill your mind with sensations (how the nubs of his elbows fit exactly into your cupped palms, how his sleeping breath stirs the small hairs on your arm) until its echoes dissipate.

So when the phone rang very early that Tuesday morning you thought nothing of it. You pulled sleep like a furry blanket over your head, and even when you half heard his voice, suddenly formal, saying *just one moment, please,* you didn't get it. Not until he was shaking your shoulder, handing you the phone, mouthing the words silently, *your mother.*

Later you try to remember what you said to her, but you can't quite get the words right. Something about a wonderful man, getting married soon (although the only time you'd discussed marriage was when he had told you it wasn't for him). She'd called to let you know that cousin Leela's wedding was all arranged—a good Brahmin boy, a rising executive in an accounting firm. Next month in Delhi. The whole family would travel there. She'd bought your ticket already. *But now of course you need not come.* Her voice had been a spear of ice. Did you cry out, *Don't be angry, Mother, please?* Did you beg forgiveness? Did you whisper (again that word) *love*? You do know this: you kept talking, even after the phone went dead. When you finally looked up, he was watching you. His eyes were opaque, like pebbles.

All through the next month you try to reach her. You call. The *ayah* answers. She sounds frightened when she hears your voice. *Memsaab* has told her not to speak to you, or else she'll lose her job.

"She had the lawyer over yesterday to change her will. What did you do, Missybaba, that was so bad?"

You hear your mother in the background. "Who are you talking to, Ayah? What? How can it be my daughter? I don't *have* a daughter. Hang up right now."

"Mother . . ." you cry. The word ricochets through the apartment so that the hanging shivers against the wall. Its black center ripples like a bottomless well. The phone goes dead. You call again. Your fingers are shaking. It's hard to see the digits through the tears. Your knees feel as though they have been broken. The phone buzzes against your ear like a trapped insect. No one picks it up. You keep calling all week. Finally a machine tells you the number has been changed. There is no new number.

Here is a story your mother told you when you were growing up:

There was a girl I used to play with sometimes, whose father was the roof thatcher in your grandfather's village.

They lived near the women's lake. She was an only child, pretty in a dark-skinned way, and motherless, so her father spoiled her. He let her run wild, climbing trees, swimming in the river. Let her go to school, even after she reached the age when girls from good families stayed home, waiting to be married. (You know already this is a tale with an unhappy end, a cautionary moral.) *He would laugh when the old women of the village warned him that an unmarried girl is like a firebrand in a field of ripe grain. She's a good girl, he'd say. She knows right and wrong. He found her a fine match, a master carpenter from the next village. But a few days before the wedding, her body was discovered in the women's lake. We all thought it was an accident until we heard about the rocks she had tied in her sari.* (She stops, waits for the question you do not want to ask but must.) *Who knows why? People whispered that she was pregnant, said they'd seen her once or twice with a man, a traveling actor who had come to the village some time back. Her father was heartbroken, his good name ruined. He had to leave the village, all those tongues and eyes. Leave behind the house of his forefathers that he loved so much. No, no one knows what happened to him.*

For months afterward, you lie awake at night and think of the abandoned house, mice claws skittering over the floors, the dry papery slither of snakes, bats' wings. When you fall asleep you dream of a beautiful dark girl knotting stones into her *palloo* and swimming out to the middle of the dark lake. The water is cool on her heavying breasts, her growing belly. It ripples and parts for her. Before she goes under, she turns toward you. Sometimes her face is a blank oval, featureless. Sometimes it is your face.

The Word Love

Things are not going well for you. At school you cannot concentrate on your classes, they seem so disconnected from the rest of your life. Your advisor calls you into her office to talk to you. You stare at the neat rows of books behind her head. She is speaking of missed deadlines, research that lacks innovation. You notice her teeth, large and white and regular, like a horse's. She pauses, asks if you are feeling well.

"Oh yes," you say, in the respectful tone you were always taught to use with teachers. "I feel just fine."

But the next day it is too difficult to get up and get dressed for class. What difference would it make if you miss a deconstructionist critique of the Sonnets? you ask yourself. You stay in bed until the postal carrier comes.

You have written a letter to Aunt Arati explaining, asking her to please tell your mother that you're sorry. *I'll come home right now if she wants.* Every day you check the box for Aunt's reply, but there's nothing. Her arthritis is acting up, you tell yourself. It's the wedding preparations. The letter is lost.

Things are not going well between him and you either. Sometimes when he is talking, the words make no sense. You watch him move his mouth as though he were a character in a foreign film someone has forgotten to dub. He asks you a question. By the raised tone of his voice you know that's what it is, but you have no idea what he wants from you. He asks again, louder.

"What?" you say.

He walks out, slamming the door.

You have written a letter to your mother, too. A registered letter, so it can't get lost. You run outside every day when you hear the mail van. Nothing. You glance at the carrier, a large black woman, suspiciously. "Are you sure?" you ask. You wonder if she put the letter into someone else's box by mistake. After she leaves, you peer into the narrow metal slots of the other mailboxes, trying to see.

At first he was sympathetic. He held you when you lay sleepless at night. "Cry," he said. "Get it out of your system." Then, "It was bound to happen sooner or later. You must have known that. Maybe it's all for the best." Later, "Try to look at the positive side. You had to cut the umbilical cord *sometime*."

You pulled away when he said things like that. What did *he* know, you thought, about families, about (yes) love. He'd left home the day he turned eighteen. He only called his mother on Mother's Day and, if he remembered, her birthday. When he told her about you she'd said, "How *nice*, dear. We really must have you both over to the house for dinner sometime soon."

Lately he has been angry a lot. "You're blaming me for this mess between your mother and yourself," he shouted the other day at dinner although you hadn't said anything. He shook his head. "You're driving yourself crazy. You need a shrink." He shoved back his plate and slammed out of the apartment again. The dry, scratchy voice pushing at your temples reminded you how he'd watched the red-haired waitress at the Mexican restaurant last week, how he was laughing, his hand on her shoulder, when you came out of the rest room. How, recently, there had been more late-night calls.

When he came back, very late, you were still sitting at

the table. Staring at the hanging. He took you by the arms and brought his face close to yours.

"Sweetheart," he said, "I want to help you but I don't know how. You've become obsessed with this thing. You're so depressed all the time I hardly know you anymore. So your mother is behaving irrationally. *You* can't afford to do the same."

You looked past his head. He has a sweet voice, you thought absently. A voice that charms. An actor's voice.

"You're not even listening," he said.

You tried because you knew he was trying, too. But later in bed, even with his lips pressing hot into you, a part of you kept counting the days. How many since you mailed the letter? He pulled away with an angry exclamation and turned the other way. You put out your hand to touch the nubs of his backbone. *I'm sorry*. But you went on thinking, something *must* be wrong. A reply should have reached you by now.

The letter came today. You walked out under a low, gray-bellied sky and there was the mail-woman, holding it up, smiling—the registered letter to your mother, with a red ink stamp across the address. *Not accepted. Return to sender.*

Now you are kneeling in the bathroom, rummaging in the cabinet behind the cleaning supplies. When you find the bottles, you line them up along the sink top. You open each one and look at the tablets: red, white, pink. You'd found them one day while cleaning. You remember how shocked you'd been, the argument the two of you'd had. He'd shrugged and spread his hands, palms up. You wish now you'd asked him which ones were the sleeping pills. No matter. You can take them all, if that's what you decide to do.

You'd held the letter in your hand a long time, until it grew weightless, transparent. You could see through it to another letter, one that wasn't written yet. His letter.

You knew what it would say.

Before he left for class this morning he had looked at you still crumpled on the sofa where you'd spent the night. He looked for a long time, as though he'd never really seen you before. Then he said, very softly, "It was never me, was it? Never love. It was always you and her, her and you."

He hadn't waited for an answer.

Wind slams a door somewhere, making you jump. It's raining outside, the first time in years. Big swollen drops, then thick silver sheets of it. You walk out to the balcony. The rain runs down your cheeks, the tears you couldn't shed. The nasturtiums, washed clean, are glowing red. Smell of wet earth. You take a deep breath, decide to go for a long walk.

As you walk you try to figure out what to do. (And maybe the meaning of what you have done.) The pills are there, of course. You picture it: the empty bottles by the bed, your body fallen across it, a hand flung over the side. The note left behind. Will he press repentant kisses on your pale palm? Will she fly across the ocean to wash your stiff eyelids with her tears?

Or—what? *what?* Surely there's another choice. But you can't find the words to give it shape. When you look down the empty street, the bright leaves of the newly-washed maples hurt your eyes.

So you continue to walk. Your shoes darken, grow heavy.

Water swirls in the gutters, carrying away months of dust. Coming toward you is a young woman with an umbrella. Shoulders bunched, she tiptoes through puddles, trying hard to stay dry. But a gust snaps the umbrella back and soaks her. She is shocked for a moment, angry. Then she begins to laugh. And you are laughing too, because you know just how it feels. Short, hysterical laugh-bursts, then quieter, drawing the breath deep into yourself. You watch as she stops in the middle of the sidewalk and tosses her ruined umbrella into a garbage can. She spreads her arms and lets the rain take her: hair, paisley blouse, midnight-blue skirt. Thunder and lightning. It's going to be quite a storm. You remember the monsoons of your childhood. There are no people in this memory, only the sky, rippling with exhilarating light.

You know then that when you return to the apartment you will pack your belongings. A few clothes, some music, a favorite book, the hanging. No, not that. You will not need it in your new life, the one you're going to live for yourself.

And a word comes to you out of the opening sky. The word *love*. You see that you had never understood it before. It is like rain, and when you lift your face to it, like rain it washes away inessentials, leaving you hollow, clean, ready to begin.

A PERFECT LIFE

Before the boy came, I had a good life. A beautiful apartment in the foothills with a view of the Golden Gate Bridge, an interesting job at the bank with colleagues I mostly liked, and, of course, my boyfriend Richard.

Richard was exactly the kind of man I'd dreamed about during my teenage years in Calcutta, all those moist, sticky evenings that I spent at the Empire Cinema House under a rickety ceiling fan that revolved tiredly, eating melted mango-pista ice cream and watching Gregory Peck and Warren Beatty and Clint Eastwood. Tall and lean and sophisticated, he was very different from the Indian men I'd known back home, and even the work he did as a marketing manager for a publishing company seemed unbelievably glamorous. When I was with Richard I felt like a true American. We'd go jogging every morning and hiking on the weekends, and in the evenings we'd take in an art film, or go out to a favorite restaurant, or discuss a recent novel as we sat out on my balcony and drank chilled wine and watched the sunset. And in bed we tried wild and wonderful things that would have left me speechless with shock in India had I been able to imagine them.

What I liked most about Richard was that he gave me *space*. I'd been afraid that after we slept together he'd either lose interest in me or start pressuring me to marry him. Or else I'd get pregnant. That was what always happened in India. (My knowledge of such things, of course, was limited to the romantic Hindi movies I'd seen. At home, we never discussed such things, and though my girlfriends in college gossiped avidly about them, they were just as protected as I from what our parents considered sordid reality.) But Richard continued to be passionate without getting possessive. He didn't mind if I went out with my other friends, or if work pressures kept us from seeing each other for days; when we met again, we slipped into our usual comfortable groove, as though we hadn't been apart at all. Thanks to the Pill and his easygoing attitude (it was a Californian thing, he told me once), for the first time in my life I felt free. It was an exhilarating sensation, once I got used to it. It made me giddy and weightless, like I could float away at any moment.

Eventually Richard and I planned to get married and have children, but neither of us was in a hurry. The households of friends who had babies seemed to me a constant flurry of crying and feeding and burping and throwing up, quilts taped over fireplace bricks for padding and knickknacks crammed onto the top shelf out of the reach of destructive little hands. And over everything hung the oppressive stench (there was no other word for it) of baby wipes and Lysol spray and soiled diapers.

I guessed, of course, that there was more to child-rearing than that. Mother-love, for instance. I'd felt the flaming rush of it when I'd gone to the maternity ward to visit Sharmila, who'd been my best friend at work before she quit (abandoned me, I claimed) to have a baby.

Sharmila had pressed her cheek to the baby's wrinkled one, to that skin translucent and delicate like expensive onion-skin paper, and looked at me with eyes that shone in spite of the hollows gouged under them. "I'd never have thought I could love anyone so much, so instantly, Meera," she'd whispered. And this from a woman who'd always agreed that the world already had too many people in it for us to add to the problem! So I knew mother-love was real. Real and primitive and dangerous, lurking somewhere in the female genes—especially our Indian ones—waiting to attack. I was determined to watch out for it.

Many of my women friends considered me strange. The Americans were more circumspect, but the Indian women came right out and asked. *Don't you mind not being married? Don't you miss having a little one to scramble onto your lap when you come home at the end of the day?* I'd look at their limp hair pulled into an unattractive bun, their crumpled saris sporting stains of a suspicious nature, the bulge of love handles that hung below the edges of their blouses. (Even the ones who made an effort to hang on to their looks seemed intellectually diminished, their conversations limited to discussions of colic and teething pains and Dr. Spock's views on bed-wetting.) They looked just like my cousins back home who were already on their second and third and sometimes fourth babies. They might as well have not come to America.

"No," I would tell them, smoothing my silk Yves St. Laurent jersey over my own gratifyingly slim hips. "Most emphatically no."

But I could see they didn't believe me.

Nor did my mother, who had for years been trying to arrange my marriage with a nice Indian boy. Every month she sent me photos of eligible young men, nephews and second cousins of friends and neighbors, earnest, mustachioed men in stiff-collared shirts with slicked-back Brylcreem hair. She accompanied these photographs with warnings (I wasn't getting any younger; soon I'd be thirty and then who would want me?) and laments (look at Roma-auntie, her daughter was expecting her third, while thanks to me, *she* remained deprived of grandchildren). When I wrote back that I wasn't ready to settle down (I didn't say anything about Richard, which would have upset her even more), she decried my crazy western notions. "I should never have given in and allowed you to go to America," she wrote, underlining the *never* in emphatic red.

In spite of the brief twinge of guilt I felt when yet another fat packet with a Calcutta postmark arrived from my mother, I knew I was right. Because in Indian marriages becoming a wife was only the prelude to that all-important, all-consuming event—becoming a mother. That wasn't why I'd fought so hard—with my mother to leave India; with my professors to make it through graduate school; with my bosses to establish my career. Not that I was against marriage—or even against having a child. I just wanted to make sure that when it happened, it would be on my own terms, because *I* wanted it.

Meanwhile I heaved a sigh of relief whenever I came away from the baby-houses (that's how I thought of them, homes ruled by tiny red-faced tyrants with enormous lung power). Back in my own cool, clean living room I would put on a Ravi Shankar record or maybe a Chopin nocturne, change into the blue silk kimono that Richard had given me, and curl up on my fawn buffed-leather sofa. As the soothing strains of sitar or piano washed over me, I would close my eyes and think of what we'd planned for that evening, Richard and I. And I would thank God for my life, which was as civilized, as much in control, as *perfect*, as a life could ever be.

The boy changed all that.

He was crouched under the stairwell when I found him, on my way out of the building for my regular 6 A.M. jog around the rose gardens with Richard. I would have missed him completely had he not coughed just as I reached the door. He had wedged himself into the far end of the dark triangular recess, so that all I saw at first was a small, huddled shape and the glint of terrified eyes. And thought, *Wild animal*. Later I would wonder how *I* must have appeared to him, a large, loud, bent-over figure in pink sweats with hair swinging wildly about her face, ordering him to *come out of there right now,* demanding *where did you come from* and *how did you get past the security door.* Only probably he didn't understand a word.

By the time I got him out, my Liz Claiborne suit was ruined, my cheek stung where he had scratched me, and my watch said 6:20. *Richard*, I thought with dismay, because he didn't like to be kept waiting. Then the boy claimed my attention again.

He looked about seven, though he could have been older. He was so thin it was hard to tell. His collarbones stuck out from under his filthy shirt, and in the hollow between them I could see a pulse beating frantically. Ragged black hair fell into eyes that stared at me unblinkingly. He didn't seem to comprehend anything I said, not even when I switched to halting Spanish, and when I leaned forward, he flinched and flung up a thin brown arm to protect his face.

What am I going to do with him, I wondered desperately. It was getting late. I'd already missed my morning jog, and if I didn't get back to my apartment pretty soon, I wouldn't have time for my sit-ups either. Then I had to wash my hair—there was a big meeting at the bank, and I was scheduled to make the opening presentation. I hadn't figured out what kind of power-outfit to wear, either. I closed my eyes and hoped the boy would just disappear the way he had appeared, but when I opened them, he was there still, watching me warily.

I unlocked my apartment door but didn't enter right away. I was afraid of what I might find. Then I said to myself, *How could it be any worse?* I'd been late to work (a first). I'd run into the meeting room, out of breath, my unwashed hair falling into my eyes, my spreadsheets all out of order. My presentation had been second-rate at best (another first), and when Dan Luftner, Head of Loans, who'd been waiting for years to catch me out, asked me for an update on the monthly statements software the bank had purchased a while back, I'd been unable to give him an adequate answer. "Why, Meera," he'd said, raising his eyebrows in mock surprise, "I thought you knew *everything!*" I smarted all morning at the memory of the triumph in his eyes, and when a customer asked a particularly stupid question, I snapped at him. "Are you feeling all right, Meera?" said my supervisor, who had overheard. "Maybe you should take the rest of the day off." So here I was in the middle of the afternoon, with the mother of all headaches pounding its way across my skull.

I'm going to spend the rest of the day in bed, I decided, with the curtains drawn, the phone off the hook, a handkerchief soaked in eau de cologne on my forehead, and strict instructions to the boy to not disturb me. When my headache gets better, I'm going to listen to the new Dvorak record which Richard gave me for Valentine's day. Everything else— including calling Richard to explain why I hadn't shown up— I'll handle later.

As soon as I opened the door I was struck by the smell. It was worse than ten baby-houses put together. I followed my nose to the bathroom. There was pee all over the floor, a big yellow puddle, with blobs of brown floating in it.

I went into the kitchen, took two aspirin, then another one. I grabbed the mop and bucket and a bottle of Pine Sol and went looking for the boy, rehearsing all the things I was going to tell him. *You little savage, didn't I explain to you how to use the toilet before I left, at least ten times, in clear sign language? That's what made me late this morning, messed up my presentation. If I don't get chosen as employee of the month like I was the last three times, it's going to be all your fault.* I was going to make him clean up the bathroom as well. But first I was going to shake him until his teeth rattled in his stupid head.

"You should have turned him over to the super that same morning," Richard would tell me later. "You should never have brought him into your apartment at all. I can't figure out why you did it—it isn't like you at all."

Richard was right, of course, on both counts. I've never been given to the easy sentimentality of taking in strays—I know my own fastidiousness, the limits to my patience. The first thought I'd had when I saw the boy was that I should call the super. Mr. Leroy, a large, not unkind man with children of his own, would have known what to do with the boy. Better than I did, certainly.

So why didn't I make that call? Did my decision have something to do with the boy's enormous eyes, the way he fixed them on my face? The way his thin shoulders had trembled, there, under the staircase, when I touched them? Did a part of me, that treacherous Indian side that believed in the workings of karma, feel that the universe had brought him to my door for a special reason? I'm not sure. But even now, as I searched the apartment angrily, I knew I couldn't send him away.

I finally found him behind the drapes in the bedroom.

He shrank against the wall when he saw me. I could hear the hiss of his indrawn breath, see his shoulders stiffen. He made a small moaning sound that seemed to go on and on.

"Oh shit." I gave a short laugh as the appropriateness of my expression struck me. "Don't look so scared, for God's sake. Just don't do it again, OK? And now I guess you'd better take a bath."

"Sharmila," I said on the phone, "what's a good place to buy clothes for kids?"

"Why d'you want to know? You planning to have one?"

"Very funny. Actually, my brother's son is visiting, and . . ." My voice trailed away guiltily. I'd never lied to Sharmila before. But the boy was my special secret. I wasn't ready to share him with anyone yet.

"Your brother! Didn't you tell me once you were an only child?"

"Did I? Maybe I'd just had a fight with him or something."

"Hmm," said Sharmila, obviously unconvinced. "Well, how old is the boy? Some stores are better for babies, and others . . ."

"He looks like he's about seven . . ."

"*Looks like?* You don't know your own nephew's age?"

"So I'm not as close to my family as you are, Madam Perfect," I shouted. "I'm sorry I asked." I slammed down the phone, then took it off the hook. Sharmila would surely call back to find out why I, who never got upset, not even the time when the bank computer suddenly swallowed the information on five hundred and sixty-three accounts, was behaving so strangely. She might even decide to drive over. And I was afraid of what she would say when she found out about the boy.

I looked over to the kitchen table and met the boy's worried eyes. "It's OK," I said. "I'm not mad at you." I smiled at him until the frown line between his brows faded. I was pleased to see that he'd eaten most of the large egg sandwich I'd fixed him and that he'd drunk all his milk. He looked a lot better after his bath, with his hair all shiny and his face clean, and weren't the circles under his eyes a little lighter?

The bath had been difficult. He wouldn't go into the tub by himself, so I had to make him. "I'm not going to hurt you," I kept saying. Still, when I took off his shirt, he struggled and trembled, with that same moaning sound, holding on to his tattered pants until I said, "OK, OK, keep them on." I put him in the tub and started soaping him, and that's when I felt them, the puckers of old burns along his back. *Cigarettes?* *Who?* I tried to imagine someone—a man? a *woman?*—holding him down, his body trembling like a caught bird's under the enormous press of that adult arm, the burning butt jabbed into his back over and over until he stopped making even that thin, whimpering sound. Then I was crying, holding him tight and crying, the lukewarm sudsy water soaking my white Givenchy blouse that I'd forgotten to change out of, and I didn't even care.

We'd made it through the bath somehow, and now he was dressed in a pair of my cutoffs tied around his middle with my kimono belt and an aquamarine Moschino shirt that hung almost to his knees. On his feet he wore my old Hawaiian sandals.

"What the heck," I said, forcing a smile onto my face. "There's a lot of folks out there dressed more weirdly than you. Let's go shopping. Ever heard of Macy's, kid?"

But all the while I was thinking, *Could it have been someone in his family? Could it have been his father? Could it —God help us all—have been his mother?*

When the doorbell rang with the two impatient double buzzes I knew to be Sharmila's, I was fixing lunch: peanut butter and jelly sandwiches and alphabet soup. I didn't know if the boy knew his ABCs yet, or if he cared for peanut butter, but generations of children on TV shows seemed to thrive on them, so they couldn't be too bad. I wondered if I could get away with not answering, but now Sharmila was pounding on the door.

"Nothing to worry," I told the boy, who'd jumped up from his chair and backed into the corner by the refrigerator. "You get started on the soup while it's hot."

"Knew you were in here," said Sharmila, pushing past me. She seemed to be carrying an entire household on her back, but on a closer look I saw it was only the baby, wrapped in a quilt and positioned inside some kind of sack that seemed to double as a diaper bag as well. "I knew something was really wrong when I called the bank and they said you'd taken a day off. You *never* take a day off."

I mumbled something about having accumulated a lot of vacation time.

"Right," said Sharmila. "And I was born yesterday.

Here, help me get this damn thing off. I swear it weighs a ton. No, Mummy's not complaining about you, *raja beta,* just your baggage." This last was to the baby, who looked like he was getting ready to scream. But before he could, Sharmila adroitly popped a pacifier into his mouth and turned toward the kitchen. "So this is the young man," she said.

"His name is Krishna," I said, struck by a happy inspiration. I needed to give him a name anyway (he didn't seem to have one), and that of a demon-destroying god who was raised by a foster mother seemed a good choice. This way, his friends at school could call him Kris.

"For heaven's sake, Meera, the boy doesn't even look Indian. Now tell me the whole story and don't you dare leave anything out."

By the time I finished, the shadows from the pepper tree outside slanted across the room. Sharmila wiped at her eyes. She picked up her baby and held him close for a long moment. The baby gurgled with laughter and Krishna, who'd been hovering around him all afternoon, reached out to touch his chubby hand. The baby grabbed his finger. Krishna, too, was laughing now—for the first time, I told Sharmila.

"Maybe he used to have a little brother or sister, poor kid," said Sharmila, watching him play with her son. Then she turned to me. "I know how you feel, Meera, but you can't just *keep* him. . . ."

"Why not?" I said, talking fast. I didn't want to hear what was coming next. I was afraid her words would echo the objections I'd kept pushing to the back of my own mind. "I can give him a good home. I can . . ."

"What if he's lost? Maybe his family's looking for him right now. . . ."

I felt a pang of guilt. Then I shrugged it off resolutely. Angrily. *So what if they were*, I thought, remembering the burn marks. But I only said, "He looked like he'd been on his own a long time."

"Even then, sooner or later he'll have to go to school, and then you'll need a birth certificate, a social security number, something to show that you're his guardian. . . ."

"What if I move someplace where no one knows us? What if I say I lost all our papers in a fire?"

"Meera," Sharmila said patiently, "you know that won't work. Maybe it would have in India, but not here, where everyone keeps records—hospitals, doctors. No, you've got to do it the legal way."

"Adoption! That's out of the question!" exclaimed Richard, so sharply that heads turned toward our table.

I pushed away my half-eaten dinner, although it was grilled salmon with a light almond sauce on the side, which I particularly like.

"Why? Why is it out of the question?" My voice was sharp, too—mostly to hide my dismay. There was a cold, leaden heaviness in the pit of my stomach. I'd expected some arguments, but I hadn't thought Richard would be so strongly opposed to my plan. In fact, I'd hoped he'd help me iron out the details, once we'd talked things over. I was shaken by how disapproving his voice sounded, how final and filled with distaste. And he hadn't even met Krishna.

We were dining at Le Gourmand, which is a bit too fancy for me with its French menu (they'll give you one in English if you ask, but grudgingly), its napkins edged with real lace (Belgian, Richard tells me), and an intimidating array of monogrammed silverware (there were four forks by my plate, not to count knives and spoons). But Richard really enjoys this kind of thing. And since I wanted to put him in a good mood, I'd invited him here.

So far the evening wasn't going well at all.

"Stupid. You did a stupid thing, Meera, bringing him into the apartment," Richard had said when I told him about Krishna. His tone made me bristle right away. No man was going to call me stupid and get away with it. And he sounded so *avuncular*, so I-know-it-all. So unlike himself. *Or was this*, an insidious voice inside me asked, *the real Richard?*

"Stupid and dangerous," he was saying now. "I can't believe you've kept him for over a week. You could get into a lot of trouble with the law. They could bring all kinds of charges against you—kidnapping, child abuse. . . ."

"And since when do you know so much about the law, Mr. Perry Mason?" I broke in. The bit about child abuse had brought back too vividly the feel of those puckered scars under my fingers. I made my voice hard because I didn't want to cry in front of Richard. "Or have you had personal experience with the charges you just mentioned?"

I guess I didn't sound like myself either, because Richard's mouth opened in a brief o that made him look astonished and indignant at the same time. I could feel hysterical laughter gathering itself inside me. We were about to have our first fight. I was surprised to find that I was almost looking forward to it.

But of course Richard is too civilized to fight. After a moment he said, his voice carefully controlled, "I can see you're too emotional to think clearly. But this can't go on. For one thing, how long can you keep him holed up in your apartment?"

I thought about it. Krishna and I had established a good routine. We ate breakfast together in the mornings and watched the news. While I was at work, he amused himself by looking through the pictures in the books I brought for him from the library. When I got back from work, we usually went to the park (we'd bought ourselves a kite) or the library, or sometimes rented a video—he liked movies about animals. After dinner we'd sit together on the couch and watch it and talk about the more exciting scenes. Actually, I was the one who did all the talking. I still hadn't got him to say anything. He wouldn't even nod or shake his head in a yes or no. But I was sure he understood everything I said. He knew the house rules and followed them carefully: no going out on the balcony where someone could see him, no opening drawers in my bedroom, no answering the door. He had learned to use the microwave oven and the bathroom, and to make himself (and me, whenever I managed to rush home for a quick lunch) sandwiches slathered with peanut butter and jelly. And at night when I fixed dinner he liked to be near me, doing little things: breaking up the spaghetti, washing the spinach leaves, slicing the salad tomatoes into neat rounds that hinted at previous experience. Perhaps he had been used to helping his mother.

His mother.

I'd made myself decide he didn't have a mother, for surely she would have stood between him and that burning cigarette, as mothers are supposed to. But she appeared in my dreams almost every night, weeping as she looked around, bewildered, for her son. Sometimes her eyes would meet mine, accusing. I would stare back defiantly. *You should have been more careful,* I'd tell her. *You shouldn't have lost him.*

"I can keep him holed up for a long time if I need to," I told Richard, though even then I must have known it wasn't possible. I lifted my chin. "And now I'd like to go home. I don't like to leave Krishna alone this late at night."

I heard the patter of his feet even before I turned the key, and when I opened the apartment door, he was waiting. He took my hand and pulled me to the couch and put into my hands the book we'd been reading earlier. When I'd picked up the book, a simple story about a mouse family that lived in a vegetable garden, I'd been afraid it would be too childish for Krishna, but he loved it. He'd sit for long minutes tracing the bright vegetables with his finger—eggplant, zucchini, beans, lettuce—as though he knew the feel of them intimately. And when we came to the part where Baby Mouse wanders off and gets lost and doesn't hear her parents calling for her, his entire body would grow still with tense attention.

We settled ourselves on the couch, Krishna leaning over the book so he could turn the pages for me. (Somehow he knew just when to do it, though I was pretty sure he couldn't read.) Usually I enjoyed reading to him, but tonight I found it hard to concentrate. I kept thinking of what Richard had said when he dropped me off.

He'd offered to accompany me upstairs, and when I'd refused (somehow I couldn't stand the thought of his eyes, cool and critical, traveling up and down Krishna), he'd gripped my shoulders and pulled me to face him. "You're obsessed with this boy, Meera," he'd said. In the flickering light of the street lamp I could see the lines around his mouth, sharp and deep like cracks in porcelain, before he bent to kiss me hard on the lips. The violent press of his mouth against mine, so unlike his usual suave embraces, startled me. Was he jealous? Was he, perhaps, not that different after all from the heroes of the Hindi screen whom I'd left behind in Calcutta?

"Maybe what you need is a child of your own," he said, trying to kiss me again.

I thought of Krishna waiting upstairs. The way a faint line would appear between his brows when he concentrated on something I was saying. "Maybe what I need is to not see you for a while," I'd snapped, pushing Richard away.

But what he said had struck deep.

Sitting on the sofa now, I tried to imagine it. My child— and Richard's, for that was what he meant. But somehow I just couldn't picture it. The details confused me. Would the baby have a thick dark mop of hair, like Indian babies do? Or would it be pink and bald, like American babies? What color would its eyes be? I couldn't picture Richard in the role of father either, hitching up his Armani pants to kneel on the floor and change diapers, walking up and down at 2 A.M. trying to quieten a colicky baby who burped all over his satin Bill Blass dressing gown.

It was much easier to picture Krishna. He is running in the park. While I cheer, he pulls the kite up in a tight purple arc until it hangs high above his head, as graceful as any bird. On the first day of school, I drop him off at the gate, hand him his lunch money with a kiss, watch him follow the other kids in. He turns at the door to offer me a tremulous smile and a wave, scared but determined to be brave. At Disneyland, we scream with delicious terror as the roller-coaster car plunges down, down, down, faster than we ever imagined anything could ever be. At baseball games I clap for him till my palms are sore. I take him to buy his first car. I help him to fill out his college applications. Late in the night we sit as we're doing right now and talk about life and death and girls and rock music or whatever else it is that mothers and sons talk about. There is no Richard in these pictures, and (I feel only a moment's guilt as I think this) no need of him.

Krishna was looking at me inquiringly. Glancing down, I saw we'd reached the end of the book—probably several minutes back.

"It's time for bed, young man," I said. When I leaned over to give him a hug, his skin smelled of my jasmine soap. It pleased me that he no longer flinched away from me, not even when, after his bath every morning, I rubbed face cream on his scars. (They were probably too old for it to do any good, but it made me feel better.) And now, though he didn't hug me back, he did tilt his cheek toward me for his customary goodnight kiss.

A Perfect Life

As I watched him bring over his sheets and blankets (all carefully folded—he was a neat boy) to the sofa where he slept, I noticed that he'd put on a few pounds. It made me ridiculously happy, more than the time, even, when I straightened out the Von Hausen account which had been missing several million dollars. He was getting taller, too. Or maybe it was just the way he walked nowadays, shoulders pushed back, head up high.

Tomorrow, I promised myself as I helped him with the sheets. Tomorrow I would start making discreet inquiries into the California adoption laws.

Sitting across the desk from Ms. Mayhew while she went through my papers one more time, I was struck again by how cheerful the Foster Homes office was. I'd expected something drab and regulation gray, with lots of metal furniture. Instead, the room was bright with hangings and rugs, and through the big window the afternoon sun lit up the play corner, which was comfortably crowded with stuffed animals and bean bags and big, colorful blocks. They had books too, even the one about the mouse family that Krishna loved. I wondered if I could take that to be a good omen.

Ms. Mayhew herself was quite different from the witchlike figure I'd conjured up, complete with horn-rimmed glasses, a thin pointy nose, and gray hair pulled into a tight, unforgiving bun. She did wear glasses, but they had thin gold rims that gave her a rather thoughtful look, and her short, fashionably bobbed hair curled attractively around her face.

She was pleasant in a businesslike way—no wasting time or getting around rules with her—which I appreciated because that's how I too was at the bank. When the county office I'd called referred me to her, she had explained that adoption was a lengthy and complicated process, but the State of California was always looking for responsible foster parents. It would be a good thing for me to try while I figured out if adoption was really for me.

Though I had no doubts about that issue, I agreed. It was the best way of keeping Krishna with me legally until the adoption could be arranged.

Surprisingly, Richard too liked the idea. I suspected that deep down he was hoping that the novelty of having a child in the house would wear out for me long before the adoption papers came through. I knew better, of course, but I didn't want to argue. Richard had been making a real effort to be nice. When I finally invited him over to meet Krishna (I was still reluctant, but I figured I had to do it some time), he'd brought him a baseball and a catcher's mitt. When Krishna refused to come out from behind the curtain where he'd hidden himself at the first sound of a male voice, he said he understood. He even offered to take him to the park to practice "once we get a bit more used to each other." I appreciated that. It didn't make me change the pictures in my head, which were still just of me and Krishna, but I started going out with Richard again.

"Well, Ms. Bose"—Ms. Mayhew was looking up with a smile—"your papers look good so far. The recommendation letters are all very positive, your fingerprints indicate you've lived a crime-free life, and I see from the social worker's home visit that you've child-proofed your apartment as required and are changing the study into an extra bedroom. Just one more week of the parenting class you're attending, and you'll be ready to be a foster mother. So now it's time for us to discuss further the kind of child you want to take in."

This part was going to be tricky. I had to say it just right.

"In your papers," Ms. Mayhew continued, "you mentioned that you wanted a boy of about seven or eight—which is a good idea since you have a full-time job. But you didn't mention ethnicity—or doesn't it matter?"

"Actually, you don't need to look for a child for me. I have one in mind already."

Ms. Mayhew's brows drew together. I'd deviated from regulations. "Where is he staying now? With relatives?"

I swallowed. "He's staying with me."

"And are you related to him?"

"No." Seeing the look on her face, I hurried to explain Krishna's situation. "I knew I probably should have turned him in," I ended, "but he was so small and so scared. . . ." Even to my own ears, my reasoning sounded weak and sentimental.

"Where was he when the social worker came to check your apartment?"

"With friends," I said guiltily. I'd deposited him at Sharmila's early that morning, not wanting to take a chance.

Ms. Mayhew was shaking her head. "What you've done is quite illegal, Ms. Bose, even though your motives may have been altruistic. I'm afraid we must ask you to bring the child in at once. We need to make every effort to locate his parents. . . ."

I wanted to tell her about the burns, but I didn't. *Later*, I thought. It would be my weapon if she really did find them.

"If they can't be located, we'll try to place him with you once you become a registered foster parent. But for now he must stay with someone else."

"It's just a week." I leaned forward, gripping the edge of her desk. "Can't you make an exception, please, just for one week? He's doing so well with me. He'll be terrified if he's moved to a strange place. . . ."

"I'm sorry. I have to follow certain rules, and this is a very important one. Actually, what you've done is quite serious. It could even prevent you from becoming a foster parent."

The edges of the room turned black.

"But I'll put a note into your file saying that you acted out of ignorance and in good faith," said Ms. Mayhew, not unkindly. "That's the best I can do."

I knew it was no use arguing any further. I answered the questions she asked me about Krishna's background the best I could, and then I said, "I'll bring him in tomorrow." I looked at her and added, "Please?"

For a moment I was afraid that Ms. Mayhew was going to insist that I bring Krishna in that very afternoon. Then she glanced at her watch and gave a sigh. "Oh, OK," she said, "since it's after three already. But mind you, be here at 9 A.M. sharp tomorrow, as soon as the office opens."

94

"Sharmila, what am I going to *do*?" I tried to keep my voice calm and low, not wanting to frighten Krishna, who was building a Lego tower in the corner. But his head jerked up sharply.

"I don't see that you have a choice. You've got to take him in tomorrow." Sharmila's voice over the phone line was sympathetic but firm. "You'll get in a lot more trouble if you don't."

"I shouldn't even have started this whole process. I should have just taken Krishna and gone back to India. . . ."

"Meera!"

"I was a fool to tell her about him! I should have just pretended I wanted them to find me a child, at least until I got the license. . . ."

"And then what? Call and say, 'Oh, by the way, guess who turned up in my apartment yesterday?' That would never have worked, Meera. They would have seen through it right away. I think telling the truth was for the best. And this Mayhew woman seems quite positively inclined toward you. . . ."

"How can you *say* that? She's the one who insists that I have to turn him over. . . ." Though I'd avoided using Krishna's name, he made a sudden movement. The Lego tower fell over with a crash. On Sharmila's end I could hear her baby crying, and I wondered if he had picked up on the tension as well.

"She's just doing her job. If you were in her place, you'd probably have done the same."

"Never," I said hotly, but I knew Sharmila was right.

"I'm sorry, Meera, I've got to go. Baby's screaming his

head off in his crib. He's been real cranky all day. I don't know what's wrong." Sharmila sounded anxious.

I felt guilty. I'd heaped all my troubles on her without even asking about her son. "You go take care of him. I'll be all right."

"Don't worry too much. It's only a week, after all. Explain to Krishna—he's a smart boy, he'll understand. Listen, I'll come with you tomorrow if you want."

"Would you?" I said gratefully. "That would make me feel so much better." I dreaded, most of all, the ride back alone, the stepping into my empty apartment.

The crying in the background had given place to angry shrieks. "Sure thing!" said Sharmila hurriedly as she hung up. "See you in the morning!"

That night I cooked Krishna's favorite dish, spicy fried chicken served over hot rice. It was one of my favorites, too, but I couldn't eat more than a few mouthfuls. A feeling of dread pressed down on me, and though I told myself I was being foolish, I couldn't shake it off.

After dinner was our regular reading time. But when Krishna brought the mouse book over to the sofa, I took a deep breath and shook my head.

"I have something to tell you first," I said.

When I explained to him where we had to go in the morning, and why, the blank expression on his face didn't change. When I told him that he must have faith in me, that I'd do my best to get him back as soon as I could, he waited politely, and when he was sure that I was done, he put the book in my lap.

As I read to him about how Baby Mouse's parents find her again, I wasn't sure what I felt more deeply, relief or hurt. Had Krishna not understood me? Was he autistic? (Richard had suggested that once, and I had denied it hotly.) Or did he just not care?

That night I couldn't sleep. I lay there watching the shadows thrown onto my wall by the street lamp outside, thinking how strange the nature of love is and how strangely it transforms people. The street noises quietened. The shadows shivered on the wall and across the vast white expanse of my bed, making me shiver too. Then I noticed that another shadow had joined them.

It was Krishna, his pillow tucked under his arm, his face as unreadable as ever.

"Can't you sleep either?" I asked.

He said nothing, of course.

"Oh well," I said, raising the corner of my blanket even though I knew that this was probably the number one taboo in Ms. Mayhew's book, "climb in."

He settled himself with his back toward me, the mattress hardly dimpling under him, he was still that thin. I touched his hair with a light finger and tried to think of something that would comfort him, maybe one of the lullabyes that my mother had sung for me when I was little, an impossibly long time ago. But I had forgotten them all. The only thing I remembered was how my mother had held me. And so I tried to do the same for Krishna, looping an arm over his body, not with my mother's easy confidence but hesitantly, fearfully, as though he might break. That's how I lay all night as his breathing deepened and his body slumped against mine in trustful sleep, his scarred spine pressed to my chest, his skin giving off the mingled odor of jasmine and spicy chicken.

The phone jangled me out of a sleep I must have just fallen into. My eyes burned with tiredness, and my body ached as though I were coming down with something. Still, as I groped for the phone, I noticed how in his sleep Krishna had moved until his head was snuggled under my chin, and how right it felt.

"Meera." Sharmila's voice sounded like she too hadn't had much sleep. "It's my baby. He cried all night. I've given him his gas medicine and his gripe water and even some baby Tylenol, but none of it seems to do any good. And now he's throwing up. I've got to rush him to the clinic."

I wanted to say something to express my concern, but all I could manage was a "Yes, of course you must."

"Meera, wake up! This means I can't go with you to the Foster Homes office."

Remembrance struck like a stone between my eyes.

"Oh God," I said. I wanted to crawl back into bed and pull the covers up over myself and Krishna. Forever.

"I'm really sorry to let you down," said Sharmila. "But I have no choice."

I wanted to tell her that I understood perfectly. The needs of children came before the needs of adults, I had learned that already. Mother-love, that tidal wave, swept everything else away. Friendship. Romantic fulfillment. Even the need for sex.

"Meera, are you listening? I don't want you to have to go there alone. Will you call Richard, please? See if he can go with you."

"OK," I said, partly because Sharmila sounded so distressed, and partly because I was still dazed. When she hung up after having made me promise once again, I obediently dialed Richard's number.

"In a few minutes I'd like to introduce you to Mrs. Amelia Ortiz," said Ms. Mayhew, smiling. In a warm brown skirt and matching jacket, she looked both efficient and charming. I felt neither and didn't smile back. But Richard, who was sitting next to me holding my hand, did.

"We tried to find someone quickly so that the child wouldn't have to go into the Children's Shelter, which isn't the most pleasant experience, and she was kind enough to agree at such short notice."

"I'm sure Meera and little Krishna appreciate that," said Richard, squeezing my hand.

I wanted to snatch my hand away and inform him that I was quite capable of voicing my own opinions, thank you. But I knew I needed to save all my emotional energy. At the sound of his name, Krishna had looked up, his eyes moving from face to adult face till they came to rest on mine. He didn't look particularly anxious, but he clutched tightly at my other hand and pushed in closer to my chair.

"I can tell the little boy is very attached to you," said Ms.

99

Mayhew. "I'll make every attempt to place him back with you as soon as it's legally possible. Meanwhile Mrs. Ortiz—here she is—will take good care of him."

I swung around to face Mrs. Amelia Ortiz, a plump, middle-aged woman in a floral print dress who was dabbing at her face with a handkerchief. "Sorry to be late. The traffic was worse than I expected," she said in a pleasant, slightly out-of-breath voice and held out her hand to me with a smile. She looked kind and wholesome and motherly, and I hated her.

"I think the boy will feel quite at home with Mrs. Ortiz, who has two children herself. However, I must ask you not to contact him while he is with her—it'll only agitate him. By the way, Mrs. Ortiz speaks Spanish, which I thought would help in case that is his native language."

"Isn't that nice," said Richard.

"*Hola, mi pequenito,*" said Mrs. Ortiz, bending down to Krishna. But when he shrank toward me, she moved back right away. "No rush," she said.

My antagonism lessened a little. "His name is Krishna," I told her. "You can call him Kris."

Mrs. Ortiz nodded at me. "I will."

"He likes books, especially that one there about the mouse family."

Mrs. Ortiz picked up the book and held it out. "Chris, would you like me to read you this book?"

Krishna looked uncertain.

I gave him a little push. "Go on," I said, and he moved hesitantly toward her.

"Well!" Richard stood up. "It looks like everything is

settled for now. Meera and I had better get back to our work. . . ."

He held out his hand to me. I had to stand up too, although I wasn't quite ready to leave.

"His clothes are in this bag—I packed enough for the week. His favorite T-shirt is the red Mickey Mouse one. And for dinner he likes to eat . . ." My voice wobbled.

"Don't worry about Chris," said Mrs. Ortiz with a sympathetic smile. "He'll be OK."

I picked up my purse. There seemed nothing left for me to do. "Goodbye, Krishna," I said and started toward the door. "I'll see you soon."

Krishna pushed past Mrs. Ortiz and launched himself at my knees. He grabbed them and held on tight.

"This is often the hardest part," said Ms. Mayhew as she and Mrs. Ortiz tried to pull him loose. "You probably won't believe it, but they often calm down right after you leave."

Krishna clung to me with unexpected tenacity. I knew I should be trying to help the women, at least by saying the right things—*Be a good boy and go with the nice lady, it's only for a little while*—but it was as though my tongue were frozen right down to its root. It was all I could do not to cling on to him too.

"This is ridiculous," Richard said after he had watched us for a few minutes. Bending, he pried Krishna's fingers loose. Ignoring the kicks Krishna aimed at his shins and deftly avoiding his bared teeth, he handed him over to the two women. While he struggled fiercely—like he had with me that first day which seemed so long ago now—Richard grabbed my elbow and pulled me toward the door.

"Mama!" Krishna cried out then. "Mama!"

I whirled around. Tears were streaming down his face. "Mama-mama-mama," he called, his voice as high and sweet as I had imagined it would be, the words pouring out as though a stopper had been removed from his throat.

"He's never spoken before," I said. No one seemed to have heard me.

"Ms. Bose, you're making things harder by staying," said Ms. Mayhew, her glasses accusingly askew.

"Please, yes, do leave," said Mrs. Ortiz, red-faced and breathing hard.

"I've got to go to Krishna one last time," I said, trying to pull away from Richard. I don't know what I had in mind—a last hug, a final kiss, some word of reassurance that would keep him safe till I saw him again. But Richard wouldn't let go.

"Take him away," he shouted to the women, and as they dragged Krishna, crying and kicking, into another room, he pushed me—also struggling—out the door and into his car.

"Phew," he said once we were in the car. "That kid's worse than a wild animal!" He fingered the torn cuff of his shirt and shook his head in a way that made me want to rip the entire sleeve off.

"I'll never forgive you for this," I said. I clenched my hands but the trembling in them wouldn't stop. "You kept me from going to my baby when he needed me most."

"For heaven's sake, Meera, don't exaggerate. He's not your baby. And besides, it's better for him that we cut the parting short."

A Perfect Life

"You don't know anything," I said. Suddenly I felt very tired. Old. An old woman. Unmarried, childless, a failure. There was a name for such women in India, *banja*, empty. I put my face in my hands and let the sounds of Richard's voice flow over me until they faded away.

For the next three days, carefully, correctly, I did all the things I was supposed to. I went to the bank, where I completed installing a new software program on the teller machines. In the study, now converted into a boy's bedroom, I arranged Krishna's books on the shelves and put up posters of animals. (There were no mouse posters available, so I had to make do with wide-eyed puppies and cats peeping from baskets.) I went to visit Sharmila, whose baby was now doing much better, though she was still too exhausted to ask me her usual sharp questions. I attended my last parenting class and received my certificate from the smiling instructor, who congratulated me on a job well done. I didn't call Amelia Ortiz, not even once, though several times each day I looked at her number in the phone book.

On the fourth day when I came back from my solitary morning jog, the red cyclops eye on the answering machine was blinking ominously. I turned the machine on with unsteady fingers, telling myself that it was stupid to get so nervous, it could be anyone, Sharmila, or perhaps Richard—he'd been leaving a lot of messages on my machine lately. But of course it wasn't.

Please come over to the office at 9 A.M., said the message.

103

I replayed it several times, trying to read the terse inflections of Ms. Mayhew's voice. Her tone didn't give much away, but I knew it was bad news, something really serious.

Krishna, I whispered. The word was a dull, dead sound in my mouth.

"I just went in for a moment," Amelia Ortiz was telling us, "just for a moment to answer the phone, and when I came back out into the backyard where he'd been helping me with the weeding, he was gone." She wiped at her tear-streaked face with a balled-up Kleenex. "At first I thought he must be in the house—the gate was still latched. But he wasn't. He must have climbed over the wall or something."

I sat in front of Ms. Mayhew's meticulous desk, stupidly silent. I kept waiting for the anger to hit me, but I felt nothing.

"Of course Mrs. Ortiz called the police right away, but they couldn't find him. They're going to keep searching for the next few days." Behind her glasses, Ms. Mayhew's eyes looked tired. "I thought I should let you know."

"Six years I've been a foster mother, this never happened to me," said Mrs. Ortiz. "And he was so good too, so quiet and neat and obedient, who would have thought . . ."

From outside the window, an eucalyptus tree that surely hadn't been here the last time was throwing an intricate pattern of light and shadow onto Ms. Mayhew's desk, onto the solid brass plaque bearing her name. The plaque, I noticed, sat at a crooked angle. I felt a crazy impulse to reach out and straighten it.

A Perfect Life

"Ms. Bose, are you feeling OK?" Ms. Mayhew leaned across the desk to touch my hand.

The feel of her fingers, warm and moist on my cold, cold hand, shattered the numbness inside me. I snatched my arm back and sprang up so fast that my chair toppled to the carpeted floor with a thud.

"Don't touch me, you bitch," I heard myself say, low and furious, in a stranger's voice. "None of this would have happened if you'd let him stay with me for a week—just one more week—instead of sending him off with this—this cow. But no, you had to be legal. *Legal!*"

"Ms. Bose." Ms. Mayhew spoke calmly enough, but her face was white. Mrs. Ortiz had clapped a shocked hand over her mouth. "I realize you're upset, but it doesn't help to point the finger at other people or call them names. Mrs. Ortiz did the best she could—she's not a jailer, after all. And though you seem to have such little regard for the laws of the State of California, I *am* obliged to follow them."

I was already at the door.

"I'm going to go look for my little boy," I shouted over my shoulder, "and if I find him, this time sure as hell I'm not going to hand him over to you." I slammed the door hard behind me and was pleased to feel the walls shake. But it was a small, hollow pleasure.

I searched for Krishna all that day, and the next, and the next. All week I drove up and down the streets of Mrs. Ortiz's neighborhood, stopping passersby to ask if they had seen him. I even went up into the foothills which were several miles from her house. I struggled through groves of eucalyptus and thorny thickets of scrub oak, calling Krishna's name. At night I ignored the stares of the other tenants and sat for hours on the front steps of my building, my legs aching, my arms stinging from the thorns, waiting and hoping.

But I didn't really expect him to turn up. I wouldn't have come back either to someone who'd taken me in only to give me up, who had loved me briefly only to betray me forever.

It's been more than a year since then, a time in which my life has returned pretty much to normal. As Richard says, you can only mourn so long. I guess he's right.

For a while though, it was touch and go. I wouldn't answer the anxious messages Richard left on my answering machine, and when he showed up at the apartment I threatened to call the police if he didn't leave me alone. Even with Sharmila I refused to discuss Krishna. I considered quitting my job—I was doing so badly I was close to being fired anyway—and returning to India. I spent a lot of time going through the photos of the Brylcreemed men my mother had sent me. At one point I wrote her a letter saying that I would consider an arranged marriage if she could find me a widower with a little boy of about seven. Such a man, I reasoned, would understand about mother-love far more than Richard— or any other American male, for that matter—ever could. But I never posted the letter. Even then, crazy as I was with anger and sorrow and guilt, I knew that would have been a bigger mistake than the ones I'd made already.

And I was right. Things are good again. Recently I received a promotion at work for debugging a data-entry program that was driving everyone crazy. Even Dan Luftner stopped by my office afterward to say thank you. I've moved to a bigger, better apartment up near Grizzly Peak, with all white carpeting and bleached Scandinavian furniture to match. From the front window I can see the entire San Francisco Bay spread out at my feet. When I get together with Sharmila—though not as often as before because she's really busy with her little boy—we have a good time, talking only about happy things.

Richard and I are back together, and last month when I finally wrote to my mother about him, she surprised me by being far less upset than I'd feared. Maybe she figured that even a foreign husband—a *firingi*—is better than no husband at all. At any rate, she's planning to attend our wedding, which is to be this June, followed by a honeymoon in the south of France. I haven't yet told her that I agreed to the marriage only on condition that we don't have children. But no doubt she'll get used to that as well. For a while Ms. Mayhew would leave messages on my machine about boys I might like to take in, now that I was an eligible foster parent. I would erase the messages right away (though her voice continued to travel through my body, insidious, deadly, like a piece of shrapnel the surgeon had missed) and after some time she stopped calling.

Only sometimes, once in a while, I take a day off from work. I go back to Mrs. Ortiz's neighborhood—nobody knows this—and drive through all the streets, slowly, carefully, peering at passing faces. I hike up into the eucalyptus and scrub oak, the dead bark crumbling under my feet like sloughed-off snakeskin, the thorny branches catching in my clothes, and call a name until the shadows congeal deep and cold around me. And when I come back to my apartment, I close my eyes before the last bend of the stairs that lead to my door. I hold my breath and imagine a boy in a red Mickey Mouse T-shirt sitting on the topmost step. *If I can count to twenty, thirty, forty, without letting go,* I say to myself, *he'll be there. He'll hold out his arms, and in his high, clear voice he'll call to me.* I stand there halfway up the darkening staircase feeling the emptiness swirl around me, my lungs burning, my eyes shut tight as though in prayer.

THE MAID
SERVANT'S
STORY

THE AFTERNOON SUN LIGHTS UP THE SOFT FOLDS OF Deepa Mashi's red-and-white sari as she sits back with a satisfied after-lunch sigh in her cushioned easy chair. It shines on her hair, which is still as glossy and black as in my childhood, when I loved running my fingers through it. The *ghu-ghu* birds are cooing in the calm shadows under the eaves of her house, and in the distance I can hear the faint cry of the *kulfi* vendor calling out *fresh fresh ices, sweet sweet ices*. For a moment it is as though I had never left Calcutta.

Then Mashi says, "So, Manisha, I hear you might be getting married soon."

I am not surprised by the comment. I've been anticipating something of the sort ever since I mentioned to my mother, with careful casualness, that I'd met a Bengali professor at the university in California where I taught English. Still, disappointment rises raw and bitter in my throat. I'd hoped that things would be different between my mother and myself this time.

I told her about Bijoy the very first night of my visit home. We were alone in her small flat overlooking a park filled with *kadam* trees that sent their too-sweet fragrance into the dark, moist air. We served ourselves from the dishes the day maid had cooked before she left. Rice, *dal,* a plain cauli-flower curry. My mother lives simply. Strains of Rabindra Sangeet from a neighboring radio floated on the still evening —*Ami chini go chini tomare, I know you well, woman from a distant land beyond the ocean.* It was a good time, I felt, to talk—if not as mother and daughter, at least as two intelligent, adult women.

But when I'd spoken she just glanced up sharply with a look that could have been suspicion or disapproval, or even relief that a prospect had appeared, at last, on my barren marital horizon. I never have been able to read my mother's expressions. "That must be very nice, dear," she said. Then she went back to describing the naming ceremony for my cousin Sheela's oldest son in Burdwan last year.

Deepa Mashi is waiting. So I force a laugh and raise my hands in exaggerated protest, feeling myself slip back into the habits of my childhood, hiding pain with humor. "Mashi! I've just started seeing Bijoy! No one's said anything about a wed-ding yet."

Mashi opens her silver *paan* case, carefully chooses a rolled-up betel leaf, and places it in her mouth. "Two months since you met him, no?"

When, I wonder—as I used to throughout my growing-up years—did the sisters manage to get together to discuss their errant daughter-niece? My resentment is all for my mother—it is she who should be asking these questions, not my aunt, much as I love her.

"You know for how long I met your uncle before we were married?" Deepa Mashi continues.

Of course I know. She's told me of it a hundred times. But I also know how much pleasure the retelling will give her. So I offer her a fond, expectant smile.

"Fifteen minutes during the bride-viewing, that's how long!" Mashi speaks with the plump and breathless exuberance she brings to all her stories. "And last year, grace of God, we celebrated our twentieth anniversary." She shuts her *paan* case with a victorious snap, as if she's won a major argument.

I take refuge in platitude. "Times have changed, Mashi."

Mashi waves away the intervening decades with a beringed, dimpled hand. "Oh, you Americanized girls! The really important things never change."

Perhaps she's right. I'd come back from my three years abroad feeling adult and sophisticated, determined to match my mother's distant courtesy. Over and over on the flight to Dum Dum airport, I'd promised myself that I wouldn't offer up my life for her inspection and approval, as I had so many times before. Yet I'd done it almost immediately. I guess transformations—the really important ones—require more than time and distance, and even desire.

That first night back, smarting at Mother's seeming indifference, I'd forced my way into her description of the

guests at the naming ceremony. "Bijoy teaches psychology—
it's quite unusual to find Indians in that field, at least in California."

I was angry with myself as soon as I blurted it out, callow
as any adolescent yearning for parental love—even before I
heard her responding, in the perfectly modulated voice which
I remembered so well, that he must be a most interesting
man. I felt the familiar, furious urge to say something brutal
enough to shatter her self-possession. *You're right, Mother,
he's very interesting—especially in bed.* But I swallowed them
both, the anger and the words. What good would it do? What
good had *anything* done?

Throughout high school I'd pushed myself to stand first
in exams, to win debates and drama competitions; but I never
got the praise I craved, that squeezed-breathless, delirious-
with-joy hug that other mothers gave their daughters for far
lesser achievements. For a while in college I'd tried the oppo-
site, cutting classes and running around with a wild crowd,
smoking cigarettes (an absolute taboo for an Indian girl of
good family) and even *ganja* a couple of times, letting boys
hold my hand in broad daylight in the Maidan park, where it
was certain someone would see us and report the facts back to
my mother. But all she did was look at me with a distant
sadness, as one might regard a character in a book or movie,
and say that she didn't understand why I'd want to ruin my
life this way. When, in my final attempt to shock some kind of
feeling out of her, I'd told her that I was leaving for America,
she'd merely said, "Be careful, and write if you need anything." At the airport she'd pressed a cool, dry cheek to mine
(while all around us parents clung to departing children and

let fall torrents of tears) and said, "You know I want the best for you."

The worst part was, I knew she did. She watched over my life carefully, vigilantly, if from afar. All through my childhood, everything I wanted—everything material, that is—was provided for me, often before I needed to ask. But what *she* thought, what *she* longed for, what made her cry out in her dreams (for I'd heard her, once or twice), I never knew. It was as though she'd built a wall of ice around her, thin and invisible and unbreakable. No matter how often I flung myself against it, I was refused entry.

Maybe she no longer knew how to let me. Maybe people were right when they said that the death of her husband and baby in a cholera epidemic that had struck Calcutta overnight when I was about five had killed a part of her too. (Why had that explanation always seemed too facile for me?) At any rate, she'd relinquished me to Deepa Mashi who, herself childless, enthusiastically took on the role of second mother, commending and cajoling and consoling me all those years, asking embarrassing questions and, when I refused to answer, creating vociferous scenes dramatic enough to satisfy any teenager's need for attention. Other girls might have resented the interference, but I was grateful. When I felt myself dissolving before my mother's even, passionless gaze, Deepa Mashi's voice, laughing at my follies, scolding me for my misdeeds, gave me solidity and shape. Secretly, guiltily, I wished I could have been her real daughter.

"We should plan your wedding outfit," Mashi is saying now. "Who knows when you'll come visit us next. And weddings have a habit of happening suddenly."

I want to explain to her about Bijoy. He's not like other Indians—certainly not the ones Aunt would know, engineers and accountants with responsible gold-rimmed eyeglasses and Parker fountain pens in their breast pockets—upright, virtuous, and deadly boring. On our second date he'd told me that he found me attractive and was interested in getting together, but wasn't ready to be tied down by marriage. I'd felt angry, insulted—far more so than if an American man had said the same thing. I'd taken the bus home that night, after informing him in chilled tones that we'd better not see each other again.

And we hadn't for a month, during which I thought incessantly, obsessively, of him. His utter disregard for the rules of my youth—and surely his as well—fascinated me. At the end of the month I contrived to get myself invited to a party where I knew he'd be present. I accepted his offer to escort me home. I let him kiss me, and when his lips pressed down hard on mine, his tongue forcing its way into my mouth, his hands deftly insistent on my *kurta* buttons, I told myself it was what I wanted. A liberated relationship, no strings attached. A sailing into uncharted and amazing areas of experience that someone like my mother couldn't even imagine. I'd pushed back the feeling of shame, the old voices echoing in my head, *Men don't do these things to women they respect.*

But it will only distress Mashi if I tell her I'm living with a man I'm not—and might never be—married to. Her world is constructed of simpler lines, its shapes filled in with bright primary colors that do not bleed together, as in the calendars of gods that hang on the walls of her living room. So it is much easier, as I sit under the slow-revolving ceiling fan, lulled by

the sun-warm smell of jasmine and gardenia from the garden,
by the *shhh shhh* sound of the *mali* watering the lawn, to let
myself fall into her fantasy.

"I'll wear a Benarasi silk, I guess, except I don't want any
of those traditional gaudy colors." A part of me is amused at
my own emphatic tone, as though this might actually happen.
"You know, orange and maroon, eggplant-purple, bloodred." I
realize I am thinking of my mother's wedding sari. I came
across it once, wrapped in a blanket and thrust into the bottom of a trunk, like a sordid secret. "You can't ever wear them
later, especially in America." I am pleased at the cleverness
with which I've let drop the fact—which will duly find its way
to my mother—that I'm not intending to come back to India.
Not to stay. "Maybe saffron would be nice—a pale saffron.
Yes, that's it. I want a saffron Benarasi for the wedding."

Mashi is silent for a long moment. Then in a strangely
quiet voice she says, "Oh, my dear, not saffron, not that."

"Why not?" I ask, surprised by her uncharacteristic seri-
ousness.

"Saffron is such a sorrowful color."

"Funny you should say that. I always thought of it as
rather festive—the color of beginnings."

"I guess you're right. It's just that it reminds me
of . . ." Deepa Mashi's voice disappears into a sigh.

"Of what, Mashi?"

"Oh, nothing, nothing, it's only a story," says Mashi,
twisting her fingers together. "A sad story, a bad-luck tale, not
meant for brides-to-be. Come, let me make you some cardamom tea—I remember how much you used to enjoy that."

But like most Indian women, Mashi is not good at saying no. So when, intrigued by the uneasiness in her voice, I insist, she tells me.

Once there was a young wife, the apple of her husband's eye. She was beautiful and charming and intelligent, and had been to college as well, a rare achievement for women in those days. Her husband was fond of bringing up this fact in the course of conversations with friends—especially as she didn't flaunt her education and deferred, in most instances, to his superior judgment.

The young wife, whom everyone considered a lucky woman, lived in an old and respected part of Calcutta in a marble mansion that had belonged to the family since the time of the grandfather. (The grandfather, whose portrait hung, majestically framed in antique brass, in the hall, had been famous for his charitable works—free medical clinics and slum schools—another fact that the husband liked to mention in conversations though he was not involved in any of them.) While the husband was away at work (he was an assistant manager at a very proper British bank that had stayed on in India after Independence), she occupied herself with household duties, as a wife should, telling the cook which of the master's favorite dishes to prepare for dinner, and supervising the maids as they dusted the tall armoires and wall clocks and polished the ivory and brass figurines that sat in various alcoves around the house. She took long walks in the garden and advised the *mali* on what to plant in the flower beds that edged the circular driveway. And when the *darwan*

116

The Maid Servant's Story

(who doubled as chauffeur) stood up with a smart salute from his stool at the wrought-iron gates which were kept closed at all times, she wished him good day with a smile and asked after his wife and children, who lived in the servant's quarters above the garage and whose names she always remembered.

She was additionally lucky, people said, in that she didn't have a mother-in-law to contend with, but it is very probable that she would have got along well with one. Her mother had taught her to be respectful of elders, and she took good care of her husband's aunt, an ancient and somewhat deaf widow who lived with them, in spite of the biting remarks the old woman let drop from time to time. She also took good care of her daughter, bathing and feeding her with her own hands instead of turning her over to the *ayah* as so many of the women of her class did, and reading to her in the afternoons as they lay together in the cool white nursery bed until the little girl fell asleep.

In her spare time the wife read the books which the husband picked up from the library for her on his way back from the office, and practiced her singing. (She had a good voice and an interest in contemporary music, and the husband, who liked to boast of this talent of hers as well, had hired a lady teacher who came to the house every Thursday to teach her Rabindra Sangeet.) She wrote many letters, mainly to her family, mentioning always how happy she was, how loved and protected, how blessed—especially now that she was expecting another baby. In one of them she asked her younger sister, who was still unmarried and thus without responsibilities of her own, if she could come and stay with her for a few months, just until her delivery. It was a little lonely at times in this great big house where voices echoed and footsteps rang hollow down the corridors. Maybe it would be a little boy this time, she ended, like her husband wanted, a charming fair-skinned boy with curly hair and bright eyes, to delight their hearts and carry on the family name.

The maid servant arrived soon after that.

The two sisters were walking under the fragrant *neem* trees in the early evening, taking advantage of the cool breeze before the sun disappeared behind the coconut palms and mosquitoes invaded the garden. For the younger sister had come right away, pleased and even a little gratified that the sister she had looked up to all her life, who everyone said was prettier and smarter and sweeter-natured and who had married so much better than she herself could hope to, actually needed her. Besides, her annual exams were over and the prospect of summer in provincial Burdwan stretched ahead of her, long and barren and parched like the fields she stared out at each morning from the windows of her father's house. In Calcutta there would be shops to visit and movies to see, the grounds of the Maidan and the Victoria Memorial to promenade in, and musical soirees to attend. And even the Kalighat temple, noisy with chanted prayers and the frantic bleating of sacrificial goats, where her sister took the aunt every Tuesday, was an exciting change from the small Shiva shrine back home. She liked her brother-in-law too, though she was a bit in awe of him—especially when, on workday mornings, he appeared at breakfast dressed in suit and tie, his shoes spit-shiny and the stiff collars of his shirts precisely ironed. He

118

made her uncomfortable (although she never would have said it to anyone) with his easy charm as he asked after her health, with his sophisticated jokes that she didn't understand. With the look that flickered briefly, hotly in his eyes when her sister wasn't around.

The woman was standing outside the wrought-iron gates, perfectly still, her head haloed by the setting sun, so that when the sister first caught sight of her she seemed dazzle-bright, a forest goddess materialized out of a children's fairy tale. But of course she wasn't. She was only a poor woman in a coarse, green-bordered sari, with high, hungry cheekbones and shadows in the hollow of her throat. She was good-looking enough in a primitive *adivasi* way, but no one would have mistaken her—at least on second look—for anything except a working-class girl who'd been out of work awhile.

"Mistress," she said in a broad rural accent when she saw the women staring at her, "do you need a maid?"

The sister expected the wife to say no. Things like this had happened before, in spite of this being a neighborhood that housed the cream of the Calcutta families. Sometimes tramps would wander up to the gates, ragged bearded men who wanted food in exchange for a day's work and turned sullen when told they weren't needed. Street urchins would try to climb over the wall to get at the mango tree, even when the fruit was green and hard and bitter. The beggar women were the worst. They would grip the wrought-iron spears of the gate with clawlike fingers and cry that they had hungry children at home, could the little mother let them have just one cup of rice. But of course you couldn't, as the husband

119

always reminded them, because news of it would travel along the beggar grapevine and the next day a hundred others would descend on them.

The sister paused for the wife to call the *darwan,* who was washing the black Studebaker at the other end of the driveway, and ask him—as she had done on those other occasions—to make the woman leave. So she was surprised when instead she heard her ask the woman what she could do.

"Anything," said the woman. "If you show me how to, I'll learn. I'm a good worker—I won't be any trouble to you." Her voice, though respectful, wasn't obsequious like that of most servants. Bell-clear, it resonated in the evening air in spite of the way her collarbones rose sharp and fragile from her flesh.

"Do you have family?" asked the older sister.

"Yes," said the woman after a slight pause, "the kind it's better not to have." She didn't offer explanations.

"Where will you go if I say no?"

The woman shrugged, her face calm with the look of a lake over which many storms have passed.

The young wife thought for a while. Then she lifted the gate latch and motioned the woman to follow her. The sister, concerned, tried to tell her that it wasn't a good idea, that her brother-in-law would surely be displeased. But the wife had begun a casual discussion about baby quilts—whether a lining of imported satin, which the husband favored, would be better than the traditional red *malmal* that was supposed to bring good luck to newborns—and she didn't get a chance.

The Maid Servant's Story

The sister was right, of course. There was a scene at dinner when the husband found out that his wife had hired a woman to be her personal maid without consulting him.

"First of all you don't need another servant. As it is, Ayah doesn't have enough to do. And then, where will she stay? The servant's quarters are full already."

"She could stay in the house," the wife said in her soft voice. "We have so many empty rooms."

"In the house! You want to put her in the house! What d'you know of this woman? She could be a thief or, worse still, the spy for a gang of *dacoits*. Remember what happened at the Dasguptas last year, the whole family murdered in their beds, and later the police found out that the maid had let the killers in."

"That's right," said the old aunt (for she could hear well enough when she wanted to). "Asking for trouble, you are. Half those women are prostitutes anyway."

"I don't think this girl's like that," said the wife. She folded her hands over the swell of her belly, fixed her luminous eyes on her husband, and waited until he said, grudgingly, "Let me take a look at her."

So the woman was summoned. The husband's eyes slid over the dark glow of her new-washed face, the neatly pulled-back hair that brought out the arresting shape of her cheekbones. The slim, straight body, the taut belly, the sinuous curve of breast and hip that the old green sari didn't quite hide. (But perhaps the sister was only imagining this.) Then he said in a voice which still sounded annoyed that he was willing to try her out for a month or so, but only if his wife took full responsibility for anything that went wrong.

"I will," said the wife, giving him a smile of grateful brilliance and clasping his hand in hers, though she knew that the old aunt frowned on such forward behavior on the part of wives. But the sister, who sensed that the husband was not really annoyed at all, crossed her fingers under the table to avert bad luck and said a prayer for her sister.

That was how the maid—let us call her Sarala—came to the house.

The maid was as good as her word. Quick and alert, in a few weeks she learned all that the wife showed her, from embroidering baby diapers to mixing medicinal oils according to the special recipe passed down to the wife by her mother. And she was a hard worker. Up at dawn, she would be waiting on the balcony with a pot of the basil tea considered particularly beneficial for pregnant women by the time the wife emerged from the bedroom. Once the husband left for work, she dusted the wife's dressing table, lovingly lining up the combs and brushes, the little pots of *kumkum* and *sindur* and *kajal*, and arranging in their velvet cases the jewelry the wife was increasingly too tired to put away. She washed her fine cotton saris by hand and dried them in the shady part of the terrace so they would smell sun-fresh without the colors fading. She massaged the wife's swollen feet with the medicinal oil and never tired of running down to the kitchen to bring her up a glass of chilled *nimbu-pani* whenever she felt nauseous. Even in the hot afternoons when the rest of the servants disappeared for their siestas, she would sit in the passage outside her mistress's bedroom, hemming one of her petticoats or letting out a blouse, and keeping the little girl, who often woke early from her nap, occupied with tales and rhymes so she wouldn't go in and disturb her mother's sleep.

Sometimes the wife would call out in her gentle voice, "Why don't you go and lie down for a bit, Sarala? I don't mind if Khuku comes and plays on my bed."

But the maid would always say, "Oh no, Didi (she had taken to calling her *elder sister*, just as her own sister did), I'm not tired. You please rest. Khukumoni is no trouble at all."

At first the sister regarded the maid's devotion to the wife with suspicion. (And yes, it must be admitted, even some jealousy. She didn't like the business of the maid calling her sister *didi,* a title that was rightfully hers to use. A hot resentment pricked at her when she heard the wife speaking to the maid in the same affectionate tone she used toward her own sister.) She had never come across a servant quite like her. Even the old ones who had been in her father's family for years were, though loyal, always taking advantage of their seniority to ask for favors—a new shawl at Durga Puja time, gifts of money for the marriage of their children, longer vacations to visit family. The sister watched the maid intently for a slip —a glint of the eye, a twist of the lip, a careless word dropped to a fellow servant that would reveal her real motives. But there was nothing. Though polite to the other household help, the maid didn't gossip with them. When the wife asked her if she needed anything—clothing, soap, another blanket—she said no. The sister noticed, too, how she took care to stay out of the husband's way without making it obvious. How she pulled her thick hair back in a style she must have known was unattractive (for she was smart, this maid—the sister had seen that right away) and kept her sari modestly pulled around her shoulders at all times. How she chose, for her sleeping space, not the big alcove with the ceiling fan, as the wife had suggested, but a cramped and airless storeroom which could be locked from the inside.

After a month the sister was forced to admit to herself that she had been wrong. The maid loved the wife in the way intelligent animals love their keepers, with a ferocious and total loyalty, a forgetting of self. (The sister had heard tales of such beasts—cheetahs and house snakes and the great gray wolf-dogs that rajahs sometimes kept—killing for their masters, dying for them.) Perhaps it was because the wife was the first person to be truly kind to the maid, with a kindness that expects nothing in return.

One evening the sister watched the maid bring a footstool and a glass of honey-milk to the wife as she sat on the balcony. She saw the gracious smile with which the mistress took the drink from the maid, and the desperate bright joy that flashed across the maid's face in response, and she forced herself, finally, to wipe the last traces of jealousy from her heart. *When I am gone*, she told herself, *there will still be someone in this house to look after my sister.*

"We must teach Sarala to read and write," the wife told the sister one day. Turning to the maid, who was combing out her hair with long, sweeping strokes, she asked, "Would you like that?"

The maid's face was that of someone who, after being in a dark room all her life, sees a window opening and the brilliance she'd only heard about till then pouring in. "Oh yes, Didi." Then her voice faltered. "But do you think I can?"

"Of course," said the wife. "You're a clever girl."

"But Dadababu—he may not like it. I don't want him to be angry with you."

The wife did not deny what the maid said about the husband, and the sister, surprised, thought, *She knows more than I realized.*

"Dadababu need not know," said the wife after a moment, smiling again. "It can be our secret."

And so the lessons began.

The wife bought the maid a slate and chalk and a primary reader, and in the hot hushed afternoons when she couldn't sleep (for she was increasingly uncomfortable nowadays with the great growing swell of her belly pressing up into her chest, making it hard to breathe), she taught her the Bengali alphabet. The sister would sit in one of the cushioned chairs in the dim bedroom, smelling the damp grassy odor of *khush-khush* screens lowered against the heat, and watch as the wife helped the maid shape the letters. She would look at her sister's fingers—fragile, almost translucent—curving over the maid's sturdy dark ones, she would listen to her soft, clear voice enunciate the sounds—*cha, la, bha, sha*—and the maid's faltering echo, and love for her sister would sweep through her, ferocious as a fire or flood. But beneath the love would be a prick of apprehension, a voice in her heart saying, *Where will this lead?*

News traveled, of course, in spite of the closed bedroom doors, as it always does in a house full of servants. Down to the kitchen, in jealous whispers, then up again to the old aunt, who had her informers. And the aunt, who had never really liked the wife in spite of her many kindnesses (or perhaps because of them, for that is how the human heart sometimes works), who had often complained to her friends—other old women living in bitterness on the charity of relatives—that she was too modern and uppity and not a fit daughter-in-law for the Bandopadhyay family, said casually one night at dinner, "So now you're teaching that woman to read and write."

"Yes," said the wife. Her voice was composed enough—experienced in the ways of large households, she must have expected this to happen sooner or later—but a slight flush tinged her cheeks.

"What's this now?" said the husband. When the wife explained, his lips pressed together in displeased thinness. "Don't you think you should have asked me before you started all this?"

"When," said the aunt, "did she ever ask anyone."

"I didn't think you'd be interested," said the wife. "It is a small thing, after all."

"Small things lead to big problems," said the aunt.

The sister felt the rage rise in her like a wild wind, but she bit down on her tongue to keep herself quiet. Anything she said, she knew, would only harm her sister's case.

"Aunt's right," said the husband. "Things like that give ideas to the lower classes, especially the women. Makes them want to rise above their station."

"Next she'll be asking for a higher salary," the aunt began. "Then more vacation time, then . . ."

For the first time the wife interrupted. Speaking only to her husband she said in a clear voice, "They're so exploited, our people, because they're illiterate. The women most of all. And Sarala—she's such a smart girl. It would be a great pity to waste her intelligence. I know your grandfather would have felt the same way." Her eyes were like diamonds, with a chiseled spark to them.

Faced by that resolute shine, the husband seemed at a loss for words. Finally he said, "Oh, very well, go ahead. But you remember what we told you, Aunt and I. You watch out for that maid."

Later in private he told the aunt, "We don't want to upset her, not at this time. I'll take care of things later."

The maid was as good at the lessons as at everything else. Soon she learned her letters and was able to decipher simple words. After a while she could even read a few nursery rhymes aloud to the little girl, who was quite excited by this turn in events and annoyed the old *ayah* terribly by saying that she liked Sarala better and wanted to play only with her.

Writing came harder. Callused and unschooled, the maid's fingers found it difficult to form the twists and turns of the *sha,* the sharp angles of the *ra,* the tight curls of the *la.* But she wouldn't give up. Every night on her way to bed the sister would see her sitting under the corridor light outside the storeroom, head bent in concentration, wiping, with the edge of her sari, the erratic, disobedient lines that slashed the slate again and again.

Finally one day the maid presented to her mistress the slate across which was written, in crude and barbaric letters, yes, but clearly enough, her name. The wife stood up and

127

pulled her close for a hug, saying, "Sarala, that's beautiful, I'm so proud of you." The slatted sunlight from the window illumined the faces of both the women, the tears glistening on their lashes, and the sister, whose eyes had filled too, felt blessed, as though for a moment she had been allowed to look into the heart of grace.

The next morning, after the black Studebaker had disappeared with the husband down the newly washed driveway that smelled of lemon blossom, the wife called the maid into the bedroom and opened the mahogany *almirah* that held her clothes. She pulled out the bottom drawer, which was filled with colorful silks, and the scent of sandalwood from the sachets that nestled between the saris filled the room.

"I want you to choose a sari—any one," she said to the maid. "It's my gift to you for learning so well."

The maid shied away, a scandalized look on her face, for the saris were expensive and far above her station. The sister, who had been sitting on the bed, watching, drew in her breath in sharp dismay, for it seemed to her that the wife was making a serious error.

"Go ahead," said the wife encouragingly. Looking at the maid's expression she added, "Don't worry, these saris are quite old, and Dadababu thinks they're dreadfully out of style. I'll probably never wear any of them again. So no one should mind."

The sister stared at the wife's face, wondering if she really believed what she was saying. Plenty of people, she knew, would mind. Her sister's enormous innocence made her feel at once sad and envious.

"Didi," she ventured, "I don't think it's such a good idea. Perhaps instead you can give her . . ."

The wife whirled to face her with unusual anger (though the sister could see, even then, that the anger wasn't directed at herself). "These saris are mine," she said. "From before marriage. No one else has the right to say what I should do with them."

The sister realized that she had made a mistake in judging the wife as too innocent.

After much persuasion, the maid timidly picked out one of the simpler pieces, a saffron silk with a thin gold border worked in the shape of *peepul* leaves.

"Good choice," said the wife approvingly. "Saffron is one of my favorite colors, too. Here, see, it has a matching blouse. Go wash up and put it on so I can see how it looks on you."

The sister's brief hope that the unfortunate sari would lie at the bottom of the maid's box until her sister forgot about it died. She tried again to stop her, to say that perhaps another day would be better, but the wife, her face like marble, turned from her and said, "Now."

So the maid went and put on the sari. Perhaps she had intended at first merely to show herself to her mistress and then, using the excuse of work, change back into her regular clothes. But when she felt the silk against her skin, softer even than the petals at the heart of a lotus, something seemed to come over her. She searched in her box till she found a broken piece of mirror and held it up for a long moment to see how the fabric glowed like dawn against her ebony skin. Then she combed out her hair and tied it into a braid that swung against her hips. And finally—can you blame her? she was not much older, after all, than the sister—she went into the little girl's room and took some of the homemade *kajal* that is believed to be good for children's eyes and applied a tiny bit of the lampblack to her lashes.

"You look very nice," said the wife when the maid knocked shyly on the door. "You should always wear your hair like that." She was lying on the bed, which was unusual for her this early in the day, with her swollen feet propped on a folded quilt. Against the pillowcase embroidered with turtle doves her smile flickered tiredly, as though she'd been pushing an enormous weight uphill. "I think I'll rest for a few hours now. Maybe you can bring me up a little sweet yogurt for lunch, Sarala. And if you"—turning to her sister a trifle apologetically—"could supervise Khuku's bath and make sure she takes her nap, you know how naughty she can be sometimes. . . ."

"Of course I will," said the sister with a reassuring smile as she drew the curtains. "You just rest and don't worry about any of it." But inside she was thinking how her sister didn't look well at all, how as soon as he came home she must ask her brother-in-law to send for old Dr. Hazra. She was also thinking of a tactful way of telling the maid to take off the saffron sari and tie her hair up the old way, but before she could find the right words the girl had run down to the kitchen to fetch her mistress a glass of cold pomegranate juice.

130

The Maid Servant's Story

In the kitchen the cook's jaw dropped as the maid entered, and the bearer-boy who ran errands pursed his lips in a low whistle as he watched that braid swing against the slim waist. The *ayah,* who was squatting by the door chewing *paan,* drew in her breath so sharply that a sliver of betel nut caught in her throat and she coughed and coughed until the cook hurried over and thumped her on the back.

The maid hid a triumphant smile and went about her task in her usual reserved way, peeling pomegranates and crushing the pods in the juicer until a deep red liquid filled a glass.

The *ayah,* who had recovered by now, stated acidly that it was well known that when ants grew wings, the time of their doom had arrived.

The maid filled the glass calmly with ice chips, not letting a drop of juice spill to the silver tray on which it sat, but when she left her chin was up just a bit straighter, her braid swung a little more than before, and she continued to wear the saffron sari (which she had been intending to put away) for the rest of the day.

Later the sister would think back to this day as the highest point on a wheel—the wheel of luck, perhaps, or karma, the moment of balance when everything was as perfect as it can be in this flawed world. Perhaps, by its very nature, such a time cannot last but must topple into darkness as the wheel continues to turn. But the sister blamed the sari for what happened next, that ill-fated sari around which wisps of disaster (which might otherwise have dissipated) coalesced and took shape. The sari that burned through the afternoon like a taunt to the gods with its thoughtlessly cheerful tint, its gay, gold *palloo* fluttering behind the maid as she played tag with the little girl around the tall oleander bushes.

Darkness was falling—suddenly, violently, as it always does in the twilightless tropical evenings of Calcutta. Smoke from the charcoal *chula* the cook had lit in the backyard hung in the air, heavy, acrid as a premonition. The wife slept on, stretched unmoving on the high white bed like someone drugged or dead. From her own bedroom window the sister crinkled her eyes through the purplish haze to see the two figures weaving among the bushes, a flicker of burnished gold, then her niece's child-voice rising querulously as her pursuer caught up with her, *No, no, I don't want to go inside yet.*

The sister was about to call down an admonition when she noticed the husband—the chauffeur must have just let him out at the front porch—walking toward the two of them. The maid and the girl, their backs toward him, were busy arguing. So the sister was the only one who noticed how his gait took on the predatory lope of a wolf—or was it a jackal? Before she was able to force a cry out of the dry tightness of her throat, his arm was around the maid's waist, pulling her hard against him. Shock stiffened the maid's body for a moment. Then she was struggling, pushing fiercely, mutely at the husband's chest, while the little girl tilted up her curious head —her large luminous eyes so like her mother's—to watch them.

He let her go at once, of course. From where she

gripped the edge of her window, the sister could hear the laugh low and deep in his throat, the smooth murmur of his words as he bent to pick up his daughter. She knew what he was telling her as he stared after the disappearing figure of the maid. *A mistake. I thought it was your mother.*

It was certainly not impossible. It was almost dark by now, and the maid *had* been wearing the wife's sari. But the sister stood at the window for a long time after, her head against the bars, her eyes squeezed shut, feeling the cold rust fleck off on her forehead, the thick, muddy fear clog her heart.

The next day the wife was worse. Her face was the color of *chapati* dough, and the flesh around her eyes was soft and puffy. She complained of a dull ache low in her abdomen, and when the aunt suggested a poultice of warm turmeric, she didn't say no. Watching her lie there submissive and motionless, eyes closed, while the aunt rubbed the yellow paste on her belly, the sister thought for a moment, *She's dead.* And though she tried to pluck the bad-luck words out from her mind, they wouldn't go.

"I want to call the doctor," she said.

"What for?" said the aunt. "This poultice is the best thing for pregnant women—didn't I tell you how my sister-in-law . . ."

"Where's the number?" the sister asked.

"You'd better wait till Babu comes home and ask him if he thinks it's really necessary," said the aunt.

"The number," said the sister, leaning over the wife, and

the wife lifted her hand to point at the bureau and let it fall heavily again.

When she finally got through to the doctor's office, the sister found out that he couldn't be reached—he was at the hospital performing an operation. She had to be satisfied with the assistant's assurance that he'd written down everything she'd said, and that the doctor would come over as soon as he could, probably sometime that night.

The sister stood outside the wife's room for a while, biting her lip, listening to her sister moan. It was a low, hopeless animal sound that distressed her more than the sharpest cry of pain would have. She finally decided to call the brother-in-law, although yesterday she had thought she would never be able to speak to him again. But the operator at his firm informed her that he wasn't back yet from lunch.

"Choto-didi." It was the hesitant voice of the maid. "Do you think I might have the afternoon off?"

The sister looked up at her distractedly. Even through her worry, a part of her mind was pleased to note that the maid had gone back to her usual mode of dress. Her hair was pulled back more tightly than before, making the edges of her eyes slant slightly upward, giving her face a quality of alienness. She was surprised, though, that the maid would choose *this* day to want to go somewhere. It wasn't like her. The other servants were always manufacturing elaborate excuses for why they *must* have a day off, but the maid had never asked for a vacation since she'd been hired, so that the sister had supposed that she didn't know anyone in the city.

"I guess it's all right," she said. It would have been more correct for the girl to ask the aunt for permission, but she couldn't blame her. From the bedroom she could hear the old woman's nasal voice telling the wife that a glass of black tea with a sprig of *tulsi* seeped in it would be just the thing for her cramps.

"Be sure to come back fast," she said over her shoulder as she hurried to protect her sister from more of the aunt's home remedies.

"Oh yes, Choto-didi, I will."

Only later, when the wife, fretting, asked, "Where's Sarala? I want her to rub my legs," did the sister realize that she had forgotten to inquire where the maid was going.

The maid didn't return till the shadow of the *peepul* trees slanted shivering across the lawn to the veranda, where the family was having evening tea and biscuits. The wife, claiming she felt a little better—though her face still looked drawn, with dark half-moons under the eyes that gave them a bruised look—had joined them. ("Told you that turmeric poultice would take care of your cramps!" declared the aunt.)

The husband thanked the sister for having called the doctor. "You did the right thing. I don't want to take any chances with your sister's health." He wore, like always in the evening, an immaculate *kurta*, white as just-picked *shiuli* flowers and fastened with gold buttons that shone. When he leaned forward to touch her hand—but lightly, respectfully, with a brother's touch—his eyes, too, shone, and with such sincerity that for a moment the sister believed she had imagined yesterday's episode.

That was when the maid came hurrying down the drive,

135

holding a packet in her hands. She stopped when she noticed the husband sitting there. The sister thought she saw a brief tremor run through her body.

"Sarala," called the wife. "Where have you been?"

"I went to the Kalighat temple, Didi, to offer a prayer for you." The maid held out a crumpled banana leaf with some flowers and *kumkum* and a graying sweetmeat. "I brought you some *prasad*. Mother Kali, she's very powerful— she can cure anything."

"Thank you, my dear." The wife's eyes were warm as she took the package and touched it to her forehead.

"I've nothing against Kali," said the husband, not looking at the maid as he spoke, "and it was a nice thing for the girl to do. But I don't think you should eat any of that stuff."

"One little bit can't do any harm, especially when it's blessed by the goddess," said the wife calmly, and she broke off a piece of the sweet and put it in her mouth.

"Babu. . . ."

It was the *darwan,* looking uncomfortable.

"What is it?"

"There's a woman outside, demanding to be let in. I tried to turn her away, but she claims she's"—he pointed to the maid—"her mother. She's making a lot of noise. Shall I ask the bearer-boy to come help me get rid of her?"

The sister looked at the maid, who stood beside the wife's chair, stricken into stillness.

The husband, who had also been watching the maid, spoke slowly, consideringly. "No. Bring her in. I think we should hear what she has to say."

The Maid Servant's Story

They could hear the woman's voice long before she appeared around the bend of the drive, its broad peasant accent the same as the maid's, but crude and grating in a way hers had never been. "So this is where she ended up, the little slut. Who would've thought it!"

And the *darwan's* outraged, scolding whisper, "Watch your mouth, old woman. This is the house of *bhadralok,* decent people, not a *bustee* like you come from."

The woman's laugh was gravelly with contempt. The maid winced from it as though it were something solid, flung across the evening at her face. "Don't talk to me about *bhadralok!* I know more about them than you ever will. I've seen the inside of a lot of mansions in my time—palaces, even —and I'm not talking about drawing rooms and dining halls either."

At first when she saw her, the sister was surprised that this woman should be the mother of the maid. In her garish yellow sari and cheap silver jewelry, she seemed to belong to a lower order of humanity, her lips pulled back from her teeth in a predatory smirk. And yet, in the creases of that face which had long since given up all claim to innocence, the sister could see traces of a certain ruined beauty. It struck her that at one time men must have forgotten to breathe when they watched the mother walk down the street.

"So," said the mother, advancing on the maid. "You've been hiding out here, have you, you sly thing, while I'm going crazy looking everywhere for you. And so's Biru." Addressing

137

the husband with an obsequious bow, she explained, "They had a little tiff, husband and wife, and my silly daughter here, she ran away."

"He's not my husband," the maid said through stiff lips.

The mother ignored her. "It's lucky I was at Bappi's Tea Stall across from the temple bus stop today. The goddess's grace, what else can you call it. I'd just started on my *kima paratha* when Kamala lets out a yell that just about makes me choke. *Ai*, Lakkhi-Pishi, she says, isn't that your girl, the one that's missing. I didn't even finish my *paratha,* I tell you, I jumped right up—couldn't take a chance on losing my daughter again, could I—and ran out. She was already on the bus, but fortunately another one came right away. And here I am." Her grin brown and smug in her seamed face, she turned to the maid. "So if you'll just gather your things, we'll thank the *babu* and his good wife here, and be on our way."

"I'm not going," said the maid, her voice small but definite.

"What?"

"I'm not going."

"Oh yes you are, even if I have to drag you by your hair every step of the way."

The sister took a swift, shocked breath and turned to the wife, who sat as though in a dream, as though none of this were really happening. The maid, too, turned to her. "Please, Didi, don't make me go." She gripped the handle of the wife's chair with white fingernails.

"I'm your mother. I have the right."

Looking only at the wife, the maid said, "She sends men to my room at night, her and Biru, for the money."

The Maid Servant's Story

There was a sudden hush in the air, as before the *baisakhi* storms that rip the sky open. The sister saw that the *darwan*'s mouth had fallen comically open, and that the aunt's eyes glittered with victory. But the look on her brother-in-law's face she couldn't read.

"That's a lie, a stinking, bare-faced lie, you bitch. You'd better stop babbling and come with me right this minute. . . ."

The wife's chair fell over with a crash as she stood up, and the packet of *prasad* dropped from her lap, the sweet-meat rolling on the ground until it came to rest next to the husband's *chappal*. She swayed a little, hand pressed to her belly. The sister noted with alarm that her lips were ash color, and she too rose.

"Get rid of this—creature," said the wife to the husband in a slurred, sleepwalker's voice. She waited until he nodded at the *darwan*, and then held out her hand for the maid. "Sarala," the words came out jerky, disjointed. "Help me to my room."

As the sister rushed to take her other arm, she heard the mother shout behind her, "Creature—who's she calling *creature?* And, *babu*, don't think you can get rid of me so easily. I know my rights. You might be rich, but I can get a hundred people from the *bustee* to come back here with me tomorrow. Make a stink like you won't believe." Her voice dipped knowingly. "Don't think I can't see the real reason you're keeping my girl on—that pregnant wife of yours isn't much good for anything else right now, is she?"

And the *darwan,* shoving her before him, "Get out, get out, you filthy-minded witch, before I bash your head in.

Threaten the *babu* in his own home, will you? Just you try coming back. . . ."

"Break a stick across her back when I do get hold of her . . ." screamed the mother.

"Out, out this minute. . . ."

And the husband leaning smoothly back in his chair, the dark pooling around his bone-white *kurta*, a curiously pleased expression on his face.

By the time Dr. Hazra arrived, the wife was delirious with fever, and the ache in her belly was worse. She tossed on the bed, throwing off the covers they tried to keep on her, hitting out when the aunt tried to put on another poultice, and when her husband leaned over to ask her how she felt, she didn't seem to know him. The doctor gave her a shot and called the hospital, for she would have to be moved right away.

"We'll probably keep her there for the next few weeks, until it's safe for the baby to be born. She needs supervision. But most of all"—he looked accusingly at the rest of the household—"she needs to be kept from getting agitated."

"I can't go," the wife spoke in a tired whisper. "Who'll take care of Khuku? Who'll . . . ?"

"My dear," said the husband, taking her hands solicitously between his, "if the doctor says you must go, then of course you must. None of us like the thought of you being away, but we have to think of whatever's best for you—and the baby. You need not worry—your sister is here after all. And the maid."

"Yes, please, don't worry," said the sister, pushing back a

damp strand of hair from the wife's forehead, though every muscle in her body tightened at the thought of remaining in this house without her sister.

The wife beckoned the sister closer, until her ear was close to her mouth. "Promise me you'll stay until I get back," she said in the faint tones of one who is already far away. "Promise me you'll take care of Khuku. And, Sarala—promise me you'll take care of her too."

"I promise," said the sister, trying to keep the doubt from her voice. She felt weak and incapable, weighed down with misgivings. But what else could she say?

In the week after the wife was hospitalized, the sister was amazed at how smoothly everything at home continued to run. The *mali* watered and fertilized and mowed as usual, and even trimmed, without having to be told, the mango branches that were blocking the light from the living-room window. The cook performed magnificently, fixing a Mughlai lamb dish that the husband claimed was better than anything he had done before; the bearer-boy came to work on time; and the *ayah* didn't get into a single fight with the other servants all week. Even the little girl didn't cry for her mother, as the sister had worried she might. She went for her bath unprotestingly and let the sister comb out the tangles in her hair without kicking or screaming. She ate a good lunch and took her nap, and in the evenings she played checkers with her father quite cheerfully until bedtime.

The sister was relieved, but her relief was tinged with dismay. At first she'd interpreted this sudden spate of good

141

behavior as a temporary, shocked reaction to the wife's absence, but as the weeks passed she saw that she had been wrong. The household had closed over the departure soundlessly, without sorrow, the way the fluted leaves of the water hyacinth close over the surface of a pond after the bathers have left. As though it were the most natural thing. Would it be the same if—she couldn't keep the thought from her mind though she tried hard to push it away—her sister were dead? Is this, finally, all a life amounts to, all the mark it makes on others, she asked herself as she turned restlessly—but carefully, so as to not wake the others—on the large pallet that had been put together by joining two mattresses on the nursery floor.

The pallet was in the nursery because there had been a problem with sleeping arrangements. The wife had asked that the aunt sleep in the nursery with the little girl, while the maid slept on the floor of the sister's bedroom (for what reason the sister thought better not to ask). But from the second night on, the little girl had refused, insisting that the sister sleep with her instead.

"She snores," she said, pointing to the old woman. "And she smells too."

The aunt, bristling, had said that the wife had asked her specifically to sleep in the nursery, and no one was going to stop her from carrying out the poor sick woman's wishes.

They'd reached a compromise by having the sister join the other two in the nursery, but when she'd asked if the maid could sleep there too, the aunt had put her foot down quite firmly. The room was too small, and besides, she wasn't going to sleep in the same space as a servant girl, especially one with questionable morals. (After the mother had shown up, there had been lengthy and heated discussions about the maid's morals throughout the house, though not in the wife's hearing. In the dining room the aunt had held forth on how it was a scandal that a decent family should be asked to put up with a woman who was, by her own admission, no better than a call girl. And in the kitchen a vindicated *ayah* had told everyone how she knew, just *knew,* right from the first that the girl was *evil.*)

So the maid slept, as before, in the storeroom. And she was probably better off there, thought the sister, sighing, as for the tenth time she pushed the little girl's foot off her stomach and clamped a pillow over her ear to block out the aunt's vigorous snores.

The sister had never been a heavy sleeper. And now, what with the new sleeping arrangements and worry over the wife's health and that of her unborn child, she spent long stretches of the night lying awake. Staring at the walls streaked with moonlight, she thought of her last visit to the hospital. How the wife had lain in the narrow military-green cot she was confined to at all times by the doctor's orders, her face leached of animation, pale as old ivory. How in spite of the open windows her room had smelled faintly of urine (for she wasn't allowed to get up to go to the bathroom) and another odor the sister couldn't quite place but thought of as the smell of helplessness.

Lying awake, the sister grew familiar with the night noises of house and garden, the *jhi-jhi* insects chirping in the honeysuckle, the owls hooting mournfully from the distant *ata* tree, the geckos calling *tik-tik-tik* as they slithered over the whitewashed corridor walls. The watchman's shoes clattered on the cobbles outside the gate as he patrolled the streets with his baton, raising his voice periodically in the cautionary *kaun hai.* The dripping faucet in the bathroom sounded as though someone were impatiently tapping his fingers along a table; the door frames creaked and settled with the noise of knuckles being cracked; and the halting *shhk-shhk* of the ceiling fan was disturbingly like a person shuffling along in bedroom slippers.

But on this night in the beginning of the second week the sister heard a different sound, one that made her sit up in bed with a hand pressed against her pounding chest. It was a very soft padding, as of naked feet on marbled mosaic, coming down the corridor. What frightened the sister was the fact that it was the sound of someone trying to be quiet.

She looked down at the sleeping child beside her, the old woman breathing loudly with her mouth open. She wanted to lie down again, to plunge, like them, into an uncomplicated rest. But she couldn't. She slipped off the mattress cautiously, in spite of the voice in her head that cried *no, no, no.* She pulled her sari tight across her chest, unlatched the bedroom door, and looked out through the crack.

A man was disappearing around the bend of the corridor. She didn't recognize him. Only a little moonlight seeped into the passage, and he was dressed in the sleeveless *genji* and white *dhoti* that most Bengali men wear on hot nights. Could it be one of the servants? Did the maid have a "friend"

after all? The sister followed, keeping to the shadows, though she knew that she shouldn't. *Unwise, dangerous*, screamed the voice in her head. *What does it matter who he is?* But something about the man drew her on. When she stopped at the corner to peer into the gloom, she saw that he was knocking on the door of the storeroom, muffled, urgent beats that the sister could barely hear above the thudding of her heart.

"Who is it?" she heard the maid call, her tone wary. "Who is it?"

The man—she couldn't see his face yet—whispered something the sister couldn't catch, but she heard the latch click open. The maid appeared in the doorway, face swollen with sleep, hair and clothes disarranged. "Khuku's ill? Where is she? What's wrong? I'd better go help Choto-didi right away. . . ." And then more loudly, as the man tried to push her back into the storeroom, "No, I beg you, no, stop it, let me go, please. How can you be like this with Didi sick in the hospital?"

"Don't act so virtuous," the man hissed. "Once a whore, always a whore."

The sister recognized the voice. Dizziness swept through her—or was it terror, mixed with rage on her sister's behalf—and she had to hold on to the edge of the wall.

The man tried to clamp a hand over the maid's mouth but she twisted away. "Don't worry, no one will know. I'll make it worth your while," he said with a laugh that struck the sister like a shard of ice. "And it'll be a lot more fun with me than it was with those stinking peasants at the *bustee*."

"Let me go, Dadababu." The maid was kicking at the

man's shins now. When the man didn't release her, she clawed at his face, her voice rising threateningly. "Or else I'll scream loud enough to wake everyone in the house."

The man swore, low and vicious, clapping a hand to his cheek. He shoved the maid backward, and the sister heard her body thudding against the wall. "Bitch! You'll be sorry."

The sister caught a glimpse of her brother-in-law's rage-engorged face. And then she was running faster than she ever had in her life to get back to the bedroom before he saw her.

For years afterward, she would ask herself why she'd felt so ashamed, so guilty, as though *she* had been the clandestine one. She would wish that she'd stayed and confronted him, if only with a look. She would wonder if that might have made a difference to what happened later.

The next day the sister sat with a late-morning cup of tea on the balcony, thinking. The idea of facing her brother-in-law's polite inquiries at the breakfast table—*Is everything all right, Did you sleep well, Is there anything I can get you on my way back from the office*—had filled her with nausea, and she had stayed in bed, complaining of a headache, until he left home. Now as she listened to the maid reading aloud to the little girl, her voice rising and falling melodiously, with no trace of the night's turbulences in it, she wondered what she should do. Should she indicate to her that she knew what had happened and try, together, to figure out a plan so that it didn't occur again? Should she approach her brother-in-law with her dangerous knowledge and blackmail him into good behavior? Should she tell her sister? She remembered the wife's face,

white against the white hospital pillow, her eyes that passed
without curiosity over people's faces, as though they were part
of a distant past which no longer held meaning for her—and
knew she couldn't. Nor could she undertake the other actions
—she was not the type. Youngest in the household and a girl
besides, she'd always had people making decisions for her, or
at least telling her what to do, praising her for being tractable
and obedient, which as everyone knew were the cardinal vir-
tues of womanhood. The thought of acting on her own, of
setting in motion some uncontrollable force that might eventually shatter her sister's marriage (for she wasn't tractable,
her sister, not like her—who knew what she might take it in
her head to do if she found out what had happened?) filled
her with dread.

And besides, she told herself, staring down at the dappled sunlight playing over the red and gold dahlias that edged
the driveway, perhaps she was overreacting. These things happened—even in her sheltered provincial existence she'd heard
of them often enough. At least her brother-in-law didn't have
a "keep," a mistress set up in a separate household, as affluent
Bengali men often did. He didn't go off with his friends for
"musical" weekends which featured, as everyone knew, sing-
ers and dancers who were happy to provide other services as
well. In his way he loved his wife and was a good father to his
little girl. Perhaps the best thing would be to forget what had
happened, to forgive him his moment's lapse (he was a man,
after all, with those uncontrollable male urges she'd been
warned of time and again). To pray it wouldn't recur.

"Choto-didi! Choto-didi!"

Startled, the sister looked down to see the *darwan's*

daughter, who lived in the servant's quarter by the gate, running toward the house, panting.

"Choto-didi, there's a crowd of people at the gate, along with that one's mother." (Here she jerked her chin at the maid, who had let the book fall to the floor.) "They're trying to get in. My father's still at the office with the car, and the bearer's gone to the market. What shall we do?"

Now the sister—she'd been too deep in thought earlier —could hear the rattling of the locked gate, the angry yells that grew louder even as she listened, and then a clanging, as of rocks being thrown. Soon they'd break the lock and be on them.

The sister stood up, her whole body trembling. She had to do something—and soon. But what? She tried to think of what her sister would have done—not the woman who now lay in the hospital as though at the bottom of a lake, with all that stagnant water pressing down on her, but her vibrant earlier self. She closed her eyes to remember the wife's strong, sweet voice, the confident grace of her gestures, and when she opened them she told the *darwan*'s daughter to fetch the *mali* and the cook.

"Take Khuku to her room," she said to the maid, "and stay there, no matter what."

The maid stared at her as though she hadn't understood.

"Go!" snapped the sister, suddenly furious with her, and the maid moved away, holding the little girl's hand. There was something odd about her walk, but the sister, rushing to call the police, couldn't tell what it was. Years later, as she watched a film about migrating birds, it would strike her that the maid had moved with the stiff gait of lost seabirds that find themselves in a landlocked field far from home.

The sister felt a little better after she had reached the police.

"They'll be here right away," she told the anxiously waiting *mali* and cook. "Now you come with me to the gate."

The cook twisted the dishcloth hanging from his shoulder. "Don't you think we should just stay in the house, Choto-didi, with the doors and windows locked? Don't you think you should call Dadababu?" Oily drops of sweat beaded his upper lip and the sister realized that he too had never faced anything like this before. Curiously, it made some of her fear dissipate.

"No," she said, answering his first question. (She wasn't ready to deal with the second, which really meant *why haven't you called him.*) "We must show them we're not afraid. *Now.* Once they break in we won't be able to control them, but if we act right away we still can." She was surprised at how calm she sounded, how logical, as though she really believed in what she was saying.

The three of them made their way to the gate, and when they were there the sister saw that the massive iron sheets were dented by rocks and the wrought-iron carvings of spears hung bent in unnatural shapes, like broken arms and legs. She looked at the faces on the other side, seeing them piecemeal —the rotted, tobacco-stained teeth, the flared nostrils, the corners of mouths turned down in hate so strong that she could smell it as clearly as their sweat. The eyes glazed with the euphoria of destruction. They weren't people, *real* people. Try as she might, she couldn't put their fragmented features together to form an entire human face. The cold, quicksilver terror flooded her veins again, making her voice shake as she asked what they wanted, and from their wolfish grins she could see that they too sensed its presence.

"We want the girl. Give us the girl."

"Her mother wants her back, and so does her man. You got no right to keep her."

"Up to no good we hear, you folks. Taking advantage of a young girl like that."

"All you rich people, all alike, think you own the earth."

Clumps of onlookers had gathered at the edges of the mob by now, street vendors and sweepers, passersby on their way to work, servants from some of the neighboring houses. The sister searched their faces for support but found only elation at the prospect of drama, the rich folks finally getting what they deserve. She bit down on the inside of her cheek until she tasted blood, salty, metallic. The throbbing pain took away some of her fear.

"No one's keeping Sarala against her wishes. She doesn't want to go back to her mother, or her"—with a mental apology to the maid, she forced herself to say the word—"husband."

"Sarala! Is that what she's calling herself nowadays!"

"What's this about her not wanting? Everyone knows a daughter belongs to her parents, a wife to her husband. *Sahibi* talk like this is what's making our families fall apart."

"Look, miss, you better not stick your finger in what isn't your business. We got no quarrel with you. Just call the girl to the gate. We'll take her and be off."

"Shall I go get her?" whispered the cook.

The wife's face floated into the sister's vision. It was the palest yellow, as though, having been underwater a long time, it had taken on the color of lake sand. Strands of uncombed hair tangled around it like water weeds. The eyes were closed, in death or resignation.

"No," she said. "No!"

An angry sound, half roar, half hiss, rose from the crowd, and they moved closer. Someone began to rattle the gates again.

"You'll be sorry." She recognized the mother's voice, strangely happy, though in the melee she couldn't find her face.

A clod hit her shoulder, and something else—hard, abrasive—struck her cheek. They were throwing whatever they could get their hands on—mud, clumps of grass, pebbles. She could hear the pounding of stone on metal as someone attacked the lock again. She put up an arm to shield her face and heard the sharp crack as the lock gave. Someone—the *mali* perhaps—pushed her out of the way against the *hasnahana* bushes as the gates opened and the crowd pressed forward with a cry of jubilation.

And then she heard the sirens.

"Imagine!" said the aunt at the dinner table that night. "The police and everything, in *our* compound. Vans, sirens, handcuffs. The whole neighborhood gathered around, gaping. What shame! In my seventy-two years I've never seen anything like this. The *hasnahana* bushes by the gate all trampled —it'll take years to grow them back. We should have got rid of that bad-luck girl a long time back, like I said."

"We should have," said the husband, fingering the strip of sticking plaster that ran down the side of his face. "I should have been firmer about it." There were white lines around his mouth, thin, tight lines that the sister tried to decipher, but couldn't quite. All she knew was that it wasn't just anger, nothing simple like that.

"And have you seen the gate?" said the aunt. "Completely ruined. That ironwork was from your grandfather's time. We'll never be able to replace it."

"Mr. Chowdhury from next door phoned this evening," said the husband, "to ask me what was the reason for such disgraceful goings-on. Those were his words. I've never been so humiliated."

The aunt clucked sympathetically.

"And worst of all, you're hurt," he added to the sister, indicating the bandage on her cheek. "I feel responsible for that."

"Please," said the sister through dry lips, for she could see where this was leading. "Don't worry about me."

"But think what might have happened if the police hadn't arrived just then!" said the husband. He gave a shudder, as though even the imagining of such a possibility was too much for him. Then he turned to the cook, who had been listening avidly from the doorway, and asked him to summon the maid, and when she arrived he told her, in his kind, reasonable voice, that he appreciated her difficulties but had to think of the reputation and safety of his household. Surely she could see why he couldn't keep her on. All of this was very bad for the little girl, who was already upset by her mother being in the hospital; the people next door had complained, and rightly, that events like this were intolerable in a neighborhood that had been written up in *The Statesman* as one of the best in Calcutta; and look what had happened to Choto-didi—attacked and maybe scarred for the rest of her life.

"I'm fine," insisted the sister. "It's only a scratch." But no one paid her any attention.

"I have no doubts about your moral character," continued the husband. "However, I have no choice but to let you go."

The maid did not weep or plead to be kept on. From her unsurprised face the sister could see that she had known—perhaps for a long time—that this was going to happen.

"I'm sure you understand," said the husband.

"I understand," said the maid. There was something in her tone—an irony, perhaps—that made the husband lose his composure for a moment. But he recovered almost immediately and told her, in his customary benevolent tones, that of course she would be paid for the full month. And since it was dark already—he wasn't an unreasonable man—she could stay the night, as long as she was gone first thing in the morning.

In the middle of his sentence, the maid left the room.

"What impertinence," said the aunt. "Really, the lower classes today, I don't know what they're coming to. In my father's day, a servant would have been whipped for acting like that. Why . . ."

"You can't just send her away!" the sister cried. "It's not her fault."

"No one said it was," said the husband. Beneath the softness in his voice lay a razor edge of warning.

But the sister continued, "Her life will be ruined if she leaves here—her mother's bound to get hold of her again. And she was doing so well, learning to read and . . ."

"My first responsibility is the welfare of my family. That woman has caused nothing but trouble since the day she came."

The sister tried to garner strength from her morning's victory over the mob, to say something devastating that would make him choke on his hypocritical words. *I know why you're really getting rid of her.* But she wasn't ready for what such a comment might unleash. Besides, it was one thing to face a ragged bunch of intruders from the *bustee* and another to stand up against the suave power of her brother-in-law. Hating the conciliatory words even as she spoke, she said, "At least wait until Didi gets home—she was so fond of Sarala. . . ." She noticed with dismay that she was speaking in the past tense, as though the maid were gone already.

The husband, who had also noticed the slip, gave a victorious smile. "All the more reason for her to go right now. We wouldn't want your sister to go through another trauma right after she comes back from the hospital, would we? And you know just as well as I that your sister, dear woman though she is, is prone to get overly emotional."

"Please," the sister tried once more, because she had promised her sister. But she knew it was no use.

The husband held up his hand.

"Credit me with a little intelligence. I know what's best

for my household. You *will* agree that I'm still the head of this household, no?"

The sister felt as though a fist were squeezing her chest, leaving no room for breath. As she pushed away her half-eaten dinner and rose to leave, she heard the husband's voice saying, from very far away, "If I were you, I wouldn't agitate your sister by telling her any of this. In her unstable condition, something fatal may well occur. . . ."

And so the wife knew nothing of what happened until she came home with her new baby, who was born full-term and healthy—which was more than people had hoped for—and was, besides, a boy. She was swept up into a flurry of congratulatory visits and general jubilation. (Even the aunt had only good things to say about her ability to mother such a charming, bright-eyed son, and with so much hair, too, just like his father when he'd been a baby.) But one afternoon she called the sister into her bedroom, where the new air conditioner which the husband had bought for the baby hummed comfortingly, and asked her what exactly had gone on while she'd been away.

The sister looked away from the wife's eyes, their dark, penetrating gaze, to where the baby slept. She stared at his dimpled knees, his little fisted hands that twitched from time to time, his impossibly tiny, perfect mouth that was puckered as though ready for a kiss. She loved him so much already that every time she looked at him she felt a tugging pain in her chest. He was so defenseless. Without a father, he would be more so. And Khuku with her luminous, wondering eyes—she would lose all chances for a good marriage if the scandal of a broken home stained her life. And the wife herself, what future was there for women who, no matter how pressing the reason, left their husbands' homes?

The night the husband dismissed the maid, the sister ran from the dinner table all the way up to the storeroom, where the maid was gathering her things.

"You're not leaving tonight?" the sister asked, distressed, and then, "But where will you go?"

"I'm not sure," the maid said, and for the first time her voice trembled. In the passage light her face looked young and afraid.

"I'm sorry," the sister said, clasping the maid's hand in her own. "I'm really sorry. I wish I could do something."

"Nothing to be done now," the maid said, gently disengaging her fingers. And the sister realized that the maid knew that she knew, and that she forgave her for not accusing the husband, for not using his lapse to help the maid's case.

"Tell Didi . . ." the maid started, then broke off, so that for a long time after the sister would wonder what she had wanted the wife to know. About the husband's actions? About her own fidelity to the woman who had taken her in? About injustice and ill chance? Whatever it was, she knew she couldn't tell it to her sister. But she did tell her the last thing the maid said, with a sigh, before she disappeared around the corner of the passage. *I wish I could have seen her one last time.*

"I wish I could have too," the wife replied. She wiped her eyes with the edge of her sari and, leaving her sleeping baby, went to the storeroom which no one had entered since the maid's departure. Following her, the sister saw something she hadn't noticed that night. The maid hadn't taken all her belongings with her. Piled neatly in the far corner of the tiny room lay the slate and chalk box and the readers the maid had studied with such passionate care. When the wife picked them up, the women noticed something else—at the bottom of the pile was the saffron sari.

"Poor Sarala," the wife said after a long silence, smoothing out the delicate, crushed fabric. "Poor, poor girl." She put the small pile back just as it had been and closed the door of the storeroom behind her. In the few remaining days of the sister's visit, she did not mention the maid again.

It was over a year later when the sister returned to Calcutta, this time to pick out her wedding trousseau, for her marriage had recently been arranged. It was a good match. Her husband-to-be was an engineer for Ralli's Fans and lived in a large company flat in Khiddirpore, a fairly decent Calcutta neighborhood, and owned his own scooter—all of which, everyone agreed, was a fine achievement for a young man not yet thirty. He wasn't bad-looking either.

Perhaps it was the excitement of the coming wedding and all the shopping to be done, or perhaps the pleasure of seeing the children who crowded around her, the little one tripping over his feet in his excitement, shouting *mashi, mashi*. Or maybe it was the glowing joy with which her sister embraced her saying, "My dear, I'm so glad. He seems like a really nice man. Besides, we'll practically be neighbors. We'll be able to see each other all the time—I can send the car for you in the afternoons when the men are at work—and gossip to our hearts' content. And our children can grow up together." At any rate, the sister found herself enjoying hugely the visit she'd looked to with some dread. Even conversing with her brother-in-law, who was as debonairly charming as ever, was less difficult than she'd feared.

This night, for example, on their way to a housewarming ceremony at the new home of a business associate, he was jovially discussing her husband-to-be. The poor man had no chance, he said. She would control every waking moment of his life, and probably his dreams as well, just like her *didi* did with *her* husband. It was the fate of married men.

In the back of the car—it was a new one this time, a powder-blue Rolls Royce, because the husband had recently been made manager of his branch—the wife smiled and shook her head indulgently. She looked at her sister over the heads of the children, who were dressed, according to the husband's instructions, in elaborate party clothes befitting his new position. "He likes to joke, your brother-in-law," she said as she straightened the little boy's silk *kurta* and tucked a curl into the girl's filigreed gold headband.

"Dadababu." It was the driver, sounding anxious. "There's a *michil* up ahead. If we get caught in it, we'll be stuck for hours."

"Damn!" said the husband with a scowl. "These strikers and union-*wallahs*, always blocking the roads with their flags and their shouts, their unreasonable demands. Messing up the lives of decent folks. They should be thrown in jail, the lot of them, like when the British were here. Teach them a lesson."

To the driver he added, "Take another road, and make sure we get to the ceremony on time."

"The only other way is through the *mandi*," said the driver hesitantly.

"We'll have to take it then," the husband said, annoyed. He waved an impatient hand at the driver. "Go on, what are you waiting for?"

The sister leaned forward, staring, as the car turned sharply and entered an alleyway barely wide enough for a vehicle to pass. She'd never been in this part of the city. She noticed that the pavements were more crowded here, and with a different kind of people. There were, of course, the usual vendors who spilled onto the street with their wares of sweet-smelling jasmine garlands, colorful glass bangles, and hot onion *pakoras*. And the ubiquitous *chai*-boys hurried back and forth with racks of tea glasses from which steam rose and mingled with the vapor from the gas street lamps. But what about the men—large numbers of them, dressed in embroidered *kurtas* with glittering buttons, garlands wrapped about their hands—who sauntered up and down the street, seemingly going nowhere? And the women who crowded the balconies of the narrow buildings lining the road, their lips red with betel juice, thick lines of *surma* smearing their eyelids? They jangled their bracelets as they waved to the passing men and let the *palloos* of their gauzy nylex saris slide artfully from their bosoms. The sister's cheeks grew hot as she realized who they were.

"Can't you hurry?" the husband asked the driver in an irritated tone.

"Sorry, Dadababu—there's just too many people—and

you know how they are nowadays, ready to smash the car windows if you even touch them with a fender."

The wife had been trying to divert the children's attention from the street with a game of rhymes, but as the car lurched to a halt at a corner, she glanced up. Three women were standing on the pavement, and when the car stopped one called out something to the men in front and blew them a kiss, while the other two burst into raucous laughter.

"Disgusting," said the husband, turning away, but the wife, who'd been staring at the woman who had spoken, drew her breath in sharply.

"Isn't that Sarala?" she said, and started to roll down her window.

"What the hell are you doing!" exclaimed the husband. "Are you crazy? Don't you realize that these are . . . ?"

"It's Sarala, I'm sure it is," said the wife, and leaning out of her window she called breathlessly, "Sarala! Sarala!"

"Put up your window this minute," shouted the husband. And to the driver, furiously, "Get out of here. Right now. I don't care how you do it."

In the back seat, the children, scared by the shouting, had started to cry, but the wife didn't seem to hear them. Or the sister, who was tugging at the *palloo* of her *zari*-embroidered sari, pleading for her to sit back.

"Sarala," she called again. She was struggling with the lock now, trying to open the door as the car inched forward.

The woman creased her eyes and bent to peer into the car's dark plush interior. The sister stared, fascinated, at the gaping neck of her low-cut blouse, the white powder layering the cleavage between the breasts. Fumes of cheap perfume and alcohol filled the car. The face—was it the maid's? How could the wife seem so certain? She herself couldn't see sufficiently past the plaster of makeup, past the jaded droop of eyelid and mouth, to be sure.

The husband reached across from the front seat and grabbed the wife's arm, his mouth taut with anger or fear.

But the wife reached out through the window with her other hand, its pale, cool fingers shining with her wedding rings, toward the woman. "Sarala," she said, "it's me, Didi."

The woman stared at her for a moment, then spat. A bloodred wad of betel leaf splattered against the wife's palm. She sat there looking at it, long after the woman had swung away, long after the husband had jerked her away from the window and ordered the sister to roll it up. After the driver, finding a fortunate gap in the crowd, had roared forward. After the sister, with shaking fingers, had scrubbed and scrubbed at her hand with a lace-edged handkerchief until no trace of the stain was left.

"That was stupid," the husband snapped as the car, having made it back to the main road, picked up speed. "Those women—they're no better than animals. She could have done worse—snatched your rings, your bangles, anything."

"It was Sarala, I know it," the wife said in a voice of toneless calm which frightened the sister more than any hysterical outburst.

The husband's mouth was an ugly gash in his face. "That was a whore, do you understand, a *whore*." But his voice, thought the sister, shook the tiniest bit.

Next morning the wife called the *ayah* to the storeroom and handed her the things the maid had left behind.

"Burn them," she said.

"Everything?" asked the *ayah,* her voice high with shocked disapproval. "Even *this?*" She ran a longing hand over the flawless, petal-soft surface of the saffron sari, finer than anything she ever hoped to own.

"Especially that," said the wife. Her face seemed composed entirely of planes and angles, as though it would never soften into a smile again.

"But it's so beautiful—it would be such a waste," said the *ayah.* A note at once accusing and cajoling crept into her voice. "You could maybe let me have it?"

"Burn it," shouted the wife. The *ayah*, who had never before heard her mistress raise her voice, backed away in fear. "Didn't you hear me? Burn it right now if you want to keep your job."

("Imagine!" the *ayah* would later say indignantly to the other servants, who had, of course, been given a full account of the evening by the driver. "She threatened to fire me. *Me,* who's been working for this household twenty years, long before she came into it. And all over a sari she'd given to that slut."

"Shows you what strong *jadu* that girl worked in the short time she was here," the cook responded, making a sign to ward off the evil eye.)

The wife shut herself in her room and did not open the

door all day and all night, not when the sister called her for lunch, not when the children, crying at naptime, came looking for her. Even when the husband, back from work, rattled the knob and said, *What nonsense is this now,* she remained inside, so silent that the sister wondered apprehensively if she had done something to harm herself.

But in the morning she rose and took her bath and combed her long wet hair neatly down her back. She put on a sunrise-red *bindi* and a freshly ironed *dhakai* sari and set out office clothes for the husband (who, forced to sleep for the first time in his life in the guest room, had submitted to this indignity with surprising meekness). She summoned the cook and told him what to make for lunch and dinner, reminding him to drain the fried *brinjal* on newspapers before serving it, warning him not to put any chili paste in the children's chicken curry, nor any *dhania* leaf either, because it always made the little boy throw up. She played Ludo with the children until they went for their nap, then called the sister to come and choose a suitable design, from the Sheffield catalogue that the husband ordered each year from Britain, for the silver dinner set that was to be their wedding gift to her. In the evening she sat on the veranda with the family and served tea in the fragile Wedgewood cups that had been part of her dowry and wiped the children's mouths and made conversation in a voice calm as the just-watered jasmine bushes that lined the steps.

And it was like this every day till the end of the sister's visit, as though that brief upheaval of household had never been. As though no one had seen that woman with her tawdry clothes, her lewd, painted face. Her contempt-filled eyes that came back to haunt the sister—and surely the husband?—when they lay defenseless under the onslaught of sleep. Everyone breathed a sigh of relief that things were back to normal—it had been so discomfiting to have the wife behave in that crazed manner, even for a day.

But sometimes in the heat-encrusted afternoons when the wife looked up from a piece of embroidery to stare through the window bars at the blank yellow sky, the sister felt that something was gone, irrevocably, from her face. How much had she guessed of the maid's story? It was impossible to tell. A patina of hardness that kept the sister from looking in had descended on her. Over the years it would thicken (though no one except the sister seemed to notice) into a burnished mask that gave away nothing. Watching, the sister would shiver, as though she felt the cold hardening of her own arteries. She would grieve silently and, yes, guiltily (no matter how often she told herself that it wasn't her fault) for that eager embracive grace which had once made her sister a rare and magical being.

Night has taken over the lawn by the time Deepa Mashi finishes the story. We sit in the dark room, held by the echo of her words, until she reaches over to switch on the lamp. Her cheeks glimmer wetly in the sudden light.

"Mashi, you're crying."

Mashi laughs embarrassedly, dismissively. "Oh, you know me, I'm too emotional. No wonder Uncle is always scolding me about it. Any sad story can make me cry. Remember the time we went to see that movie about the kidnapped girl, what was it, *Umrao Jaan,* at the Globe—I went through three handkerchiefs. . . ."

But there's something more. I feel it in the uneasy silence that has gathered in the corners of the room, among the houseplants and knick-knacks and wall hangings that look suddenly dusty and sad, as though they embodied some unendingly futile human endeavor—a search for beauty, a belief in luck. A hope that happiness will endure. My aunt's beleaguered world is not the simple one I have always taken it to be.

"Mashi," I ask, "why did you tell me this story?"

Mashi fidgets, uncomfortable with the bald, western habit I've acquired of going at things head on. It isn't proper, womanly, safe.

"I don't know," she finally says, not looking at me.

She's not telling me everything, I sense it. Is this a cautionary parable for brides-to-be? An ancestral tale taken from some outlying branch of our convoluted family tree? Then it strikes me—but without surprise, as though the realization had lain in my subconscious throughout the telling. The events could have happened to my own mother. The child that died of cholera, along with my father, was a boy. He could well have been the baby in the story, and I the little girl.

I try to push aside the cobwebbed years to get at those pre-epidemic days before my mother moved with me to the small flat (more suited to a widow's lifestyle and finances) where I grew up, the home where she still lives, the home which appears in all my dreams of childhood—and my nightmares. And now it seems I remember an old house—long marble halls, bright magenta bougainvillea trailing the balcony, the cool whirr of fans in high-ceilinged bedrooms. Once unleashed, the images will not stop: afternoon games of Ludo and checkers, my father's cologne-scented kiss as I run down the graveled driveway, dodging the *mali*'s hose, to the black Studebaker that brought him home. Lullabies sung in a country accent haunting as the moonlight that glimmered in the palm trees.

I tell myself that it's only my aunt's storytelling taking root in my overfertile imagination. But I'm sure they happened to me, those sun-filled balcony mornings when I sat at the feet of a woman with a smile sweeter than palm-honey. Her hands were a gentle wind in my hair. When she lifted me onto her lap—*come, Khuku*—awkwardly, around the growing curve of her belly, I never wanted her to set me down. A woman so different from the mother I know that I want to hit out at someone, to shatter something, to scream until I have no breath left. For a moment I feel the burden of guilt my aunt must bear and wonder if her loving of me, all these years, has been in part an attempt at reparation.

The others, they existed too—the cranky *ayah* with her bark-wrinkled face, the deaf aunt whose snores cut through my sleep like a raspy saw, the sweaty cook who made the divinest rice pudding, thickly studded with sugared almonds and fat golden raisins. The slim girl with long hair who played catch with me in the gloom of evening under the *lichu* trees and read to me of jinns and water witches in a shivery, silvery voice.

The Maid Servant's Story

And that last evening—I'm not just giving form to my aunt's words when I see it again. The forbidden street filled with the bitter scent of drying marigold and jasmine. A woman's lips twisted in a sneer that is perhaps her defense against heartbreak. A man's dark face where fear battles rage. My mother curling her fingers around the red stain in her palm as though around a wound that will never heal, while the brightness drains from her face.

"It's my mother's story, isn't it," I say to Mashi.

"Oh dear!" Mashi wrings her hands in agitation. "What an idea! It's just a story—I should never have brought it up."

I know she will not tell me any more. It's how we survive, we Indian women whose lives are half light and half darkness, stopping short of revelations that would otherwise crisp away our skins. I'm left alone to figure the truth of the story, to puzzle out why it was given to me.

And then, along the illogical byways of thought, Bijoy's face flashes against my raw, aching eyelids, handsome and charming and full of laughter, but also—I have never admitted this before—implacable. I wonder if the story (though not intended as such by my aunt) is a warning for me, a preview of my own life which I thought I had fashioned so cleverly, so differently from my mother's, but which is only a repetition, in a different *raga*, of her tragic song. Perhaps it is like this for all daughters, doomed to choose for ourselves, over and over, the men who have destroyed our mothers.

"It's late," says Deepa Mashi. "I'd better start dinner. Uncle will be *so* annoyed if he finds out how I've been wasting the afternoon away on silly stories." But she doesn't move, and

167

when I reach for her hand, she holds tightly to my fingers. We sit like this, two women caught in the repeating, circular world of shadow and memory, watching where the last light, silky and fragile, has spilled itself just above the horizon like the *palloo* of a saffron sari.

THE
DISAPPEARANCE

AT FIRST WHEN THEY HEARD ABOUT THE DISAPPEARANCE, people didn't believe it.

Why, we saw her just yesterday at the Ram Ratan Indian Grocery, friends said, picking out radishes for pickling. And wasn't she at the Mountain View park with her little boy last week, remember, we waved from our car and she waved back, she was in that blue *salwaar-kameez*, yes, she never did wear American clothes. And the boy waved too, he must be, what, two and a half? Looks just like her with those big black eyes, that dimple. What a shame, they said, it's getting so that you aren't safe anywhere in this country nowadays.

Because that's what everyone suspected, including the husband. Crime. Otherwise, he said to the investigating policeman (he had called the police that very night), how could a young Indian woman wearing a yellow-flowered *kurta* and Nike walking shoes just *disappear*? She'd been out for her evening walk, she took one every day after he got back from the office. Yes, yes, always alone, she said that was her time for herself. (He didn't quite understand that, but he was happy to watch his little boy, play ball with him, perhaps, until she returned to serve them dinner.)

Did you folks have a quarrel, asked the policeman, looking up from his notepad with a frown, and the husband looked directly back into his eyes and said, No, of course we didn't.

Later he would think about what the policeman had asked, while he sat in front of his computer in his office, or while he lay in the bed which still seemed to smell of her. (But surely that was his imagination—the linen had been washed already.) He *had* told the truth about them not having a quarrel, hadn't he? (He prided himself on being an honest man, he often told his son how important it was not to lie, see what happened to Pinocchio's nose. And even now when the boy asked him where Mama was, he didn't say she had gone on a trip, as some of his friends' wives had advised him. I don't know, he said. And when the boy's thin face would crumple, want Mama, when she coming back, he held him in his lap awkwardly and tried to stroke his hair, like he had seen his wife do, but he couldn't bring himself to say what the boy needed to hear, *soon-soon*. I don't know, he said over and over.)

They hadn't really had a fight. She wasn't, thank God, the quarrelsome type, like some of his friends' wives. Quiet. That's how she was, at least around him, although sometimes when he came home unexpectedly he would hear her singing to her son, her voice slightly off-key but full and confident. Or laughing as she chased him around the family room, Mama's going to get you, get you, both of them shrieking with delight until they saw him. Hush now, she would tell the boy, settle down, and they would walk over sedately to give him his welcome-home kiss.

He couldn't complain, though. Wasn't that what he had specified when his mother started asking, When are you getting married, I'm getting old, I want to see a grandson before I die.

If you can find me a quiet, pretty girl, he wrote, not brash, like Calcutta girls are nowadays, not with too many western ideas. Someone who would be relieved to have her husband make the major decisions. But she had to be smart, at least a year of college, someone he could introduce to his friends with pride.

He'd flown to Calcutta to view several suitable girls that his mother had picked out. But now, thinking back, he can only remember her. She had sat, head bowed, jasmine plaited into her hair, silk sari draped modestly over her shoulders, just like all the other prospective brides he'd seen. Nervous, he'd thought, yearning to be chosen. But when she'd glanced up there had been a cool, considering look in her eyes. Almost disinterested, almost as though *she* were wondering if he would make a suitable spouse. He had wanted her then, had married her within the week in spite of his mother's protests (had she caught that same look?) that something about the girl just didn't feel *right*.

He was a good husband. No one could deny it. He let

171

her have her way, indulged her, even. When the kitchen was remodeled, for example, and she wanted pink and gray tiles even though he preferred white. Or when she wanted to go to Yosemite Park instead of Reno, although he knew he would be dreadfully bored among all those bearshit-filled trails and dried-up waterfalls. Once in a while, of course, he had to put his foot down, like when she wanted to get a job or go back to school or buy American clothes. But he always softened his no's with a remark like, What for, I'm here to take care of you, or, You look so much prettier in your Indian clothes, so much more feminine. He would pull her onto his lap and give her a kiss and a cuddle which usually ended with him taking her to the bedroom.

That was another area where he'd had to be firm. Sex. She was always saying, Please, not tonight, I don't feel up to it. He didn't mind that. She was, after all, a well-bred Indian girl. He didn't expect her to behave like those American women he sometimes watched on X-rated videos, screaming and biting and doing other things he grew hot just thinking about. But her reluctance went beyond womanly modesty. After dinner for instance she would start on the most elaborate household projects, soaping down the floors, changing the liners in cabinets. The night before she disappeared she'd started cleaning windows, taken out the Windex and the rags as soon as she'd put the boy to bed, even though he said, Let's go. Surely he couldn't be blamed for raising his voice at those times (though never so much as to wake his son), or for grabbing her by the elbow and pulling her to the bed, like he did that last night. He was always careful not to hurt her, he prided himself on that. Not even a little slap, not like some of the men he'd known growing up, or even some of his friends now. And he always told himself he'd stop if she really begged him, if she cried. After some time, though, she would quit struggling and let him do what he wanted. But that was nothing new. That could have nothing to do with the disappearance.

Two weeks passed and there was no news of the woman, even though the husband had put a notice in the *San Jose Mercury* as well as a half-page ad in *India West*, which he photocopied and taped to neighborhood lampposts. The ad had a photo of her, a close-up taken in too-bright sunlight where she gazed gravely at something beyond the camera. WOMAN MISS-ING, read the ad. REWARD $100,000. (How on earth would he come up with that kind of money, asked his friends. The husband confessed that it would be difficult, but he'd manage somehow. His wife was more important to him, after all, than all the money in the world. And to prove it he went to the bank the very same day and brought home a sheaf of forms to fill so that he could take out a second mortgage on the house.) He kept calling the police station, too, but the police weren't much help. They were working on it, they said. They'd checked the local hospitals and morgues, the shelters. They'd even sent her description to other states. But there were no leads. It didn't look very hopeful.

So finally he called India and over a faulty long-distance connection that made his voice echo eerily in his ear told his mother what had happened. My poor boy, she cried, left all alone (the word flickered unpleasantly across his brain, *left, left*), how can you possibly cope with the household and a child as well. And when he admitted that yes, it was very difficult, could she perhaps come and help out for a while if it wasn't too much trouble, she had replied that of course she would come right away and stay as long as he needed her, and what was all this American nonsense about too much trouble, he was her only son, wasn't he. She would contact the wife's family too, she ended, so he wouldn't have to deal with that awkwardness.

Within a week she had closed up the little flat she had lived in since her husband's death, got hold of a special family emergency visa, and was on her way. Almost as though she'd been waiting for something like this to happen, said some of the women spitefully. (These were his wife's friends, though maybe acquaintances would be a more accurate word. His wife had liked to keep to herself, which had been just fine with him. He was glad, he'd told her several times, that she didn't spend hours chattering on the phone like the other Indian wives.)

He was angry when this gossip reached him (perhaps because he'd had the same insidious thought for a moment when, at the airport, he noticed how happy his mother looked, her flushed excited face appearing suddenly young). Really, he said to his friends, some people see only what they *want* to see. Didn't *they* think it was a good thing she'd come over? Oh yes, said his friends. Look how well the household was running now, the furniture dusted daily, laundry folded and put into drawers (his mother, a smart woman, had figured out the washing machine in no time at all). She cooked all his favorite dishes, which his wife had never managed to learn quite right, and she took *such* good care of the little boy, walking him to the park each afternoon, bringing him into her bed when he woke up crying at night. (He'd told her once or twice that his wife had never done that, she had this idea about the boy needing to be independent. What nonsense, said his mother.) Lucky man, a couple of his friends added and he silently agreed, although later he thought it was ironic that they would say that about a man whose wife had disappeared.

As the year went on, the husband stopped thinking as much about the wife. It wasn't that he loved her any less, or that the shock of her disappearance was less acute. It was just that it wasn't on his mind all the time. There would be stretches of time—when he was on the phone with an important client, or when he was watching after-dinner TV or driving his son to kiddie gym class—when he would forget that his wife was gone, that he had had a wife at all. And even when he remembered that he had forgotten, he would experience only a slight twinge, similar to what he felt in his teeth when he drank something too cold too fast. The boy, too, didn't ask as often about his mother. He was sleeping through the nights again, he had put on a few pounds (because he was finally being fed right, said the grandmother), and he had started calling her "Ma," just like his father did.

So it seemed quite natural for the husband to, one day, remove the photographs of his wife from the frames that sat on the mantelpiece and replace them with pictures of himself and his little boy that friends had taken on a recent trip to Great America, and also one of the boy on his grandma's lap,

175

holding a red birthday balloon, smiling (she said) exactly like his father used to at that age. He put the old pictures into a manila envelope and slid them to the back of a drawer, intending to show them to his son when he grew up. The next time his mother asked (as she had been doing ever since she got there), shall I put away all those saris and *kameezes*, it'll give you more space in the closet, he said, if you like. When she said, it's now over a year since the tragedy, shouldn't we have a prayer service done at the temple, he said OK. And when she told him, you really should think about getting married again, you're still young, and besides, the boy needs a mother, shall I contact second aunt back home, he remained silent but didn't disagree.

Then one night while cooking cauliflower curry, her specialty, his mother ran out of *hing*, which was, she insisted, essential to the recipe. The Indian grocery was closed, but the husband remembered that sometimes his wife used to keep extra spices on the top shelf. So he climbed on a chair to look. There were no extra spices, but he did find something he had forgotten about, an old tea tin in which he'd asked her to hide her jewelry in case the house ever got burgled. Nothing major was ever kept there. The expensive wedding items were all stored in a vault. Still, the husband thought it would be a good idea to take them into the bank in the morning.

But when he picked up the tin it felt surprisingly light, and when he opened it, there were only empty pink nests of tissue inside.

He stood there holding the tin for a moment, not

breathing. Then he reminded himself that his wife had been a careless woman. He'd often had to speak to her about leaving things lying around. The pieces could be anywhere—pushed to the back of her makeup drawer or forgotten under a pile of books in the spare room where she used to spend inordinate amounts of time reading. Nevertheless he was not himself the rest of the evening, so much so that his mother said, What happened, you're awfully quiet, are you all right, your face looks funny. He told her he was fine, just a little pain in the chest area. Yes, he would make an appointment with the doctor tomorrow, no, he wouldn't forget, now could she please leave him alone for a while.

The next day he took the afternoon off from work, but he didn't go to the doctor. He went to the bank. In a small stuffy cubicle that smelled faintly of mold, he opened his safety deposit box to find that all her jewelry was gone. She hadn't taken any of the other valuables.

The edges of the cubicle seemed to fade and darken at the same time, as though the husband had stared at a lightbulb for too long. He ground his fists into his eyes and tried to imagine her on that last morning, putting the boy in his stroller and walking the twenty minutes to the bank (they only had one car, which he took to work; they could have afforded another, but why, he said to his friends, when she didn't even know how to drive). Maybe she had sat in this very cubicle and lifted out the emerald earrings, the pearl choker, the long gold chain. He imagined her wrapping the pieces carefully in plastic bags, the thin, clear kind one got at the grocery for vegetables, then slipping them into her purse. Or did she just throw them in anyhow, the strands of the necklace tangling, the brilliant green stones clicking against each other in the darkness inside the handbag, the boy laughing and clapping his hands at this new game.

At home that night he couldn't eat any dinner, and before he went to bed he did thirty minutes on the dusty exercise bike that sat in the corner of the family room. Have you gone crazy, asked his mother. He didn't answer. When he finally lay down, the tiredness did not put him to sleep as he had hoped. His calves ached from the unaccustomed strain, his head throbbed from the images that would not stop coming, and the bedclothes, when he pulled them up to his neck, smelled again of his wife's hair.

Where was she now? And with whom? Because surely she couldn't manage on her own. He'd always thought her to be like the delicate purple passion-flower vines that they'd put up on trellises along their back fence, and once, early in the marriage, had presented her with a poem he'd written about this. He remembered how, when he held out the sheet to her, she'd stared at him for a long moment and a look he couldn't quite read had flickered in her eyes. Then she'd taken the poem with a small smile. He went over and over all the men she might have known, but they (mostly his Indian friends) were safely married and still at home, every one.

The bed felt hot and lumpy. He tossed his feverish body around like a caught animal, punched the pillow, threw the blanket to the floor. Even thought, for a wild moment, of shaking the boy awake and asking him, *Who did your mama see?* And as though he had an inbuilt antenna that picked up his father's agitation, in the next room the boy started crying (which he hadn't done for months), shrill screams that left him breathless. And when his father and grandmother rushed to see what the problem was, he pushed them from him with all the strength in his small arms, saying, Go way, don't want you, want Mama, want Mama.

After the boy had been dosed with gripe water and settled in bed again, the husband sat alone in the family room with a glass of brandy. He wasn't a drinker. He believed that alcohol was for weak men. But somehow he couldn't face the rumpled bed just yet, the pillows wrested onto the floor. The unknown areas of his wife's existence yawning blackly around him like chasms. Should he tell the police, he wondered, would it do any good? What if somehow his friends came to know? *Didn't I tell you, right from the first*, his mother would say. And anyway it was possible she was already dead, killed by a stranger from whom she'd hitched a ride, or by a violent, jealous lover. He felt a small, bitter pleasure at the thought, and then a pang of shame.

Nevertheless he made his way to the dark bedroom (a trifle unsteadily; the drink had made him light-headed) and groped in the bottom drawer beneath his underwear until he felt the coarse manila envelope with her photos. He drew it out and, without looking at them, tore the pictures into tiny pieces. Then he took them over to the kitchen, where the trash compactor was.

The roar of the compactor seemed to shake the entire house. He stiffened, afraid his mother would wake and ask what was going on, but she didn't. When the machine ground to a halt, he took a long breath. Finished, he thought. Finished. Tomorrow he would contact a lawyer, find out the legal procedure for remarriage. Over dinner he would mention to his mother, casually, that it was OK with him if she wanted to contact second aunt. Only this time he didn't want a college-educated woman. Even good looks weren't that important. A simple girl, maybe from their ancestral village. Someone whose family wasn't well off, who would be suitably apprecia-tive of the comforts he could provide. Someone who would be a real mother to his boy.

He didn't know then that it wasn't finished. That even as he made love to his new wife (a plump, cheerful girl, good-hearted, if slightly unimaginative), or helped his daughters with their homework, or disciplined his increasingly rebellious son, he would wonder about *her*. Was she alive? Was she happy? With a sudden anger that he knew to be irrational, he would try to imagine her body tangled in swaying kelp at the bottom of the ocean where it had been flung. Bloated. Eaten by fish. But all he could conjure up was the intent look on her face when she rocked her son back and forth, singing a chil-dren's rhyme in Bengali, *Khoka jabe biye korte, shonge chhasho dhol, my little boy is going to be married, six hundred drummers*. Years later, when he was an old man living in a home for seniors (his second wife dead, his daughters moved away to distant towns, his son not on speaking terms with him), he would continue to be dazzled by that brief unguarded joy in her face, would say to himself, again, how much she must have hated me to choose to give *that* up.

But he had no inkling of any of this yet. So he switched off the trash compactor with a satisfied click, the sense of a job well done and, after taking a shower (long and very hot, the way he liked it, the hard jets of water turning the skin of his chest a dull red), went to bed and fell immediately into a deep, dreamless sleep.

ACKNOWLEDGMENT: *My thanks to Claudine Ward, whose story "Fugue" inspired this one.*

DOORS

IT ALL STARTED WHEN RAJ CAME TO LIVE WITH THEM.

But no, not really. There had been signs of trouble even earlier. Maybe that was why Preeti's mother had kept warning her right up to the time of the marriage.

"It'll never work, I tell you," she had declared gloomily as she placed a neatly folded pile of shimmery *dupattas* in the suitcase Preeti would be taking back to Berkeley with her after the wedding. "Here you are, living in the U.S. since you were twelve. And Deepak—he's straight out of India. Just because you took a few classes together at the university, and you liked how he talks, doesn't mean that you can live with him."

"Please, Ma!" Preeti paused halfway through emptying out her makeup drawer. "We've been over this a hundred times. Don't you think it's time to stop, considering the fact the wedding's tomorrow?"

"It's never too late to stop yourself from ruining your life," her mother said. "What do you *really* know about how Indian men think? About what they expect from their women?"

"Now don't start on that again. You and Dad have had a happy enough marriage the last twenty-four years, haven't you?"

"Your father's not like the others. . . ."

"Nor is Deepak."

"And besides, he's mellowed over the years. You should have seen him when we first got married."

"Well, I'm sure with all the training you've given me, I'll be able to mellow Deepak in no time!"

"*That's* your problem!" Preeti's mother flared. "Making a joke of everything, thinking the world will always let you have your own way. I wish I *had* trained you better, like my mother did me, to be obedient and adjusting and forgiving. You're going to need it."

"Is this the same mother who was always at me to marry a nice Indian boy! The one who introduced me to all her friends' sons whenever I came home from college!"

"They were all brought up here, like you." Her mother refused to be charmed. "Not with a set of prehistoric values."

"Mom! Deepak is the most enlightened man I know!" Preeti spoke lightly, trying to push down her rising anger because she knew her mother's concern came from love.

"I want you to know you always have a home with us." Preeti's mother lowered the lid of the suitcase with a sigh, as though she were closing up a coffin.

"Enough of all this doom and gloom!" Preeti had given her mother a determined hug, though deep down she felt a twinge of fear at her ominous tone. "Let's not argue anymore, OK? Deepak and I love each other. We'll manage just fine."

Deepak's Indian friends had also been concerned when he'd met them at the International House Cafe to share the good news.

"*Yaar*, are you sure you're doing the right thing?" one of them had asked, staring down at the wedding invitation Deepak had handed him. "She's been here so long it's almost like she was born in this country. And you know how these 'American' women are, always bossing you, always thinking about themselves. . . ."

"It's no wonder we call them ABCDs—American-Born-Confused-*Desis*," quipped another friend as he took a swallow of beer.

"Preeti's different!" Deepak said angrily. "You know that —you've all met her many times. She's smart and serious and considerate. . . ."

"Me," said a third young man, adjusting his spectacles, "I'd go for an arranged marriage from back home any day, a pretty young girl from my parents' village, not too educated, brought up to treat a man right and not talk back. . . ."

"I can't believe you said that!" Deepak stood up so abruptly that his chair fell over with a crash. "Women aren't dolls or slaves. I *want* Preeti to make her own decisions. I'm proud that she's able to."

"Calm down, Deepak-*bhai*, we're only trying to help!

We don't want you to end up with a broken marriage a few years down the road . . ." someone protested.

"Our marriage isn't going to break up. It's going to be stronger than any traditional marriage because it's based on mutual respect," Deepak had flung over his shoulder as he walked out of the cafe.

On the whole it seemed that Preeti and Deepak had been right. They had lived together amicably for the last three years, at first in a tiny student apartment in Berkeley and then, after Deepak got a job with a computer firm, in a condominium in Milpitas. Preeti, who was still working on her dissertation, hadn't been too enthusiastic about moving to the suburbs, but she'd given in when Deepak pointed out how difficult his commute had become. And it was true, like he said, that she only had to come to campus a couple times a week to teach. In return he left all the decorating to her, letting her fill the rooms with secondhand shelves crammed with books, comfortable old couches and cushions piled on the floor, a worn Persian rug and multicolored wall hangings woven by a women's art co-op to which her friend Cathy belonged. He himself would have preferred to buy, on the Sears Home Improvement Plan, a brand-new sofa set (complete with shiny oak-finish end tables) and curtains that matched the bedspreads, but he figured that the house was her domain.

When finally, having settled in, they gave a housewarming party, all their friends had to admit that Deepak and Preeti had a fine marriage.

Doors

"Did you try some of those delicious *gulabjamuns* she fixed?" said one young man to another as they left. "Deepak sure lucked out, didn't he?"

"Yes, and did you hear how she got the Student of the Year award in her department? Pretty soon she'll land a cushy teaching job and start bringing in a fat paycheck as well!" replied the other, sighing enviously.

Preeti's Indian girlfriends were amazed at Deepak's helpfulness. "I can't believe it!" one exclaimed. "He actually knows where the kitchen is. That's more than my brothers do."

"Did you see how he refilled her plate for her and brought her her drink?" said another. "And his talk—it's always, *Preeti-this* and *Preeti-that.* Maybe I *should* let my mother arrange my marriage with her sister-in-law's second cousin's son in Delhi, like she's been wanting to."

Even Cathy, who wasn't easily impressed, pulled Preeti aside just before she left. "I must admit I had my doubts in the beginning, though I didn't want to say anything—your mother was already being so negative. Just like her I thought he'd turn out to be terribly chauvinistic, like other men I've seen from the old countries. And of course I know how stubborn and closemouthed *you* are! But I think you've both adjusted wonderfully. At the risk of sounding clichéd, I'd say you're a perfectly matched couple!"

"What was Cathy saying?" Deepak asked later, after all the guests had left. They were at the sink, she washing, he drying.

"She thinks we're a perfectly matched couple!" Preeti's

187

face glowed with pleasure as she rinsed a set of mugs. Cathy's comments meant a lot to her.

"Funny, that's what my friend Suresh said, too."

"Maybe they're right!"

"I think we should check it out—right now." Deepak dropped the towel and reached for her with a grin. "The dishes can wait till tomorrow."

None of the guests had known, of course, about the matter of doors.

Deepak liked to leave them open, and Preeti liked them closed.

Deepak had laughed about it at first, early in the marriage.

"Are the pots and pans from the kitchen going to come and watch us making love?" he would joke when she meticulously shut the bedroom door at night although there were just the two of them in the house. Or, "Do you think I'm going to come in and attack you?" when she locked the bathroom door behind her with an audible click. He himself always bathed with the door open, song and steam pouring out of the bathroom with equal abandon.

But soon he realized that it was not a laughing matter with her. Preeti would shut the study door before settling down with her Ph.D. dissertation. When in the garden, she would make sure the gate was securely fastened as she weeded. If there had been a door to the kitchen, she would have closed it as she cooked.

Deepak was puzzled by all this door shutting. He had

grown up in a large family, and although they had been affluent enough to possess three bedrooms—one for Father, one for Mother and his two sisters, and the third for the three boys —they had never observed boundaries. They had constantly spilled into each other's rooms, doors always left open for chance remarks and jokes.

He asked Preeti about it one night just before bed, when she came out of the bathroom where she always went to change into her nightie. She wasn't able to give him an answer.

"I don't know," she said, her brow wrinkled, folding and refolding her jeans. "I guess I'm just a private person. It's not like I'm shutting you out. I've just always done it this way. Maybe it has something to do with being an only child." Her eyes searched his face unhappily. "I know it's not what you're used to. Does it bother you?"

She seemed so troubled that Deepak felt a pang of guilt.

"No, no, I don't care, not at all," he rushed to say, giving her shoulders a squeeze. And really, he didn't mind, even though he didn't quite understand. People were different. He knew that. And he was more than ready to accept the unique needs of this exotic creature—Indian and yet not Indian— who had by some mysterious fortune become his wife.

So things went on smoothly—until Raj descended on them.

"Tomorrow!" Preeti was distraught, although she tried to hide it in the face of Deepak's obvious delight. Her mind raced over the list of things to be done—the guest bedroom dusted,

189

the sheets washed, a special welcome dinner cooked (that would require a trip to the grocery and the Indian store), perhaps some flowers. . . . And her advisor was pressuring her to turn in the second chapter of her dissertation, which wasn't going well.

"Yes, tomorrow! His plane comes in at ten-thirty at night." Deepak waved the telegram excitedly. "Imagine, it's been five years since I've seen him! We used to be inseparable back home although he was so much younger. He was always in and out of our house, laughing and joking and playing pranks. You won't believe some of the escapades we got into! I know you'll just love him—everyone does. And see, he calls you *bhaviji*—sister-in-law—already."

At the airport Raj was a lanky whirlwind, rushing from the gate to throw his arms around Deepak, kissing him loudly on both cheeks, oblivious to American stares. Preeti found his strong Bombay accent hard to follow as he breathlessly regaled them with news of old acquaintances that had Deepak throwing back his head in loud laughter. She watched him, thinking that she'd never seen him laugh like that before.

But the trouble really started after dinner.

"What a marvelous meal, *bhaviji*! I can see why Deepak is getting a potbelly!" Raj belched in appreciation as he pushed back his chair. "I know I'll sleep soundly tonight—my eyes are closing already. If you tell me where the bedsheets are, I'll bring them over and start making my bed while you're clearing the table."

"Thanks, Raj, but I made the bed already, upstairs in the guest room."

"The guest room? I'm not a guest, *bhavi*! I'm going to be

with you for quite a while. You'd better save the guest bed-room for real guests. About six square feet of space—right here between the dining table and the sofa—is all I need. See, I'll just move the chairs a bit, like this."

Seeing the look on Preeti's face, Deepak tried to inter-vene.

"Come on, Raju—why not use the guest bed for tonight since it's made already? We can work out the long-term ar-rangements later."

"*Aare bhai,* you know how I hate all this formal-tormal business. I won't be able to sleep up there! Don't you remem-ber what fun it was to spread a big sheet on the floor of the living room and spend the night, all us boys together, telling stories? Have you become an *amreekan* or what? Come along and help me carry the bedclothes down. . . ."

Preeti stood frozen as his singsong voice faded beyond the bend of the stairs; then she made her own way upstairs silently. When Deepak came to bed an hour later, she was waiting for him.

"What! Not asleep yet? Don't you have an early class to teach tomorrow?"

"You have to leave for work early, too."

"Well, as a matter of fact I was thinking of taking a couple days off. You know—take Raju to San Francisco, maybe down to Carmel."

Preeti was surprised by the sudden surge of jealousy she felt. She tried to shake it off, to speak reasonably.

"I really don't think you should be neglecting your work —but that's your own business." She controlled her voice with an effort, not letting her displeasure color it. "What I do need to straighten out is this matter of sleeping downstairs. I need to use the dining area early in the morning, and I can't do it with him sleeping there." She shuddered silently as she pictured herself trying to enjoy her quiet morning tea and the newspaper with him sprawled on the floor nearby—snoring, in all probability. "By the way, just what did he mean by he's going to be here for a long time?"

"Well, he wants to stay here until he completes his Master's—maybe a year and a half—and I told him that was fine with us. . . ."

"You *what*? Isn't this my house, too? Don't I get a say in who lives in it?"

"Fine, then. Go ahead and tell him that you don't want him here. Go ahead, wake him up and tell him tonight."

There was an edge to Deepak's voice that Preeti hadn't heard before. Staring at the stony line of his lips, she suddenly realized, frightened, that they were having their first serious quarrel. Her mother's face, triumphant in its woefulness, rose in her mind.

"You know that's not what I'm saying." She made her tone conciliatory. "I realize how much it means to you to have your old friend here, and I'll do my best to make him welcome. I'm just not used to having a long-term houseguest around, and it makes things harder when he insists on sleeping on the living-room floor." She offered him her most charming smile, desperately willing the stranger in his eyes—cold, defensive—to disappear.

It worked. He smiled back and pulled her to him, her own dear Deepak again, promising to get Raj to use the guest

Doors

room, gently biting the nape of her neck in that delicious way that always sent shivers up her spine. And as she snuggled against him with a deep sigh of pleasure, curving her body to fit his, Preeti promised herself to do her very best to accept Raj.

It was harder than she had expected, though.

The concept of doors did not exist in Raj's universe, and he ignored their physical reality—so solid and reassuring to Preeti—whenever he could. He would burst into her closed study to tell her of the latest events in his computer lab, leaving the door ajar when he left. He would throw open the door to the garage where she did the laundry to offer help, usually just as she was folding her underwear. Even when she retreated to her little garden in search of privacy, there was no escape. From the porch, he gave solicitous advice on the drooping fuchsias.

"A little more fertilizer, don't you think, *bhavi*? Really, this bottled stuff is no good compared to the cow dung my family uses in their vegetable garden. I tell you, *phul gobis* THIS size." He would hold up his hands to indicate a largeness impossible for cauliflowers, while behind him the swinging screen door afforded free entry to hordes of insects. Perhaps to set her an example, he left his own bedroom door wide open so that the honest rumble of his snores assaulted Preeti on her way to the bathroom every morning.

"Cathy, Raj is driving me up the wall," she told her friend when they met for coffee after class.

"Tell him that!"

"I can't! Deepak would be terribly upset. It has to do with hospitality and losing face—I guess it's a cultural thing."

"Well, have you discussed it with Deepak?"

"I tried, once or twice. He doesn't listen. It's like he's a different person nowadays—he's even beginning to sound different."

"How?"

"His accent—it's a lot more Indian, like Raj's."

"Preeti, you've got to talk to him." Over the rim of her cup, Cathy's eyes were wide with concern. "I haven't ever seen you so depressed. There are craters, literally, under your eyes, and you look like you've lost weight. Surely if he knew how strongly Raj's habits bothered you, he'd do something about them."

Cathy was right, Preeti thought on the way back as the BART train's jogging rhythm soothed her into drowsiness. She needed to make more of an effort to communicate with Deepak. Maybe tonight. She was glad she had taken the time that morning, before she left for school, to fix a *bharta*, the grilled eggplant dish which was one of his favorites. When she got home, she'd make some *pulao* rice—the kind he liked, with lots of fried cashews—and after dinner when they went to bed she'd lay her head in the curve of his shoulder and hold him tight and tell him exactly how she felt. Maybe they'd even make love—it seemed like a terribly long time since they'd done that.

But when she opened the door to the house, she was assaulted by a loud burst of *filmi* music. Deepak and Raj sat side by side on the family-room couch, watching an Indian movie where a plump man wearing a hat and a bemused expression was serenading a haughty young woman. Both men yelled with laughter as the woman swung around, snatched the hat off her admirer's head, and stomped on it.

"*Vah*, look at those flashing eyes!" Raj exclaimed. "I tell you, none of our modern girls can match Nutan for style!" Noticing Preeti, he waved a cheery hand. "Oh, *bhavi*, there you are! Come join us. Deepu-*bhaiya* and I rented a couple of our favorite movies from the Indian video store. . . ."

"Yes," Deepak added, "that was a great idea of Raj's. I never thought I'd have such a terrific time watching these old videos. They bring back some really fun memories."

"I bet they do! *Bhavi*, did you know your husband used to be a regular street-corner Romeo in his bachelor days? *Yaar,* remember that girl who used to live across from your house in Birla Mansions? How you used to sing *chand-ke-tukde*—that means piece of moon, *bhavi*—whenever she waited at the bus stop . . . ?"

"That's enough, Raju! You'll get me in trouble now," Deepak said, but he looked rather pleased. "Preeti, come sit with us and I'll explain the Hindi words to you." He moved closer to Raj to make space on the couch, and Preeti noted with a twist of the heart how he casually let an arm fall over Raj's shoulder.

"I have to warm up dinner," she said through stiff lips.

"Oh, don't bother!" Deepak said. "We stopped for *samosas* at that little restaurant next to the video store—what is it—"

"Nusrat Cuisine," Raj supplied helpfully. "We're stuffed."

"We brought you back a few," Deepak said. "They're on the counter."

Preeti walked to the kitchen. Her body seemed heavy and unwieldy, as though she were moving in deep water. Emotions she didn't want to examine churned through her, insidious currents waiting to pull her under. She picked up the brown bag printed with the restaurant's logo and, without opening it, threw it in the trash can. She wanted to throw out the *bharta*, too, but with an effort she put it in the refrigerator.

As she started up the steps, she heard Deepak call behind her, "Don't you want to watch the movie?"

"No. I have a lot of schoolwork to catch up on." She knew she sounded ungracious. A party pooper, in Raj's language.

"Well, if you're sure. . . ."

"Do you think you could come upstairs soon?" She tried to make her voice bright and pleasant. "I wanted to talk to you about something."

"Sure thing. I'll be up in a bit."

This can't be happening to me, Preeti told herself as she stared into the bedroom mirror. In the dim light her face looked sallow, unwell. She tried to remember her past successes—standing on a university stage in Ohio receiving her B.A. degree from the college president, knowing that she was one of a handful of students with solid A's; opening an embossed envelope with trembling fingers to find that she'd been accepted at Berkeley; standing at a podium and hearing the roar of applause when she finished presenting a paper at a national conference. None of it seemed real. None of it seemed to have happened to the woman who looked back at her from the mirror, the skin of her face drawn tight over cheekbones that stuck out too sharply. All her life she had believed that she could do anything she set her mind to; it was what her mother had always said. Now as a sudden wave of giddiness struck her, she felt doubt for the first time. Then she drew her breath in fiercely. *I won't let him ruin my life,* she said. For a moment it wasn't clear to her if it was Raj she was referring to, or Deepak.

She changed into the lacy pink nightdress Deepak had bought her for their first anniversary. She sprayed perfume on her wrists and practiced, in the mirror, the words she would say. *Think positive,* she told herself. *Losing your temper will achieve nothing.*

It was a couple of hours before Deepak opened the door of the bedroom. He was humming a Hindi song under his breath.

"You still awake?" He sounded surprised.

"Remember, I wanted to talk to you about something." *Calmly, calmly.* But her voice trembled, thin and high. Accusing.

"Sorry," Deepak said, a little shamefaced. "The movie was so good—I forgot all about the time." Then he gave a great yawn. "Maybe we can talk tomorrow?"

"No! I have to tell you now." Preeti spoke quickly, before she lost her nerve. "I can't live with Raj in the house anymore. He's driving me crazy. He's . . ."

"What d'you mean, he's driving you crazy?" Deepak's voice was suddenly testy. "He's only trying to be friendly, poor chap. I should think you'd be able to open up a bit more to

197

him. After all, we're the closest thing he has to family in this strange country."

"Even family members sometimes need time and space away from each other. In my family no one ever intruded. . . ."

"Well, maybe they should have," Deepak interrupted in a hard tone that made Preeti stare at him. "Maybe then you'd be a little more flexible now."

After this, Preeti took to locking herself up in the bedroom with her work in the evenings while downstairs Deepak and Raj talked over the old days as the stereo blared out the Kishore Kumar songs they'd grown up on. Often she fell asleep over her books and woke to the sound of Deepak's irritated knocks on the door.

"I just don't understand you nowadays!" he would exclaim with annoyance. "Why must you lock the bedroom door when you're reading? Isn't that being a bit paranoid? Maybe you should see someone about it."

Preeti would turn away in silence, thinking, *It can't be forever, he can't stay with us forever, I can put up with it until he leaves, and then everything will be perfect again.*

And so things might have continued had it not been for one fateful afternoon.

It was the end of the semester, and Preeti was lying on her bed, eyes closed. That morning her advisor had called her into his office to tell her that her dissertation lacked originality and depth. He suggested that she restructure the entire argument.

His final comment kept resounding in her brain: "I don't know what's been wrong with you for the past few months— you've consistently produced second-rate work. And you used to be one of my sharpest students! I still remember that article on Marlowe, so innovative. . . . Maybe you need a break —a semester away from school?"

"Not from school—it's a semester away from home that I need," she whispered now as the door banged downstairs and Raj's eager voice floated up to her.

"*Bhavi, bhavi*, where *are* you? Have I got great news for you!"

Preeti put her pillow over her head, willing him away like she tried to do with the dull, throbbing headaches that came to her so often nowadays. But he was at the bedroom door, knocking.

"Open up, *bhavi!* I have something to show you—I aced the Math final—I was the only one in the entire class. . . ."

"Not now, Raj, please, I'm very tired. Dinner's in the kitchen—do you think you could help yourself?"

"What's wrong? You have a headache? Wait a minute, I'll bring you some of my tiger balm—excellent for head-aches."

She heard his footsteps recede, then return.

"Thanks, Raj," she called out to forestall any more con-versation. "Just leave it outside. I don't feel like getting up for it right now."

"Oh, you don't have to get up. I'll bring it in to you." And before she could refuse, Raj had opened the door—how could she have forgotten to lock it?—and walked in.

Shocked, speechless, Preeti watched Raj. Holding a squat green bottle in his extended hand, he seemed to advance in slow motion across the suddenly enormous expanse of the bedroom that had been her last sanctuary. His lips moved, but she couldn't hear him through the red haze that was spreading across her eyes.

A voice pierced the haze, screaming at him to *get out, get out right now.* A hand snatched the bottle and hurled it against the wall where it shattered and fell in emerald fragments. Dimly she recognized the voice, the hand. They were hers. And then she was alone in the sudden silence.

The bedroom was as neat and tranquil as ever when Deepak walked in. Only a very keen eye would have noted the pale stain against the far wall.

"Are you OK? Raju mentioned something about you not feeling well." And then, as his glance fell on the packed suitcase by which Preeti was standing, "What's this?"

"I'm leaving," she said, her voice very calm. "I'm going to move in for a while with Cathy. . . ."

She watched, eyes expressionless, as Deepak swore softly and violently.

"You can't leave. What would people say? Besides, you're my wife. You belong in my home."

She looked at him a long moment. Somewhere in the back of her mind was a thought. *Mother, you were right.* Oddly, it caused her no sorrow.

"It's Raju, isn't it? You just can't stand him, can you,

although he's tried and tried, poor fellow." Deepak's voice was bitter. "Very well, I'll get him out of your way. For good."

She listened silently to his footsteps fading down the stairs. A long, low murmur of voices came from the living room. Then she heard sounds of packing from the guest room. She realized that she was still standing and moved to sit on the bed. Her limbs felt stiff and wooden, and she had trouble bending her knees. Sometime later—she couldn't tell how much—from outside her bedroom door, Raj thanked her and wished her luck in the hushed voice people reserve for the very ill. The front door banged behind the men.

She was still sitting on the bed when Decpak returned and told her that Raj would be staying at a motel till he found a room on campus.

"Hope you're happy, now that you have the house all to yourself," he ended acidly. And then, "I'm going to sleep in the guest room."

From the master bedroom, Preeti could hear his awkward bed-making efforts, the muffled sound of pillows thrown on the floor, the creaking bedsprings. A part of her cried out to go to him, to apologize and offer to have Raj back. To fashion her curves to his warm body and let his lips—so familiar, so reassuring—soothe her into sleep.

Instead, for the first time, she lay down alone in the big bed they'd bought together the week before their marriage. She closed her eyes and tried to recall the happiness of that day, but there was only a black square filled with snow and static, as when, while watching a video, one comes across a portion of the tape that has been erased by accident. She lay there, feeling the night cover her slowly, layer by cold, clean layer. And when the door finally clicked shut, she did not know whether it was in the guest room or deep inside her own being.

THE
ULTRASOUND

MY COUSIN ARUNDHATI AND I ARE BOTH PREGNANT WITH our first babies, a fact which gives me great pleasure. Although she's in India and I'm here in California, we've kept close track of each other's progress. Each week we compare notes on the nausea (I have it worse than Runu, not just in the morning but through the entire day), the crippling sleepiness of the early afternoon (particularly hard on Runu since that's when she has to fix tea snacks for her in-laws), the depressing weight gain (we have no waists at all); the exhilarating sense of unrealness which makes us write, at the end of each letter, "Is this truly happening?"

We keep in touch mostly through letters. International calls are too expensive for my slender budget, since I'm still in school and there isn't much left of Sunil's salary after he sends money home to his parents. Still, once in a while, for a special occasion, I'll phone. Runu and I plan these calls for months in advance. Sometimes the night before I lie in the dark, too excited to sleep, and think of the moment when I'll hear Runu's voice with its dear, familiar breathlessness, as though she's run all the way to the phone.

Next week is one of those special times. Because that's when (we planned it this way, changing my date to match the one her mother-in-law arranged for her) we get the results of our amniocentesis tests.

"Just one more day now for the results!" I fold my knitting, an impossibly tiny red sweater, and smile up at Sunil, who has just walked in. He sets his briefcase down and leans over the recliner to give me a hug.

"Are you nervous, Anju?" he asks. There's a history of birth defects in my family—just one or two, but it's enough to worry us.

"Not really. Well, maybe a bit. Actually I was thinking of Runu. It'll be so nice to talk to her again, to find out how she's doing. To know if she's having a boy or a girl. That way we can plan matching names. . . ."

Sunil scowls. "I don't know why *you* have to be the one to call every time."

"Now don't be mean! You know Runu would call if she could. But her mother-in-law doesn't believe in spending money on long-distance calls. She doesn't even let Runu call her mother in Calcutta. . . ."

"Why can't you just write?" mutters Sunil as he heads for the kitchen. Above the clang of lids, I hear him say, "It's not as though we're millionaires." In my prepregnancy days he would have scolded me, his voice sharp with justified anger, while I lowered my eyes and picked guiltily at the border of my sari. *Is that why I'm killing myself, sweating from dawn to dusk so you can fritter the money away?* But now he lets the matter drop.

Sometimes I suspect that Sunil is jealous of Runu. Perhaps it's because we go so far back together, to the time when we were both seven and Pratima-auntie, Runu's widowed mother, moved to the apartment behind our house in Calcutta soon after my own father died. Perhaps it's the memories we share, which Sunil can never feel as we do no matter how carefully I paint them for him. Perhaps he guesses, though I'm careful not to give him cause, that in some ways she's still the most important person in my life.

Runu's due date and mine are within a week of each other, in about five months. I wasn't really surprised, though, when I called Calcutta to tell her about my baby and she, laughing— but a little shyly, as though someone were close by, listening —replied that she too had some good news for me. Because for as long as I can remember, we've always done everything together.

In grade school we would race each other to the bus stop, identical gray uniform skirts slapping against identical knobby knees, our vapor-breath mingling in the cold morning air. The loser had to buy *panipuris* for us both from the street vendor who stood outside the school gates each afternoon. (Sometimes I lost on purpose, because Runu never had much pocket money. But I had to be careful about it because she had a lot of pride.) We would gulp down the crisp spicy rounds filled with sweet and sour potatoes, glancing around to make sure no one who knew our parents was around. (Both our mothers were convinced that eating street food would give us the most horrible diseases.) Then, after inspecting each other's mouths carefully to make sure no telltale traces remained, we would make our way home, united further by our act of wickedness.

Later we would play truant together and go to the movies. (We both liked the same kind, historical romances where turbanned heroes on horseback rescued damsels with pouting rosebud mouths, wearing jeweled saris.) On our way to college we would discuss boys. That Suresh in History class, with the crooked smile, wasn't he a heartbreaker? And that one, the one with the thick sideburns whose name we didn't know, who always waited at the same bus stop and sometimes (oh shocking) winked at us. What would we do if he actually approached us, asked us to meet him at the coffee house or at the Rabindra Sarobar lake? But all the while we knew it was just talk, because after graduation, like good Indian girls, we both allowed our mothers to arrange traditional marriages for us. The only thing we insisted on was a double wedding.

I'm not saying there weren't differences. Money for one. When my father died, Mother had taken over the family business, a bookstore in a prime College Street location, and surprised everyone by managing it with shrewd efficiency. Runu's father, dying after a long illness, had left only debts behind, and Pratima-auntie, like most genteel Bengali widows, was always struggling to make ends meet. Runu never had new dresses and shoes like me, or large plush teddy bears or wind-up dolls from America that could dance and say hello. Or, later, silk saris or gold earrings with matching bracelets for her birthdays. But she wouldn't let me give her any of my things, even though it would have made me happy, and after a few fights I stopped trying.

Somehow she never did as well academically either, though I believed she was quite as intelligent as I was. Encouraged by my mother to be competitive, I went on to win spelling bees and debate contests, and later in college to grapple with Chaucer and Thomas Hardy and W. B. Yeats in my English Honors classes. I browsed through our bookstore and the USIS library, reading Hemingway and Kerouac and Willa Cather and longing to visit the places they wrote of. Runu took up Home Science, which everyone admitted was the major that the dullest girls chose. She seemed to enjoy it, though, all that knitting and crocheting and cooking that would have driven me crazy. She would turn out elaborate dishes like *biriyani* and *patisapta* that took days to prepare. When I carelessly tore my sari borders, she would mend them with stitches so tiny they were almost invisible. And she made the best mango chutney I ever tasted.

So maybe it's fitting that Prajapati, the winged and capricious god of marriage, set us down in such different places—me here in San Jose with Sunil, and her in provincial Burdwan, the eldest daughter-in-law of a large, traditional brahmin family.

My feet are really swollen today. Again. My legs look puffy, boneless, like flesh-colored nylons stuffed to bursting. When I press down on my shins with my thumbs, they form oval, purple-tinged hollows that refuse to disappear. Nothing hurts, though, because it's all numb.

When Sunil comes home from work he takes one look at my legs and makes me lie down on the couch with my feet up. He massages them with pine oil until a little feeling comes back into them. I take in a deep breath of the strong pungent odor I've come to love and smile at him. "I feel much better," I say, and really I do.

Sunil smiles back and leans over to kiss my stomach lightly. "How's Peace-and-Joy?" he asks.

"Fine," I reply.

This is our little private joke. If we have a son, we're going to call him Anand, which means joy in Bengali. If we have a daughter, her name will be Shanti, peace. Until the amnio results reveal the baby's sex, we call him (her) Peace-and-Joy.

"Will you be just as happy if it's a girl?" I ask Sunil, my voice trembling a bit though I try to control it. This is a conversation we've had many times before.

"Of course, silly," he replies patiently, smoothing my hair.

"And your parents . . . ?"

"They will too. And even if they're not at first, they'll get over it. So stop worrying!"

Then we're both silent, thinking about the other thing, the one we don't talk about. What we would do if something turned out to be wrong with the baby. I think of the drooling boy with albino eyes who used to be kept hidden in a small room in the dark and crumbly Calcutta mansion where another aunt lived. I'd come across him by accident one afternoon, exploring the forbidden parts of the house while the grown-ups were drinking tea downstairs. I hear again the grunting sounds he'd made, see his fingers beckoning to me from between the iron grills of his window, soft and fat and a pale pinkish-brown, like earthworms. No one ever told me what happened to him. I slip my hand into Sunil's and he grips it tightly. We sit like this until night darkens the room.

Sometimes when I'm dressing, I glance up at the mirror and am surprised once again by the changes—the dark line of hair pointing downward from my navel, the nipples dark and glistening as the prunes I soak in water overnight for my constipation, the pearlike swell of abdomen and breast, at once luscious and obscene. I cannot decide if I am gorgeous or revolting. I wonder what Runu looks like. I don't have any recent photos of her. I guess her mother-in-law doesn't believe in taking photos either.

The last time I saw Runu was a month before I came to America. I had gone down to Burdwan to visit her in the big brick and marble mansion in which her husband's family had lived, her mother-in-law proudly informed me, for seven generations. Was there just a hint, in her voice, of how lucky Runu was to be chosen into such a household?

Runu had been waiting for me just behind the front door, in the looming shadow of the heavy teak panel carved with fierce-looking house gods, *yakshas* and *yakshinis*. (It wasn't fitting that the bride of the Bhattacharjee family should come to the station where common people could stare at her.)

Her eyes sparkled as she threw herself into my arms, repeating over and over how delighted she was to see me, how wonderful I looked, just like on our marriage day (which was the last time we'd seen each other), and how much she had to tell me.

I was about to say that she too seemed exactly the same. The wedding *sindur* on her forehead and the red-bordered sari wrapped around her slight, girlish form only made her look like she was playing at being a grown-up. But right then Runu's mother-in-law called from the kitchen, her voice pleasant but firm, "Arundhati, are you coming to roll out the rotis?"

"Coming, Mother," Runu answered. Turning to me apologetically, she said, "Why don't you rest for a while, Anju dear?" As I stared at her back disappearing hurriedly down a corridor, I realized that many things had changed.

Next afternoon we sat in the backyard, under the shadow of an old *neem* tree, Runu sewing buttons onto a pair of pants that belonged to one of her brothers-in-law. There were three of them. I'd met them at dinner last night. And though they'd been properly respectful, calling her *boudi*, older sister-in-law, and complimenting her on her new fish *kalia* recipe, I'd felt a pinprick of anger as I watched Runu serve them and clean up their spills and remove their dirty dishes with a smile that never faltered.

"Don't you get bored when your husband is gone?" I asked. Runu's husband Ramesh worked for Indian Railways and had to travel several weeks out of the month.

"Oh no! There's always so much to be done! Early in the morning I have to supervise the maid as she milks the cows.

Then I make tea for Mother, she's very particular, I have to get it just the right color. Then I tell the maid what to get from the market. After that there's vegetables to cut, and breakfast and lunch and dinner to cook."

It sounded terribly dreary to me.

"And when the brothers come back from school I make them something nice to snack on, maybe some hot fried *singaras* or some *rasogollahs*," Runu proudly continued, "and in between there's quilts to be put out on the terrace in the sun, you won't believe how musty everything gets. . . ."

I couldn't stand it any longer. "Wait, doesn't your mother-in-law help with *any* of it?"

"Oh yes, but I tell her not to. She's getting old and frail, poor lady, and she's worked so hard her entire life. It's only fair that she should rest now."

To me Runu's mother-in-law looked tough as alligator hide and fit enough to outlast us both by decades. But I didn't say anything.

"There are servants to do some of the heavier work," Runu was saying. "But you know how it is." She shook her head wisely, almost like her mother-in-law might have. "They'll steal the clothes off your back if you don't watch them like a hawk."

I thought of how, when we were growing up, Runu would meet me secretly on the roof on summer nights so we could watch shooting stars and make up stories about them. We believed that if we saw one falling exactly at midnight, we could wish on it and the wish would be granted.

Even the night before we were to be married, we had gone up to the roof together at Runu's urging.

"Oh, I do hope there'll be a midnight star for us to wish on," Runu had whispered.

I didn't believe in shooting stars anymore. I knew they were merely burning meteors that had no power to help anyone, not even themselves. But I heard the longing in Runu's voice and hoped there would be a star for her.

And now, just one year since then, that wistful girl seemed to be gone forever. In her place was a pragmatic housewife concerned only with mildewed quilts and lazy servants.

I sat there in that backyard watching the sun's rays falling dappled and golden over Runu and her mending. Through the dust motes that hung in the heavy afternoon light, her small, animated face seemed suddenly far away, beyond reach, like something at the bottom of the sea which might at any moment, if the current changed, blur or even disappear. It frightened me.

But I pushed back the feeling of having been betrayed and told myself, *She's happy, that's all that matters.*

And so for the rest of the visit we spoke only of innocuous things: the fun-filled times of our childhood, new recipes Runu had learned from her mother-in-law, the shopping I'd done in preparation for America. When I left we hugged each other, promising that we'd never lose touch even though I was going so far away. But once I was on the train I leaned my head against the hard wooden seat back and stared out at the parched afternoon sky and thought of the little things that disturbed me, things I would have ordinarily told Runu about. The way her mother-in-law would sometimes appear in the middle of our conversations so that I'd look up to find her watching me and Runu from the door. The way one of Runu's brothers-in-law had made a rude comment when she'd burnt the rice pudding. The way Ramesh, who'd returned from his business tour a couple of days before I left, had scolded her, his voice rising in irritation, *Arundhati, how many times have I told you not to mess up the newspaper before I've read it.* I wondered if my husband in America would speak to me the same way.

The train gave a sudden lurch as it changed tracks, causing me to bump my head hard against the wood bench. The beginnings of a headache gripped my skull so fiercely that I ground my knuckles into my eyes. And when the tears came I couldn't tell whether I was crying from tiredness or pain or fear of what the future held for us both.

But of course I was being adolescent, melodramatic. Four years have passed since and we are happy enough. Our husbands are kind and dependable and take good care of us. In the Indian culture, that is the same as love.

I feel additionally fortunate because in Sunil I've found a friend, someone to discuss the perplexities of America with, someone who understands on evenings when I look up and the skyline with its palm-tree silhouettes is so like home that my throat tightens with loneliness. Oh, we've had our quarrels —mostly about money, of which Sunil is far more careful than I. Sometimes when I bought something I shouldn't have, he shouted that I was a spendthrift, letting money flow through my fingers like water. *Your mother should have married you to a maharajah, not a mere working man like myself.* Sometimes he stormed out of the house and didn't come back till late at night. I cried on those nights, sitting in the kitchen, keeping his dinner warm in the oven, waiting. Still, I know I have it better than most of the girls I grew up with.

Sunil was the one who urged me to go back to school to get a degree in education. He didn't mind fixing dinner when I had evening classes. He let me practice abysmally inept model lessons on him and stayed up with me those nights before exams when I was too nervous to sleep. At the graduation ceremony next year, I know he'll be in the front row, cheering, as I go up to receive my diploma. Though Runu looks forward to going back to her mother's house for the delivery, as is the custom, and laments the fact that I can't, I'm not unhappy. In India they don't let husbands into the labor room. And I know that I'll need Sunil with me, holding my hand, sharing the pain and the triumph of our baby's birth.

Runu doesn't say much about her husband. Sometimes I'll ask and a shy note will come into her voice, and she'll change the subject. Even in her letters she is cautious, understated, writing only about tangibles—the jasmine she planted underneath their window last spring because he likes the smell, how tall it's grown; the intricate design, cream and red and navy-blue, of the new sweater she knitted for him. (Like a good wife, she never calls him by his name, even in letters.) How pleased he's been because his mother's cough improved after she started taking the herbal tablets Runu had sent away for. It is hard for us Indian women to talk openly of love.

The Ultrasound

But she's happy, I'm sure of it. I would sense it otherwise. I feel her growing into her household, spreading her tendrils like the jasmine she has planted, dispensing fragrance and shade enough to win anyone's heart.

And now, to make everything perfect, the babies are coming.

The doctor's waiting room is decorated in pastels, pale blues and pinks designed to soothe the anxieties of expectant mothers and fathers. They have no effect on Sunil and me as we fidget in our plush pastel chairs. The doctor is forty-five minutes late. Complications with a delivery, the nurse assures us smilingly. But I'm certain his delay has to do with the test results we're waiting for. He's probably sitting in his office right now, head in his hands, agonizing over how to tell us. I glance at Sunil, but he's no help. He dabs at his upper lip, then clutches my palm damply.

What will I—we—do if . . . ? But my mind, freezing on that thought, refuses to proceed further. I stare at the cover of the magazine on the table in front of us until I think that the face of Princess Diana will be etched forever in my memory.

But once again I've tortured myself needlessly. The doctor breezes in, smiling plumply and waving a sheet. All is well with our baby—and it's a boy! We follow him with sheepish, relieved grins to the examination room where he measures my abdomen, declares himself pleased with my progress, and invites us to listen to our baby's heartbeat. It sounds like a runaway engine, full of furious energy. I cry, and even Sunil looks away and wipes at his eyes. The doctor pats us indulgently and tells us to come back in a month.

On the way home, we stop at the China Lion, our favorite restaurant, to celebrate. We splurge on hot and sour soup, spring rolls, eggplant in black bean sauce, sweet and sour shrimp, and pork chow mein. Recklessly, I eat a whole plateful of the extra spicy kung pao chicken which always gives me heartburn. But I know nothing can go wrong today. The fortune in my cookie reads, *A wonderful event is about to occur in your life soon.*

Before we sleep, we make love. When Sunil kisses the curves of my breasts and hip and thigh, I cry again. In spite of my bloated body, I know I am beautiful. I cannot remember how unhappiness feels. Afterward, I lie nestled in the warm hollow of his shoulder, listening to the rhythm of his slow, deep breathing. I place my palm over my belly and picture my baby sleeping inside, curled up and as large (I know this from my pregnancy book) as a lemon. I think I feel a special warmth, a tingly yellow sunshiny warmth, radiating into my hand. I must ask Runu if she feels it too. But it's still too early to call India.

Sometimes in the middle of the most mundane activities—driving or washing dishes or doing pelvic tilt exercises to strengthen my back—a wave of thankfulness surges through me, so powerful that I have to stop whatever I'm doing. I whisper a prayer of gratitude that my baby has come to me so easily—almost unasked, like grace—as soon as Sunil and I started thinking that it would be nice to have a family. I know the stories. Women chastised, even beaten, because they couldn't have children. Women whose husbands stopped loving them because they'd reneged on the unspoken wedding contract. Women from whose faces people averted their eyes because they were bad luck.

I love my baby with a fierce abandonment that I find amazing. Already I am willing to die for him. To kill. But I have a feeling that Runu loves her baby even more intensely, with a passion that I can only guess at, a desperate tenderness. This is because she's been trying to get pregnant ever since her marriage.

Five years might not seem that long to people in America, but where we come from, it is. Marriages can be broken in half that time, and barren wives sent back to their parents' home in shame. Runu's in-laws, of course, weren't like that. Still, I felt the growing tension between the words of her letters, in the pauses of her voice. And once in a while my mother would write about things. Runu's mother-in-law had taken her to the shrine of Shasthi, goddess of childbirth. The family priest had asked Runu to wear a good-luck amulet on a copper chain around her waist to appease the angry planets. They'd taken her for a medical checkup to make sure there were no "problems" with her system.

The day I received the last piece of information, I was so furious that I called my mother even though I'd just phoned her the previous week. I really wanted to call Runu, but I was afraid it would get her into trouble.

"Did her husband go for a checkup too?" I shouted over the crackling line.

My mother, who is usually an outspoken woman, was strangely silent. Then she'd said, "That's how they do things here, Anju. Have you forgotten?"

"Why is it always taken to be the woman's fault?" I fumed to Sunil when he came home that night. "If I were Runu, I'd just pack my bags and leave!"

I'd expected him to be shocked and angry, like myself. Sympathetic. But he merely shrugged and said, "It's a man's world in India. Runu's in-laws are a lot better than some others I could name. And anyway, where would Runu go if she left?"

There was a disturbing tone in his voice. *See how lucky you are to have a husband like me, to live in this free and easy American culture,* it seemed to say. *You'd better start working harder at being a good wife. Or else.*

"You shouldn't have called India twice in two weeks," Sunil was saying. "Don't you remember how huge the phone bill was last month?"

Indignation—for myself as well as Runu—had made me bold. "You're such a penny-pincher, I can't believe it!" I snapped in a tone I'd never used with him before. "Such a tyrant. You're no different from all those men in India. A woman is nothing but a baby machine to you."

"You need a reality check, Anjali," said Sunil in a tone cold with displeasure. I knew how angry he was by the fact that he used my full name. "Then perhaps you'd be a bit more grateful."

I'd retreated with a pillow and blanket to the family-room couch, where I wept long, hot tears at the unfairness of a world which insisted not only that women had to have husbands but that they had to be grateful to them. But all the time I felt guilty for saying the things I had, and when Sunil called me to come to bed I'd wiped my eyes carefully and gone back.

All that's behind us, though, now that the babies are on their way. Sunil has grown so loving that sometimes I tell him —and I'm only half joking—that I wouldn't mind being pregnant forever. In the early months when I suffered from nausea and couldn't stand the smell of cooking, he took over the kitchen. I remember him going through piles of cookbooks trying to find something that would tempt me to eat. Even now each week he drives to Mumtaz Cuisine, clear at the other end of town, to get *rasogollahs*, my favorite sweet. He massages my back and brings me hot milk in bed. Sometimes when I wake at night I find his hand resting on my stomach, careful and cupped, as though to protect us both.

And it's the same with Runu. Nothing is too good for her. At mealtimes she's served first, with the biggest, best portions—the coveted fish heads stewed with lentils and sprinkled with lemon, the creamy top layer of the sugary rice pudding she loves. New saris every time her husband comes back from a trip. Perfume, chocolates, recently even a pair of gold earrings. She gets to sleep in late, to lie down in the afternoons. Her brothers-in-law are not allowed to pester her with demands for new dishes. And her redoubtable mother-in-law, usually so stringent with money, has actually bought imported prenatal vitamins which she urges Runu to take every morning at breakfast!

The shrilling of the alarm startles me from sleep. I shut it off and lean over Sunil, who moans in protest, to reach for the phone. It is 1 A.M., early afternoon in India, our agreed-upon time. I know Runu will be waiting by the phone. I smile with the delicious anticipation of telling her everything that's happened.

But when I finally get through, Runu isn't the one who picks up the phone. Someone whose voice I don't recognize— one of the brothers-in-law, perhaps—tells me she's resting. He hesitates when I insist I must talk to her, then tells me to hold. He's gone a long time. I chew on the inside of my cheek and try not to think of the phone bill.

Finally Runu's on the line. She sounds dreadfully tired, her voice a dead monotone I hardly recognize.

"Are you sick?" I ask, frightened. "Shall I call some other time?"

"No," she says, then adds, with obvious effort, "How's your baby?"

"Fine," I say, "he's fine." There's an awkward silence full of all the things I want to tell her, the question I am afraid to ask but finally must.

"My baby's OK too," she replies, then makes a small choking sound. "Can't talk anymore now," she says.

The line goes dead.

I sit there holding on to the phone. The muted dial tone buzzes in my ear for a while, then the metallic bleeps, then a female American voice instructing me in polite tones to replace the receiver. Obediently, woodenly, I do as it says. Something's very wrong, but I can't figure out what. If Runu's OK, and her baby's OK—could it be Ramesh? I want to slap myself for not having asked. My mind had been too full of the babies, the lacy fins of their limbs undulating within our wombs. I dial India again.

This time I have to try for an hour before I get the long-distance connection. My eyes are burning with tiredness. I can hardly keep them open.

"Go to bed," Sunil wakes up and tells me. "You'll make yourself sick. What's so important that it can't wait till tomorrow?"

I glower at him in silence as I continue to dial.

But when I get her, my mother doesn't know what it is either. It can't be a death or a major accident, or someone would have informed her.

"Go to sleep now," she says. "I'll call you if it's something really serious. Stop crying so much, it's bad for you—and for my grandson."

Her grandson. I quieten myself to consider the statement. This little life inside me, which I'd always thought of as totally mine, already belongs to so many other people. Grandson, cousin, son of his father. And it's the same with Runu's baby.

Into the silence my mother says—mostly to console me, I think—"Maybe it's nothing. You know how pregnant women get emotional for no reason."

I don't believe it, but it's what I repeat to myself as I lie down, pushing my aching spine against Sunil, who is asleep again. Without waking he puts out his hand, finds my hip, and strokes the stretch marks that line it like silken seams. His breath ruffles the small hairs on the back of my neck until I, too, sleep.

The next morning I don't go to school although I know I'll miss my psychology midterm with Professor Warner, who doesn't allow makeups. I'm afraid to leave the phone even to go to the bathroom, though by now it's past midnight in India. But I imagine Runu tiptoeing down the dark staircase of the sleeping house and lifting the receiver with trembling fingers. I have to be here for her.

By evening I'm exhausted from waiting. My shoulders ache as though I've been pushing a huge rock uphill. All I've managed to eat all day are some saltines dipped in milk.

Sunil's face grows heavy when he returns from work to find me curled up on the sofa by the phone, still in my night-gown, wads of damp Kleenex strewn around me. "Anjali," he says, "I know your cousin is really important to you, but this kind of obsessive behavior isn't helping either you or her."

He pushes me into the shower, promising to call me if the phone rings. "Take a long, hot one," he commands. He hands me a new bar of the Mysore sandalwood soap that we save for special occasions and the blue silk kaftan Mother sent for my last birthday. By the time I come out, he has dinner ready—fried rice with shrimp, tofu with stir-fried green beans, and lemon chicken, all in the gay little red-and-white take-out containers from the China Lion.

"Voilà!" he says with a sweeping bow.

I have to laugh. "Wrong language," I say, suddenly ravenous.

The Ultrasound

I'm having a nightmare, one of those where you know you're dreaming, but that doesn't make it any less terrifying. In my nightmare my baby is trapped somewhere underwater, far from me. He lifts a tiny black receiver to call me for help. I hear the muffled ringing of the phone and try to run to it, but my limbs are like stone. I cannot move even a finger. A submarine wind starts to blow. The water, quiet until now, rushes swirling around my little boy, rips the phone from his fingers. It forms itself into a whirling mass around him, sucking him in. His face crumples as he goes under. *Anju*, he cries, *Anju-anju-anju* . . .

"Anju, wake up," calls Sunil. He's leaning over me, shaking me gently. "It's Runu." He puts the phone into my numb hand.

There's a lot of disturbance on the line. I can hardly hear Runu's voice as she says hello. Then I realize it's not a faulty connection. It's the background noise of some public place—bells ringing, people shouting questions, the clang of machines, the distant roar of a bus. My heart begins to pound crazily. Normally Runu would never be allowed to go somewhere like that—and certainly not by herself.

"I'm at the main post office," says Runu, her sentences short and jerky. "Couldn't talk from home. Took a cycle-rickshaw here. They think I'm in my room, sleeping."

"What's wrong, Runu? I've been worried sick. Is it Ramesh? Or your mother-in-law?"

"No," says Runu. "They're fine," she adds with venom. Then she says, "They want to kill my baby."

"*What*?" I'm sure I've heard it wrong.

"They want me to have an abortion."

223

I can't handle this alone. I motion for Sunil to pick up the extension in the family room. But already I know—how could I not have guessed earlier—what Runu is about to say. I remember the show some time back on "60 Minutes" about the increasing popularity of amniocenteses in India.

"The amnio showed that it's a girl." Runu's voice is a hollow echo against my ear. "My mother-in-law says it's not fitting that the eldest child of the Bhattacharjee household should be a female. "

"But Ramesh—what does he say?"

"He agrees, at least for this time. He says I'm young and strong. We can start trying for another baby right away. If it's a girl again, then he'll think about whether to keep it or not."

I am too stunned to speak.

"I wept and begged. I even threatened suicide. But they're adamant. . . ."

"Your time is up, madam," interrupts the operator's voice with its heavy Indian accent.

"Anju," Runu calls desperately, "what am I going to do?"

My brain is frozen, and my tongue. "Charge the call to this number," I finally manage to tell the operator.

"That'll be a collect call then, double charge."

"OK."

I hear the intake of Sunil's breath on the extension. I stiffen, sure he'll ask me to call Runu back. But he doesn't.

"Do you have anything with you, any money?" I ask Runu. I'm afraid to hear her reply. As in most traditional households, her mother-in-law handles the finances. When Runu needs something, she has to ask her for it.

The Ultrasound

But Runu surprises me.

"I have three hundred rupees—I took it out of Ramesh's desk drawer. And all my jewelry that was in the house. Just in case."

"Just in case what?" I want her to say it. I need to hear her say it.

"Just in case I decided not to go back." Runu's voice is stronger now. I think she needed to hear herself say it too.

"Well then, why don't you take the next train to Calcutta. Stay with your mother until you figure things out—maybe she can put some pressure on your in-laws. . . ."

"It's not so simple." And now Runu sounds scared again. "I called Mother just before I called you. She says it's not right that I should leave my husband's home. My place is with them, for better or worse. She's afraid they'll never take me back if I move out, and then what would happen to me? People will think they threw me out because I did something bad. They'll think my baby's a bastard. . . ." Her voice breaks on the last word.

The walls of my bedroom seem to undulate, then close in on me. Pratima-auntie is one of the gentlest and most affectionate women I know. I've always thought of her as my second mother. "Did you tell her they're determined to make you go through with the abortion?"

"I did. She thinks it's the lesser of the two evils. Anju, what shall I *do*?"

I take a deep breath. As I talk, I press my palm tight against my belly, drawing warmth from my baby. Drawing strength.

After I hang up, I sit hunched over on the edge of the

bed. I feel old and drained and sick to my stomach. I hope by God I've given Runu the right advice.

"What are you going to do now?" says Sunil from the doorway. I can see displeasure in the tight press of his lips.

"I'm going to the bathroom to throw up," I tell him. "And then I'm going to make"—I hold his eyes, daring him to protest—"another call to India."

Later in bed Sunil says, "I don't think you should have told Runu to go to your mother's house."

I bolt upright, pushing off the covers. "Why not? What was the poor girl supposed to do? Let her in-laws force her into an abortion she didn't want? Besides, my mother didn't mind. Why do *you* have such a problem with it?" My tone is deliberately aggressive. I want—I need—to attack someone.

Sunil refuses to be baited. "What could your mother say?" His voice is infuriatingly reasonable. "You told her that Runu was on her way. Besides, you were already so worked up, she probably didn't want to upset you further. . . ."

"Worked up. *Worked up!* You'd be worked up too if people were trying to kill—no, murder—your baby niece."

Sunil ignores the interruption. "But have you thought of what's going to happen to Runu now? How's she going to live? Your aunt barely has enough money to pay her own expenses."

"Runu can get a job."

"Doing what? She has no training, no experience."

"She could . . ." I think furiously. "She could supply the local boutiques with needlework. Or *salwaar-kameez* outfits. She's real good at sewing. . . ."

The Ultrasound

Sunil gives me an ironic look. "You really believe it's that easy, don't you?"

"Not easy, perhaps, but certainly possible."

"Even if that's true, what about the social stigma? Just like her mother said, there'll be a lot of gossip."

"There's always gossip. You have to ignore it."

"That's easy for you to say from here. Runu's the one who'll have to face it every day. Even if money isn't a problem, what kind of life will it be for her? She certainly won't have the chance to remarry. She'll be alone with her daughter the rest of her life, a social pariah, someone the neighbors point a finger at every time she walks down the street."

I open my mouth to protest hotly, then shut it. I'm remembering the pictures we used to draw when we were little, Runu and I, about what we wanted to be when we grew up. Mine would change from week to week—a jungle explorer, a scientist, a parachute jumper——but hers were always the same. They showed a stick-figure woman in a traditional red bordered sari with a big bunch of keys tied to the *palloo*. She wore a red marriage *bindi* and a big smile and stood next to a mustachioed man dressed in a suit and carrying a briefcase. Several stick-figure children (their sex indicated by boxy short pants or triangular skirts) would be gathered around them, arms linked, dancing. Had I taken all of that away from her by my misplaced American notions of feminism and justice? For a moment a terrible doubt rises in me like nausea, threatening to spill out.

"Maybe her mother wasn't so wrong after all," Sunil says. "Maybe the abortion *is* the lesser of the two evils."

I stare at my husband. At the dark, heavy shapes of the

words he has released into the air between us. It strikes me I know far less about this man than I had naively, romantically, believed.

"Why don't you say Runu's mother-in-law's right too. And Ramesh," I finally whisper. "Why don't you say you agree with him? Maybe *you'd* have wanted me to have an abortion if my baby hadn't turned out to be a boy."

"Anju!" Sunil's voice quivers with indignation.

I avoid his eyes and snatch up my pillows. "I'm going to sleep on the family-room couch," I say. What I've said is probably irrational, even unforgivable, but I'm in it too deep now to back away. I slam the door behind me for good measure.

I throw my pillows onto the lumpy couch and wipe my damp, shaking palms on my nightdress. I open the refrigerator and eye a large frozen pepperoni pizza. I'm tempted to pop it into the microwave oven and eat the whole thing, every last soggy forkful. I imagine newspaper headlines which read, *Pregnant woman, driven to despair by cruel husband, ends up in hospital due to pizza overdose.* That would serve Sunil right.

Instead I settle for a glass of hot milk and honey, and after I've drunk it, I try to make myself comfortable on the couch. But questions riddle me. It feels like when I have pins-and-needles in my legs, except now it's all over my body. Does Sunil love *me*, or only the mother-to-be of his son? Would he have cared for me as much if we had been in India and the baby had turned out to be a girl? What if I hadn't been able to have a baby at all? Would he be asking his parents to look for another wife for him? Pregnant-woman fancies, perhaps, but I can't stop them from coming. And Runu, who must be almost halfway to Calcutta by now. How is she feeling as she watches, from her train window, the thatched porches of village huts where women cook their husbands' lunches over wood fires while their children play around them? Will she look back on this day and curse me?

I close my aching eyes. *Please*, I pray, *please just let me sleep.*

Then the memory comes to me, so intense that I can feel once again the cold slimy jelly rubbed onto my skin, the monitor sliding back and forth over the mound of my belly as the doctor prepares for the ultrasound that will let me see the baby for the first time. At first he is a vague dark shape on the screen. Then as the image is enlarged I see the delicate curl of his perfect fishbone spine, the small bump of his sex. He waves his arms and legs in a graceful underwater dance, though as yet I don't feel any of it. The green radium blip on the screen, not unlike the stars Runu and I used to watch on those long ago summer nights, is the beat of his fierce heart.

That ultrasound had changed everything, made my baby, my Anand, real in a way that nothing else had.

I know it must have been the same for Runu.

I feel better about my decision. I still can't say, for sure, that I gave Runu the right advice. Even with decisions you make for yourself, it takes years to know. But my body begins to relax. Soften. I take a deep breath and put my hand over my belly, and feel, for the first time, a small but definite movement.

Maybe Runu can come to the U.S. with her daughter, I think. Maybe she can live close by in a little apartment and sew clothes for all the Indian ladies. She can sell chutneys and sweets and *samosas*—maybe even open her own restaurant. I can see our children growing up together, as close as their mothers were, Anand and—I give my niece a name—*Dayita*, beloved, for so she will be to us.

Anand and Dayita, I whisper aloud. Anand and Dayita. It sounds beautiful, complete, like a line from a *ghazal*.

Tomorrow I'll ask Sunil about sponsoring Runu, maybe getting her a student visa. I know he'll fight it at first, give me a hundred reasons why we can't do it. Why we shouldn't. But I'll fight back. Already I'm learning how. I'll use what I have to —my pregnancy, even. It's worth it—for Runu and, yes, myself. I'll get my way.

I know I will, I say to myself, and smiling, I drift into sleep.

AFFAIR

I was in the kitchen chopping vegetables for dinner when I found out about it. From Ashok. During a com-
mercial break on TV in the middle of the football game he was
watching.

"You know, of course," he said, raising himself elegantly
up on one elbow from his favorite position on the couch so he
could watch my face, "that Meena is having an affair?"

Just like that.

The knife slipped and nicked my finger. I watched the
blood appear as though from nowhere, dyeing the meticulously sliced carrots a deeper orange. I felt like throwing
something at Ashok, the bowl of green *lauki* squash I'd picked
up at the Indian grocery, maybe. Or maybe even the cutting
board, arcing through the air and smacking that smile off his
face.

But I didn't. I merely held up the bleeding finger and

said, in the mild, reasonable tone I'd perfected over eight years of marriage, "Now look what you made me do. I really wish you wouldn't spring things on me like this."

"Poor Abha." The look of sympathy on Ashok's face was so real that even I, who knew better, was almost fooled. Ashok's good at that. "Want me to kiss your finger and make it better?"

"No, thank you," I snapped, reaching in the drawer for a Band-Aid.

"How was I to know she hadn't told you? She *is* your best friend, after all," said Ashok. And then, "You're mad, aren't you, that she told *me* instead of you?" Triumph gleamed in his eyes.

He was right, and he knew it. But I wasn't going to give him the satisfaction of acknowledgment, so I remained silent.

Until today I'd thought I knew all about Meena's life, just as she knew about mine. We talked to each other every day—on the phone if we couldn't get together in person. She'd called me just an hour earlier, before our husbands returned from work, so we could "really talk, without the guys interrupting us." She'd told me about the office, how the new ad campaign she'd thought up had already increased their sales. And about the cutest little jacket she'd picked up at Nordstrom's, with a real fox-fur collar. She hadn't said a thing about an affair.

Feeling betrayed, I busied myself with chopping onions so I'd have a valid reason for tears.

"I bet you're dying to know who he is." Ashok's voice sparkled with malicious mischief. "I'll tell you if you ask me very nicely."

Affair

He would have, too. But I couldn't bring myself to do it. It would have meant defeat.

Angrily I dumped a couple of extra teaspoons of red pepper powder into the chicken curry. Hot food gives Ashok the most terrible heartburn. Usually I wouldn't have stooped to such an obvious revenge, but right now I was too agitated to be subtle.

Then a thought struck me. I went over and stood in front of Ashok.

"Is this a joke? Is this some kind of a sick practical joke?"

"Would I do such a thing?" Ashok was all wounded innocence. "Especially when I know how fond you are of Meena?"

"I remember the time you pretended you got laid off from work. . . ."

Ashok flashed me a charming smile that was also a challenge. "Why don't you ask Meena yourself at Kuldeep's party tomorrow?" He pressed the volume-increase button on the remote control.

"If this is a joke, you're going to be really sorry," I shouted over the blare of the TV.

Ashok blew me a lazy kiss. He loves it when he manages to get under my skin. He recrossed his legs in one liquid motion, aimed the remote, and flipped through shows (another habit of his that drives me crazy) until he found MTV, a channel I particularly dislike.

I retreated to the kitchen with its shiny rows of canisters, its racks of spices all carefully labeled, its gleaming tiles and faucets that usually made me feel sane and in control. But I couldn't escape the TV, where a very young, very blond

233

woman in a shimmery skintight outfit was sultrily singing about *how you make me feel each night.* I averted my eyes from the slow undulation of her hips, the pointy-red tip of her tongue moistening her lips. Her painted fingernails moving suggestively over her breasts. I knew Ashok was watching me, a mocking curl to his lips that seemed to say, *Still suffering from your prudish Indian upbringing, Abha?* But I couldn't help it. Sex for me was a matter between married people, carried out in the silent privacy of their bedroom and resulting, hopefully, in babies. I preferred not to think of its other aspects, and I resented American TV for invading my home with them.

I stared down at the translucent curls of the onions waiting on the cutting board. They formed an intricate pattern against the dark wood, glistening like shavings of mother-of-pearl. If I could read them, as people did tea leaves, what would it tell me about Meena? About Ashok and myself and our constant sparring? It was a depressing thought. I threw another spoon of red pepper powder into the chicken for good measure and, leaving the rest of the dinner uncooked, locked myself in the spare bedroom upstairs.

I threw myself down on the neatly made guest bed, across the scratchy Jodhpuri bedspread embroidered with good-luck lotuses which had been part of my trousseau, and cried for a while. But crying has always seemed to me to be a waste of time. All it does is make my face puff up. So I stopped and wiped my face on the edge of my sari and checked my reflection in the mirror. I looked every bit as terrible as I'd expected—swollen eyes, red nose, sallow skin. There were red crisscross marks on my forehead where I'd pressed it against the bedspread.

Even under the best of circumstances I am no beauty. If my horoscope hadn't matched Ashok's so perfectly that everyone declared our marriage must have been ordained by the gods, I doubt that his family would have chosen me. I don't have Meena's fair skin, so dramatic with her curly black hair and long lashes. My nose is broad and honest but by no means elegant, while hers, straight and chisel-sharp, looks as though it belonged on an *apsara* from classical Indian sculpture. I constantly battle the inches that accumulate almost by magic around my hips (I put on a pound every time I *look* at dessert), while Meena glides through life slim and svelte, eating whatever she wants and wearing designer bikinis. "You could look really pretty, Abha," she laments periodically, "but you don't even *try*." She's shown me how to pull in my stomach and push back my shoulders when I walk, but I invariably forget. And when I'm forced by necessity to venture into the mall, I always pick up clothing with bright flowery patterns instead of the dark solids and narrow stripes she's advised me to wear.

"It's important for *you* to dress right because you're in marketing and have to impress clients," I told her once. "Me, I just do freelance work from home, writing recipes for the Indian papers. Why do *I* need to look good?"

"Really, Abha!" Meena had shaken her head like there was no hope for me. "*All* women need to look good. Don't you want Ashok's heartbeat to speed up when he looks at you?"

The thought of it made me laugh out loud. Really,

sometimes Meena's ideas were so adolescent. I remembered my mother, who'd spent most of her life in the simple red-bordered cotton saris most Bengali mothers wore, dabbing at her plump face with its *palloo* as she hurried from kitchen to nursery to dining room. I doubted that she'd *ever* made my father's heartbeat speed up (though of course he loved her)—at least not in the last thirty years that I'd known them.

"You're starting to sound like an American, Meena! Indian marriages aren't based on such superficial things."

"That's what you think! Watch out—by the time you realize I'm right, it might be too late." Meena's tone had been joking. Still, it had reminded me how, a few evenings earlier, Ashok had looked up from a magazine he'd been reading and said, quite out of the blue, "Abha, I wish you'd do something to your hair, go get a perm maybe."

Right now, though, I had more serious problems to worry about than my looks.

I do my best thinking when I write things down, so I reached under the bed. Safe behind the suitcases we haven't pulled out in years I hide a notepad and pen for occasions like this. On the lined yellow sheet I wrote:

I. *Why is Meena having an affair (if she is having one)?*

I left some space below that, then added:

II. *How wrong is what she is doing (if she is doing it)?*

I left some more space (although I already knew the answer to this one: *very very wrong*) and went on to the third question.

III. *Should I confront her about it?*

There was another question. Needle-sharp, it pricked at

my eyelids when I closed them. But I wasn't ready to write it down.

Downstairs the doorbell rang. Who could it be so late at night? I parted the bedroom blinds and peered out. There was a Domino's Pizza van outside, its blue-and-red lighted sign twinkling festively. Damn! Ashok had outsmarted me again.

"Mmmm, sausage and mushrooms!" he was saying, his voice raised for my benefit. "Smells great!"

My stomach growled. Sausage and mushrooms are my favorite pizza toppings. But even the extra-hot chicken sitting uneaten in the kitchen would have tasted pretty good to me at this point. I'd started, halfheartedly, on another one of my diets this morning, and I hadn't eaten anything since a spartan lunch of iceberg lettuce with no dressing. But of course I couldn't go downstairs, where Ashok was lying in wait. So I gritted my teeth and went back to question one.

Why? Why? Why? I wrote. *Was she bored? Did she want to shake up Srikant? Make him sit up and stop taking her for granted? Or had she found someone she couldn't resist?*

But what kind of man would be worth giving up your principles for? What kind of man would be more important than being a good wife?

I liked Srikant, Meena's husband. He wasn't handsome and suave and clever like Ashok, but from observing him over the years I felt he had a good heart. Living with Ashok has made me particularly appreciative of good-hearted people.

Srikant wasn't a big talker. When he and Meena came over for dinner, he'd sit back and listen to Meena and Ashok laughing at each other's wickedly witty jokes, commenting on people and books and TV shows I didn't even know existed. Sometimes from the kitchen, while I fried the *samosas* I'd made from scratch, or put the finishing touches on a particularly fine *qurma*, I would notice a wistful look flit over Srikant's face. I wondered if he was thinking, as he watched their animated gestures, how well they suited each other. Others thought so too. When we went out together, Meena and Ashok entering a restaurant ahead of us with their long-legged stride, his hand possessively on her elbow, waiters often took them to be a couple. They probably made the same error about Srikant and myself, darker, shorter, quieter, hurrying to catch up, and too traditional to even touch hands.

When Srikant did have something to say, it was usually about his work. I guess he felt about it like I did about my cooking. As he described the latest software product he was developing, his voice would go deep and his eyes would shine. Forgetting awkwardness, he would sketch forms in the air with eloquent hands, and for a moment he would be almost handsome.

Then Meena would break in, laughing.

"I swear, that computer's like his second wife—no, his mistress! He spends more time with it than with me. Do you know that he's even given it a name?"

Srikant would smile shamefacedly.

"Lalita! He actually calls it Lalita!" Meena's laugh would be high and brittle.

Srikant would look down, examining his square, blunt nails.

Affair

"I used to be dreadfully jealous when we were first married. Srikant would stay on at work till all kinds of hours, even though I kept telling him I hated being alone in the house. It was so deathly quiet, not like India, where something's always going on—street vendors, servants, people dropping in to gossip. . . ."

"How horrible that must have been," Ashok would interject, his voice low and sympathetic as it never was when *I* complained about something, sending an ache through me.

I'd want to come to Srikant's defense. *It's what all of us Indian wives went through,* I'd want to tell Meena. *Why, Ashok still does the same thing.* But already she would be telling us about all the things she'd tried to get Srikant to come home early.

"I even bought a Betty Crocker cookbook and fixed him special dinners—stroganoff and soufflés and lime pies. Me! Can you imagine!"

We would all laugh because, unlike me, Meena is a terrible cook. She and Srikant virtually live on fast food and Chinese takeout.

"That's probably what drove him into Lalita's arms," Ashok would quip.

"Probably. Anyway, my cooking efforts didn't last long, and after a while I got used to being on my own. . . ."

"And now no doubt you've discovered that there are advantages to your husband not being around."

"No! What could they be?" Meena would ask in her most ingenuous voice, fluttering her lashes.

"Remind me to tell you sometime when Srikant and

Abha aren't around," Ashok would say with a wink. And the two of them would burst into laughter, with Srikant and me joining in just a few seconds late.

That's how they always kidded around. Until today, I'd never let it bother me, because I was Meena's special friend, her only confidante. She might joke with Ashok, flirt even. She might be the life of the parties we attended—the best amateur stand-up comic, as one of our friends (a man, naturally) said. But it was me she turned to when she was unhappy.

I knew things about Meena that no one else did—how she still turned on the TV evenings when Srikant was late coming back so she wouldn't have to listen to the silence, how she slept with the light on when he went out of town. I was the one who held her and tried to calm her when, after her miscarriage last year, the doctor said that something was wrong with her uterus and she might never be able to have a baby. When her tears dampened the shoulder of my sari, I too had wept. That was another bond that held us close, the unspoken sorrow of being childless.

That's why I couldn't be resentful of Meena, not even when Ashok compared our looks. That's why I forgave her her slicing wit, even if, once in a while, she turned it on me. She needed me more than anyone in my life ever had—the way I'd hoped, when I'd got married, my husband and babies might.

But not anymore, I thought as I pressed my nails into my aching temples. Now she had a man to share her most intimate joys and fears with, and she had Ashok to tell it all to.

240

Affair

My usually pristine kitchen was a mess. Half-cooked food, unwashed dishes, vegetable peelings in the sink—and now crusts of pizza lying in an open Domino's box. I could feel the Parmesan cheese under my feet, sticky and coarse as sand. Thank God, at least, that Ashok had gone to bed. I couldn't have faced his taunting smile on top of everything else.

I considered leaving everything the way it was, but I knew I'd just have to deal with it in the morning. So I mopped the floor and washed up and took out the trash and boiled some rice for myself. It was 2 A.M. when I sat down to eat my rice and extra-peppery chicken.

I couldn't remember the last time I was up so late. I like my sleep. Usually Ashok is the night person. If there's a party that's going to run into the small hours, we either drive separately or—we've started doing this more and more—he goes alone. I'm quite happy at home by myself, listening to one of my classical music tapes—a night raga by Chaurasia, maybe, the haunting notes of his flute hanging over me as I work on next week's recipe for *The Indian Courier*. And when I go to bed I fall asleep immediately. I'm lucky in that, I guess. Meena now—she's a real insomniac, especially if she's upset. A little thing—her boss making a negative comment about her performance, or a letter from her mother about her sister's new baby—can keep her up all night. She told me once that when she's awake late she can hear the house breathing—a hushed panting, like a crouched beast's.

I listened as I sat there at the kitchen table, my mouth burning from the chicken, my diet ruined, but I didn't hear a thing except the refrigerator's hum. Still, it was eerie, all that

silence, like black snow falling around me. On an impulse I
turned on the TV.

I'm not much of a TV person. I watch a couple of cooking programs each week, and news on the days when I'm
feeling socially responsible. And on weekend mornings, for a
taste of home, I turn on the international channel where they
show song-and-dance scenes from popular Hindi movies,
though even those are getting bad, with the young girls in
skimpy skirts and low-cut blouses, letting the men touch them
here and there. I can't seem to relate to the regular American
shows, the ones Ashok watches. The people on TV—the men
with their hair cut in the latest mode and tanned faces out of
which shine eyes blue as stones, the women with their high,
high heels, their carefully made-up mouths, their tiny waists
and breasts that never sag—seem to inhabit an alien world of
romance and intrigue and designer clothes that fit perfectly.

The couple on the screen right now weren't wearing
designer clothes, though. In fact, they weren't wearing anything at all, and when I got over the shock I realized that I'd
turned on the cable channel which Ashok had ordered last
month and which he watched, in spite of the fact that I point-
edly left the room whenever he turned it on (or maybe because of it), almost every night.

My face hot, I switched off the TV. Really, the things
they'll show on the air nowadays, I said to myself indignantly
as I got up to leave. It was a good thing we didn't have kids in
the house.

Halfway up the stairs I stopped. I stood there for a
while, listening to the wall clock ticking, and then I came
down and, heart pounding, turned on the set again. I wasn't

sure why I did it. Maybe I just wanted to examine, without the inhibition of his presence, what it was that Ashok enjoyed about these shows. Or maybe it was something else.

The couple were walking along the edge of a swimming pool now, tall and unself-conscious, while the reflected light from the water shimmered over their nakedness. The woman dived into the pool and the man followed. Unhindered by clothing, their limbs cut cleanly through the blue, and when they came together bubbles broke and rose around them like silver beads. I knew intuitively that they weren't married. Their mouths and hands explored the curves and hollows of each other's bodies with a frank delight that was very different from our awkward, furtive movements in the darkened bedroom. When the man's lips closed around the tight pinkness of the woman's nipple, I watched carefully. A part of me was surprised that I felt none of the shame that would have ordinarily overwhelmed me. Perhaps the dim blue swirl of water in which they rocked, suspended, gave the act a softness, a sense of surreality. Or perhaps shame is something you feel only when someone is watching you watch. When the man's head moved lower to the half-moon of her navel, and then lower still, I clenched my fists and leaned forward. My nails dug into my palms, hard, like hers were digging into his shoulders. And when her body arched upward, shuddering, my body too gave an answering shudder.

Later I lay in bed, listening to Ashok breathe, thinking. Had I been wrong all this time, when I refused to let him turn the lights on as we made love, when I lay stiff and submissive under his thrusts until he was done with it? When I escaped thankfully to the bathroom to wash myself as soon as he moved off me? Had my mother, too, been wrong when, the night before my wedding, she had explained to me that a good wife's duty was to allow her husband to satisfy himself no matter how unpleasant she found it? For the first time I wondered how happy my father had been with her, and she with him.

I watched the dark line of Ashok's shoulder and remembered. Early in our marriage, once or twice, he'd suggested doing things differently, trying something new. He'd even bought a book—*The Joy of Sex*, I think it was called—and shown it to me almost shyly. But I'd reacted with such undisguised horror that he hadn't brought it up again.

Was that when he started turning his acid humor on me?

I put out a hesitant hand to touch his throat. His skin was warm and supple, and when I brought my face to it, it smelled of musk and maleness. Ashok muttered in his sleep, a word I couldn't catch. He made a brushing-off movement, as one might with a mosquito. The back of his hand struck my mouth as he turned away.

That night I dreamed of a man and woman underwater. I knew right away that it wasn't the couple in the movie. They ran their hands along each other's bodies with feverish haste, their muscles straining as though it was their first time together. When the swirling blue cleared and the man finally lifted his mouth from the dark patch of woman-hair fine and wavy as water grass, I saw that it was Ashok. I drew him up, up, and pulled him hard into my hips. We came together, my legs wrapped tight around him, bubbles exploding into crystal fragments around us. And then I saw my face, the way you do in dreams. It was blind with ecstasy, my mouth open in a soundless, triumphant cry, my hair spreading around my head, black and wild and maenadic. Only it wasn't my face. It was Meena's.

I noticed her as soon as I stepped into the Taj restaurant, where Kuldeep and Saroj were holding their tenth anniversary celebration. How could I not? In her sheer orange chiffon sari she flamed in the center of the banquet hall, and the men gathered around her, wearing the dark, conservative suits that successful Indians favored, seemed like bemused moths. Srikant was nowhere in sight.

"My, is that a backless *choli* she's wearing?" said Ashok. "Your friend's grown quite reckless, wouldn't you say? Maybe it's the effect of the affair. . . ."

I didn't respond. The *choli* was, indeed, very backless. I got a good view of it as Meena turned to accept a drink that someone was holding out to her. Nothing except a couple of golden strings held it together. Beside me, Ashok gave a low, approving whistle.

In spite of myself I was shocked. And furious with Meena for her foolishness. Didn't she know that every woman in the room would be whispering about that *choli?* I could already hear the comments.

Indecent.

Where on earth did she get such a thing? And to have the boldness to wear it here.

If I were her husband, I'd tell her a thing or two.

Tell! My dear, it's not telling she needs. It's a good beating.

Talk of this kind was the last thing Meena, who already
had a reputation for being different and a little dangerous,
could afford. Especially now.

So what? said a small voice inside me. Why are *you* so
concerned with what they think of Meena? Why do you feel
like you have to protect her?

I didn't have an answer to that. I guess it was something
I'd always done. Perhaps it was because, in spite of her world-
liness, Meena understood our Indian friends far less than I
did.

The men, for example, even the ones clustered around
her, laughing at her jokes, they too would have things to say
about her in the privacy of the men's room, things followed by
winks and lewd, derisive laughter. For in spite of their Bill
Blass suits and alligator-skin shoes and the sleek Benzes that
waited obediently for them in the parking lots, they still belonged to the villages of their fathers. Villages where a woman
caught in adultery was made to ride around the market square
on a donkey, her head shaved, her clothes stripped off her,
while crowds jeered and pelted her with garbage.

"Abha dear, here you are finally!"

Startled, I whirled around. I hadn't noticed Meena leaving her group of admirers. Now she leaned forward to give me
—and then Ashok—a kiss on the cheek. It was not something
Indians did as a rule—but then that was Meena. I watched
her bright lips grazing my husband's cheek and his smile as he
whispered something in her ear, and I remembered my
dream.

"Abha, you're not listening!"

Affair

It took me a moment to focus on Meena's animated face.

"They're going to have dancing before dinner. It's going to start in a few minutes. Isn't that something!"

I nodded as I watched two men wheel in assorted stereo equipment and put up strobe lights on stands and hang mirrored spheres from the ceiling. Dancing was uncommon at Indian parties, at least among our friends, whose idea of a good time consisted mostly of a bottle of Johnnie Walker and a plateful of *biriyani,* with some spicy gossip on the side.

"Kuldeep and Saroj are going all out to make an impression, aren't they?" Meena said, her eyes sparkling, her foot already tapping.

"And all this for their tenth anniversary! I wonder what they'll do for their twentieth!" said Ashok.

"That's if they're still together," I said dryly.

Meena and Ashok both turned and looked at me. They weren't used to hearing me talk like that.

"My, we're getting cynical," said Ashok. Then he turned back to Meena and gave her an elaborate bow. "May I have the first dance, ma'am?"

"Of course!" Meena's laugh was like a flock of white birds flying up into the sky all at once. "That is, if Abha doesn't mind?"

I felt a stab of disappointment. I wasn't a dancer. Still, it would have been nice if my husband had asked *me* first.

By the time I'd pulled myself together sufficiently to say it was fine with me, Ashok and Meena were gone.

I leaned against the wall and looked on as he drew her to

the middle of the surprisingly crowded floor. Maybe it was the novelty of it that made people eager to dance. Or maybe it was that the large chandelier lights had been replaced by semidarkness.

The first song was a fast number, a hit from a recent Hindi film. Under the pulsing of the strobes, the movements of the dancers took on a fragmented, disembodied quality, and faces I'd known for years looked like those of strangers. But there was no mistaking Ashok and Meena. They were without a doubt the most graceful pair on the floor. The other couples, brought up in a culture of sitar and *tabla* and years of warnings that nice girls didn't move their bodies like *that*, tried valiantly to follow the beat. But their elbows and knees stuck out at stiff, ungainly angles, and when they shook their hips and behinds, it was in an uncomfortable caricature of the film stars they had watched on their VCRs. I wondered what they thought as they watched Ashok and Meena glide by, their faces illuminated by the silver light from the revolving spheres overhead. When he spun her around, Travolta-like, until she ended up in his arms, her hair tangling around his throat like a live thing, were their eyes dazzled, like mine, by the flash and glitter of the gold strings of that backless *choli?*

No, I whispered to myself. He wouldn't have said anything to me if *he* was the one Meena was having the affair with. But my voice, weak and unconvinced, was drowned by the clamor inside my head. *Yes, yes, yes. It would be the perfect victory, the perfect revenge for all those sexless, loveless years.*

For that was what I came to realize in the banquet hall of the Taj with the broken light from the mirrored spheres

Affair

lying around me: I hadn't loved Ashok all these years, not really, though I believed I had. I'd been too busy being a good wife.

"Hope I'm not disturbing you, Abha." It was Srikant, carrying a glass of 7-Up. "I thought you might like something to drink."

"Thanks," I said, attempting a smile. It was just like him, considerate, to remember that I didn't drink alcohol. "How about yourself?"

"I've had enough," he said, leaning back by me against the wall, and when I turned to ask him where he'd been all this time, I smelled the raw whiff of it on his breath. It surprised me because Srikant, too, hardly ever drinks.

"They look good together, don't they?" he said, ignoring my question.

A slow love song was playing now. Meena and Ashok moved fluidly among husbands and wives who held each other at awkward arm's length, as they had been taught. He lowered his head to say something to her, and as she looked up to reply, it seemed to me her cheek rested for a moment on his shoulder. They didn't glance toward us. Not once.

"They do," I said heavily, watching my husband's hand on the bare skin of my best friend's back.

"You know, I'm going to India," said Srikant.

I tried, for his sake, to show some interest. "Really! Meena didn't say anything. When are you folks leaving?"

"Next week. My mother's not well. I'm going alone."

"Meena isn't coming with you?"

"No. There's no point to it."

"What do you mean?" I said, my voice sharp and too high. Did he, too, know something I didn't?

But all he said was, "She's doing so well at work, and it's their busiest season. I don't want to drag her away."

Leaning close to the mirror in the ladies' room, where we were alone for the moment, Meena touched up her lipstick—the same flame-orange as her sari—with a deft hand. She examined her eye shadow and blusher critically, then turned to me.

"Do I look OK?"

"You look fine."

In spite of all the dancing, it seemed like Meena had just arrived at the party, her hair freshly styled, her clothes un-wrinkled. She wasn't even sweating. I'd just stood against the wall drinking 7-Up, but my *kurta*, a modest, high-necked af-fair, had damp patches under the arms. My mouth was smudged and my hair, shampooed just this morning, hung limply about my face. I pulled out my lipstick, though all I wanted to do was go home and go to bed.

"Not like *that*," Meena said. "Don't scrape it across your mouth as if it's a stick of crayon. Here, let me do it for you."

Before I could say no, she'd taken the tube from me. She filled in my lips with one smooth stroke, then took a little of the lipstick on her finger and rubbed it onto my cheek-bones. Her touch was soft, the brush of a bird's wing. Did her hands move over her lover's body—Ashok's body?—with the same lightness? The thought made me want to weep.

250

Affair

"What is it, Abha?"

"Nothing." I tried to keep my voice steady, to look past her at the Taj Mahal poster hanging on the wall, where under a huge golden moon a man and a woman stood holding hands and looking at the majestic marble structure that symbolized eternal love.

"You're upset about something. Tell me."

I shook my head. "We should get back to our table—they must have served dinner already."

"Is it my *choli?*"

"You want to dress like that, it's your business."

Meena smiled faintly. "I knew you wouldn't like it—but I wanted something different. I was so tired of doing the same things, the *proper* things. . . ."

Is that why you're having an affair? I wanted to spit out. But I couldn't. I'd been too well trained, all my life, in holding in anger and heartbreak.

"Are you mad because I danced with Ashok?"

As we'd walked from the dance floor to our table, Ashok had said, "That was great, Meena. How about some more after dinner?"

"Maybe Abha would like to dance this time."

"Oh, you know Abha, she *never* dances."

The dismissive sureness of his tone had made me furious. *Yes, I want to dance,* I'd almost said. But I knew I'd only embarrass us both on the floor with my stumbling stiffness.

You stay away from my husband, I wanted to scream at Meena now.

"He's just a good friend, you know that, don't you?" Meena said, looking at me closely. In the flickering neon tube lights of the ladies' room, her irises were a deep purple-black flecked with gold.

"How is it that you don't tell me what's going on in your life anymore?" I blurted out.

"What do you mean?"

I looked at the surprise on her face. It seemed so genuine, the wide eyes so distressed, I was ashamed. Maybe Ashok had lied after all.

"Srikant told me his mother's sick—he's going to India . . ." I stammered.

"Oh *that*. We just decided on it today—I didn't get a chance to tell you." She linked her arm through mine as we made our way back to our table and lowered her voice conspiratorially. "Personally I think he's making a big deal out of nothing—she isn't really that sick. It would be quite OK even if he didn't go."

"So, Mrs. Mitra, what do you think? Mrs. Mitra . . . ?"

I looked up with a start from the pad where I'd been doodling. "I'm sorry," I said.

"I knew I'd lost you there, the last few minutes," said Suren Gupta, the editor of the Lifestyle section of *The Indian Courier*, the paper for which I wrote recipes every week. He gave me a not unsympathetic smile. "Something on your mind?"

I gave him a small smile back. *One of them is lying to me,* I'd been thinking. *Ashok or Meena?* I didn't know which possibility was worse.

I had known Suren—if one could call our brief, infre-

Affair

quent meetings at the *Courier* office knowing—for a couple of years. Usually I just mailed him recipes, but once in a while, for Diwali or Baisakhi or some other important festival when he was planning a special issue, he'd ask me to come in to see him. Sometimes I'd just stay on at the office and work until I had a menu that fitted his theme. Suren always asked me out to lunch on those days, and I always declined. Rich and single and good-looking, he had a bit of a reputation in the Indian community as a playboy.

Today, though, he had a different kind of proposition for me. The *Courier* wanted to put out a cookbook—glossy cover, color pictures, the whole bit—of selected dishes from all the Bay Area Indian restaurants. Several Indian businesses had agreed to sponsor the project, and of course the restaurant managers were enthusiastic about the publicity. Would I be interested in compiling the book?

"As I was saying," Suren repeated, "it'll mean visiting the restaurants, sampling the menu, choosing the best dishes for the book, observing how they're prepared, and writing up a simplified version suited to the western lifestyle and palate. Of course you'll be suitably paid. . . ."

"Sounds very interesting," I said, battling the heaviness in my heart. And indeed, it was. I'd been wanting to put together a cookbook for a long time, and this way I'd learn a lot about professional Indian cuisine. It would also keep my mind off things I didn't want to think about.

"Why don't I fill you in on the details over lunch?"

I started to say no. Then I took a deep breath. "Lunch would be lovely."

If he was surprised, Suren didn't show it. "Let me help

you with your shawl," he said, rewarding me with a brilliantly suave smile.

I'd been afraid that Suren would take me to one of those ostentatiously expensive San Francisco restaurants with lace tablecloths and dim lighting and snobbish waiters and I'd feel terribly out of place. But the little place in Chinatown that we went to was bright and crowded, its walls covered with good-luck signs and dragons painted on red brocade. The waiters were friendly and didn't speak much English, which, together with the disposable chopsticks in their cheerful paper wrappers, put me at ease.

So did Suren. I'd been afraid, too, of how he'd behave, given his reputation. But he was quite charming. He pointed out his favorites from the menu and told me funny stories of his experiences at the *Courier* and didn't ask any awkward questions. Slowly I relaxed. It was fun to be out with a man who wasn't my husband. In my entire life I'd never done that. I enjoyed the little courtesies I wasn't used to—someone to pull back my chair and refill my cup of Chinese tea before it was empty, someone to ask if I liked the food. When Suren said he'd tried some of my weekly recipes—the *rogan josh*, the *pista kulfi*—and liked them, I was surprised and flattered. As we talked, I found myself wishing that I were wearing something more elegant than a *kurta* printed with big sun-flowers that suddenly seemed blowsy. That I'd taken the time to put on some makeup.

So when Suren ordered me a glass of Chablis, I didn't say no. And when he leaned across the table to pat my wrist, saying, "I know you'll be perfect for the job, Abha. I look forward to working with you." I didn't snatch my hand away like I would have done at any other time. And if, when he placed my shawl around my shoulders, his fingers lingered a moment longer than necessary, I didn't care. *So what,* I thought defiantly, remembering Ashok's palm pressed against Meena's bare back. *So what.*

I looked up at Suren, my smile as brilliantly suave as his, and said, "I'd be happy to take on the project."

I bought the robe that afternoon, on my way back from the *Courier.*

In general I hate shopping. The large department stores confuse me, and the exclusive boutiques with salesgirls in slinky outfits that cost more than what I make in a whole month intimidate me. But today I wanted to celebrate my new job. Or maybe it was because, as I drove through the city, I was aware as never before of all the billboards with women in strapless evening gowns raising glasses of Smirnoff vodka to their glistening lips. All the storefront windows with slim-hipped mannequins elegant in their swimsuits and wedding dresses and white linen skirts, their holiday jackets slung over casual shoulders.

Anyway, I found myself in the big Macy's at Union Square, wandering through the lingerie department. I wasn't looking for anything particular, but as soon as I saw the peach robe, all silk and lace with a deep scooped neck and the thinnest spaghetti straps that crossed in the back, I knew it was what I had come in to get. And though it was prohibitively expensive, like most things at Macy's, for once I didn't care. When the young woman at the cash register held it up so that light shone through the translucent material and said *oooh, sexy,* I didn't blush or stammer.

"Yes, isn't it," I told her with a cool smile.

After dinner that night I went upstairs and changed into the robe. I brushed my hair till it shone and left it loose, and I put on some matching peach lipstick that I'd also bought at Macy's, smoothing it onto my lips and cheekbones the way Meena had the other night. When I walked back into the family room where Ashok was looking over a report he brought home from the office, my heart flung itself wildly around in my chest. I felt like I was about to start a revolution —and perhaps I was.

"The *Courier* has offered me a new assignment," I announced. "A cookbook. It's something I'm really excited about. But it'll mean a lot of driving around, watching chefs at work. . . ." I waited expectantly.

I don't know what I thought Ashok would say. Maybe I feared he'd turn macho on me. *My wife, hanging around in restaurant kitchens with cooks and waiters? Never.* Maybe I hoped for acknowledgment. *Great, Abha! I knew, sooner or later, someone would notice what a good job you've been doing with that weekly food column. And by the way, what's that gorgeous outfit you've got on?*

But all he said absently as he turned the pages of a report he'd brought home from work was "that's very nice."

I crushed the folds of my new robe in my fists. Even a taunt—*So you think you're going to be the next Julia Child*— would have been better.

Affair

"I had lunch with Suren Gupta today," I told him now. "You know about Suren—they say he's quite a ladies' man."

Ashok didn't even look up. "It's good for you to move around a bit in society, meet people." His voice held that same absentminded kindness. "Smarten you up some." Then he added, "Why don't you go on up to bed. I've got to finish studying this by tomorrow."

I swallowed my disappointment and my pride.

"Do you like my new robe? I picked it up at Macy's today."

That made him raise his head, finally. "Macy's, huh?" For a moment his eyes glinted with their usual malicious amusement. "What is this, your answer to the backless *choli?*" He examined me critically for a moment. "The design's pretty, Abha, but frankly I don't think it was made quite with you in mind. And the color makes you look anemic."

I moved through a haze all next morning. My usual activities —fixing bed tea for Ashok, setting out his clothes, squeezing fresh orange juice for his breakfast, making blueberry pancakes from a new recipe I'd seen in *Good Housekeeping* (I prided myself on my international repertoire)—seemed monotonous and meaningless. The thought that I'd be doing them for the rest of my life pressed down on me like a suddenly unbearable weight. Thank God Ashok was too busy marking up his report to notice how I sat across from him in silence, pushing the food around on my plate.

Maybe if I started on the project I would feel better.

So after Ashok's car pulled out of the driveway, I took a

shower and put the peach robe on again. It was cool and silky against my skin, and in the morning light from the bedroom window, the fabric glowed and shimmered. It made me feel strangely elegant. Queenly. And I wasn't going to let Ashok's comments spoil it for me. Defiantly, I sat down at the dressing table to apply makeup.

I was getting better at it already, I could see that as I outlined my lips in deep peach, darkened my eyes, and brushed blusher onto my cheeks. I sprayed myself generously with the Chanel No. 5 that Ashok had given me for my first anniversary and that I'd been saving all this while and, on impulse, slipped on my one pair of really high heels. I even put on a pair of dangly crystal earrings. I felt a bit embarrassed when I saw myself in the hall mirror as I came down the stairs, a bit silly, a girl dressed up in her big sister's fancy clothes. But it did give me an added confidence. And when I spoke to the manager of the first restaurant on the list Suren had handed me, I was surprised at how pleasantly businesslike my voice sounded, as though I'd been doing this kind of thing forever.

An hour later I was feeling a lot happier. The managers of the first three restaurants I'd phoned were eager to be part of the project, and I'd set up appointments to visit them in the next two weeks. The fourth one, the owner of a San Francisco restaurant that specialized in Mughal cuisine, one of my favorites, sounded flustered but not unfriendly. His head chef had suddenly quit, and he needed to find a replacement right away. Could I check back with him in a week? I certainly could, I graciously assured him.

Not bad for a morning's work, especially for a novice.

Affair

That's when the doorbell rang.

I didn't answer it right away. It was probably someone trying to sell something—a cleanser that would magically remove every spot on my carpet, a fertilizer that would turn my miniature daisies into giant double chrysanthemums. Maybe they would just leave if I stayed where I was and made no sound.

But the person was knocking now, a polite yet persistent knock. I sighed and opened the door a crack, bracing myself to say no.

Then I saw who it was.

"Srikant!" I was too shocked for a polite greeting. "What are you doing here?" In all the years I'd known him, he'd never visited our house without Meena, and certainly not when Ashok was away. It was not the kind of thing done by Indians brought up the way we'd been.

Srikant looked down, fidgeting with his keys. "I'm sorry if I disturbed you, Abha. I needed to talk. . . ." His voice trailed away, apologetic.

"Please," I said, motioning him in, though I felt uneasy about being alone in the house with a man I wasn't related to, even one I'd known for years. But all the familiar rules were breaking around me. What was one more?

"You look nice," said Srikant as he followed me in.

I flushed, sneaking a quick look at him. Was he being sarcastic? No, Srikant wouldn't do that. Still, I was horribly aware of the unsuitableness of my attire—the thin robe that clung to me, the lipstick that seemed suddenly garish, the high heels that made me stumble on the thick shag carpet.

"Can I get you something—a drink, or maybe a snack?"

Maybe, under cover of making tea, I could run upstairs and change into something more proper. But Srikant shook his head.

We sat stiffly on the edges of our chairs in the living room, I trying to make polite conversation while he examined the pattern on the curtains as though he were seeing them for the first time.

Then he said, "Meena and I are getting a divorce."

The erratic pounding of my heart made me forget my appearance. "When?" I whispered. But what I really wanted to ask was *why?*

"As soon as I get back from India. That's part of the reason I'm going, to break the news to my mother." He was silent for a long moment, but I could tell he wasn't done. My jaws ached with a tight fear.

"She's been having an affair for two months now. She finally told me last week, asked me to let her go." He rubbed at his face tiredly. "I'd begun to guess it was something like that—little things didn't fit, times she said she was working late, or visiting a woman friend, times in bed when . . ." He broke off.

My face grew hotter.

"You knew about it, didn't you." It wasn't a question.

I wanted to tell him that I hadn't been sure, that Meena hadn't confided in me. The hurt of it. But it was too complicated to explain. I nodded guiltily.

"It's OK. You were right to keep her secret. It's probably the best thing for us. We weren't meant for each other. Meena, she's like a falcon or something, wild and beautiful and filled with the need to soar." He paused, frowning a little as though he didn't expect me to understand. But of course I did. Perfectly. "And I"—his laugh was a sad, scratchy sound— "I guess I'm more of a penguin, waddling along my everyday path. I knew it the first time I saw her, at the bride-viewing. I should never have let my parents arrange our marriage—but she was so pretty, so *alive*. I thought some of it might rub off on me."

I wanted to say something sympathetic. But myriad images were tumbling around in my head, hot and crackling like clothes inside a dryer that's been left on too long. Ashok's taunting smile, *I'll tell you who it is if you ask very nicely*. His hand pressed to Meena's back. The *palloo* of Meena's sari flickering like a tongue of flame through the dark dance floor. Her eyes wide as a startled deer's, denying that she had kept any secrets from me. Was Ashok her lover? Was that what Srikant had come to tell me?

"Let me go make you some tea," I said, pressing my trembling hands together. "Please—I need some too."

In the kitchen I reached past the packets of Instant Lipton's that I generally used to the small metal box of Darjeeling tea my mother had sent for my last birthday. I peeled cardamom seeds and crumbled cloves and mixed them in with the cut black leaves as Indian women had for centuries, and when the water came to a boil I stirred it all in. The aroma of my childhood filled the room, calming me a little.

Behind me Srikant said, "You have a beautiful kitchen."

I whirled around. I hadn't heard him follow me in. He looked awkward and out of place, as though, like most traditional Indian males, he rarely entered a kitchen. After the divorce he'd probably have to learn how to cook for himself.

261

But maybe he'd just continue with Big Macs and Taco Bell burritos. Perhaps such things didn't matter to him.

"Everything's so clean," Srikant was saying wonderingly.

I looked around, seeing the kitchen for a moment as he must. I was proud of the blue flowered curtains that matched the airy wallpaper perfectly, the geraniums on the sill that glowed red and orange, the shiny copper-bottomed pots and pans that hung from their hooks. I would spend hours polishing those pots, lulled by the steady back and forth movement of my hands, the pungent, metallic odor of Brasso.

"Yes," I said heavily.

Srikant must have heard the bitterness in my voice, but he made no comment. Nor did he look surprised. "I've decided to let Meena have the house, though she'll probably sell it. When I get back from India, I'll get an apartment up in San Francisco."

"San Francisco! Won't it be a long commute for you?"

Srikant nodded. "Yes. But I've always wanted to live in the city," he said, holding out a cup for me to fill.

I looked at him, taken aback. His plain, dark-skinned face, his neatly combed-back hair which had been the same all the years I'd known him, except now it was thinning a little. His stolid mustache. I'd never have thought him the type. It was another reminder of how little I understood people.

"And Meena? What will she do?" I asked as I poured.

Srikant shrugged. "What will *you* do?" he asked me.

My hand shook so violently that the hot tea spilled over the edge of the saucer onto Srikant's hand, onto the cuff of his shirt. He flinched.

"I'm terribly sorry," I said, rushing to get a paper napkin. I wiped his hand and rubbed at the stains on his cuff, but all the while I was thinking, *Ashok. He means what'll I do when Ashok leaves with Meena.*

"Don't worry please, I'm fine," said Srikant, and he put his other hand over mine.

I looked down at his hand, the little hairs curling on the backs of his fingers, his honest, blunt nails. There was something unexpectedly comforting about its solidity, its warm weight. Under it, I didn't feel ashamed of my hand the way I did when Ashok—rarely now—clasped it in his manicured one.

Srikant saw me looking and removed his hand, but unhurriedly. He drank his tea and rinsed the cup and saucer and set them carefully on the drying rack.

I wanted to ask, *What did you mean by* . . . But I couldn't. I couldn't stand Srikant knowing that I didn't know about Ashok, couldn't stand the pity that would fill his eyes.

"When do you leave?" I said instead.

"Tomorrow." Srikant glanced at his watch. "Goodness, it's two already. I'd better get home and finish packing."

At the door he said, "I meant what I said, you know, about how nice you look." The lines at the corners of his eyes shone faintly, like the lines one sometimes finds deep within a block of ice. "I hope we'll still remain friends, you and I, after all this is over."

I nodded, swallowing. I wanted to say something profound and wise and reassuring to cheer him on that long, lonely flight to India, but nothing came. "Penguins are beautiful when they're in the water," I finally told him.

He laughed, and I thought he'd take my hand again,

perhaps kiss it, and what I'd do if he did. But he didn't. "I'll call you when I get back from India," he said.

That night in bed, under the protective cover of the dark, I asked, "Ashok, are you faithful to me?"

As soon as the words were out, I was embarrassed by how old-fashioned they sounded. I was afraid that Ashok would make fun of me. I was even more frightened that he'd give me a serious answer.

But he merely sounded annoyed. "What kind of a stupid question is that? I should never have told you about Meena—it's got you obsessed."

"Ashok," I persisted, "do you love me?" I held my breath and waited in the tense silence.

"It's a bit late to ask that, don't you think?" Ashok said at last with a sigh. Now his voice sounded old. Tired. We were all running out of time.

"Let's sleep, Abha. I have a meeting early tomorrow."

Sitting in my car across the street from Meena's house, I watched the leaves of the maple tree on her lawn change from green to gray to purple-black as the sun went down. I sighed, trying to stretch my legs, but there wasn't enough space for it. I'd been waiting for over an hour now—it was long past the time when Meena usually came home—and it struck me suddenly that perhaps, now that Srikant was in India, she wouldn't come home at all.

A f f a i r

Ten more minutes, I said to myself. Ten minutes and I'll leave. But I knew I wouldn't. I'd wait all night if I had to.

Then I saw her in the rearview mirror. She drove slowly, as though deep in thought, and after she'd pulled into her driveway and switched off the engine, she sat in her car for a while. She hadn't noticed me yet.

When she finally stepped out, I saw that her black skirt ended well above her knees. *Much too short to wear to work,* a disapproving voice inside me said. But another part of me noted how her legs, long and graceful and bare-looking in sheer panty hose, gleamed in the light from the street lamp.

I caught up with her at the door. The sharp click of her heels had camouflaged my footsteps, so that when I said hello she turned with a little scream. The papers she had been carrying fell, scattering all over the steps.

"Abha! What are you doing here?"

I almost laughed. They were just about the same words I'd used when Srikant showed up at my door. In all our different lives, perhaps, there were only a few situations that repeated themselves over and over, and only a few responses we had for them. I wondered how many women were lying sleepless like me through the night-dark, eyes burning from tears that wouldn't come, because their husbands were having affairs with their best friends.

"Abha?"

I watched Meena as she gathered the fallen sheets together into an untidy pile. I didn't apologize, and I didn't offer to help. When she was done I said, "Srikant came over to talk to me yesterday."

A tremor passed over her face. Was it guilt or relief? "Come inside," she said.

We sat across the dining table from each other, our glasses of juice untouched. My words, words I'd finally wrenched out of myself, hung in the silence. *How could you have done this to me, Meena?* At first I wasn't sure if I meant the affair itself, or the fact that it was with Ashok, or that she had kept it from me. Then I knew. I could have forgiven her the first one, and even the second, if only she hadn't done the third.

"How could you not tell me?" I said again.

In spite of her makeup Meena's lips looked ashy. Parched. "I was afraid to. I knew you'd be upset. You disapprove of my clothes, even. How could I tell you I'd fallen in love with another man?"

Love. The word was like a blow from a hammer of ice. It gave me a sensation of vertigo, of falling from a great, airless height. Somehow I hadn't thought of an affair quite like that.

"You've always been so *good*," Meena continued in a rush. "A good wife, a good homemaker. Perfect at all the things I didn't want to do but knew I should. Like a mother, kind of. I wanted your approval. Needed it. For a long time I told myself, I've got to stay with Srikant. What will Abha say otherwise?"

I stared at her. It was hard to take in what she was saying. Meena, beautiful Meena, whom I'd envied and admired and adored, wanting *my* approval.

"But I just couldn't keep on. Our marriage—there was nothing left in it—if there had *ever* been anything. I felt I was

266

slowly drying up inside, my blood turning to dust." She looked into my face doubtfully. "I don't think you can really understand."

But I did. It came to me that the marriage she was describing was my own. If I slit open my wrists right now, I would find only salt powder.

"And this man—he made me feel so special. He understood all the things I wanted out of life—he wanted the same things. With him I didn't feel greedy or guilty or ashamed."

I remembered the way the hard handsomeness of Ashok's face would soften when he looked at Meena. Had I too repressed him, made him feel all those negative things?

"I couldn't face trying to explain it to you—the expression I knew you'd have in your eyes. Do you know when you get really upset your eyes get opaque, like chips of slate? If I told you I needed to do this to be happy, you'd say happiness isn't as important as doing the right thing. If I told you that every night I looked at my bottle of sleeping pills and wanted to take them all, you'd say, stop being so melodramatic, Meena. So *Californian.* Pull yourself together."

No, I wanted to cry. But she was right. I would have said all those things.

"That's why I told Ashok. I wanted him to break the news to you."

"I wish you'd told me yourself," I said tiredly. "It would have hurt a lot less than having Ashok tell me that the two of you were having an affair."

Meena looked bewildered. "*Ashok* said that?"

"Not in so many words, but . . ."

"Abha, the man I was talking about works in my office. He's American. His name is Charles. We're going to get married as soon as my divorce comes through."

I waited for the relief to hit me, but it never came. I wasn't even surprised, not really. It was as if a part of me had always known.

"How could you think I'd get involved with *your* husband?" Meena was saying now, her injured eyes the color of crushed velvet. "How could you think that of me?"

As I reached out to clasp her hand, it struck me that it had been something else all this time, not Ashok, not even Meena, that I'd been so unhappy about.

"Abha! Where the hell have you been?"

I took my time answering. I liked the way Ashok's voice sounded, the sharp edge of worry in it. I hadn't heard that in a while.

"I was at Meena's. Don't tell me you waited up just for me!"

"As a matter of fact, I did."

"Well! Aren't you the one who's always saying I shouldn't get worked up when you come home late from meetings?"

"You could have phoned, at least. You know how late it is? Half past eleven."

"Poor Ashok." I was enjoying this. "Is it way past your bedtime? Why don't you go on and sleep—I have a few things to finish up."

I started up the stairs. Behind me Ashok asked, his tone

Affair

petulant, "What on earth did you have to talk about for so long, anyway?"

"Why don't you ask Meena the next time you see her," I said sweetly.

But by the time I got to the spare bedroom, my feeling of righteous triumph had evaporated. I couldn't just blame things on Ashok. It wasn't that simple.

I took out my notepad and looked at the questions that I had written—such a long time ago, it seemed. The answers to them had all changed, and so had I. It astonished me how little I'd known then, how shackled my thinking had been. Not that I'd got rid of all those chains—that would probably take the rest of my life. But I was starting.

When Meena showed me a photo of Charles, I'd been surprised all over again. I'd expected someone handsome, dashing. Maybe even a little bit like Ashok. But he was just an ordinary middle-aged man, with kind eyes and a bald spot, no better-looking than Srikant.

"I know," Meena had said, flushing a little. "He isn't much to look at." She'd wiped a dust fleck off the photo tenderly, carefully, with the edge of her handkerchief and stared at it for a moment. When she spoke again, her voice was almost shy. "But he understands me, all of me, even the bad parts. With him I can be myself, like I never could before this."

Had I ever really been myself? I didn't think so. All my energy had been taken up in being a good daughter. A good friend. And of course a good wife.

I wrote down the fourth question, the one I'd been afraid to face until now. *What are you going to do about your own life, Abha?* And suddenly I knew that that was what Srikant had meant yesterday. That was what he'd really come to ask.

Just before I left her house Meena had said, "Sometimes I still feel so guilty. I think of what my parents will say, and Srikant's mother, when they find out. *Selfish,* they'll call me. *Immoral. A bad woman.* I have to keep telling myself I'm not that. It's not wrong to want to be happy, is it? To want more out of life than fulfilling duties you took on before you knew what they truly meant?"

The face of my own mother—disappointed, sorrowful, shamed—filled my vision for a moment.

"No," I said, speaking as much to myself as to Meena. I took the edge of my *dupatta* and gently wiped the mascara streaks from her wet cheeks. "It's not wrong. This way you both get another chance."

As I drove back from Meena's, the letter I would write was already taking form in my head. The shapes of the words I'd use were foreign, their taste at once sad and exhilarating.

The old rules aren't always right. Not here, not even in India.

The headlights of the car had carved looming monster-shapes out of the familiar trees and buildings and road signs.

I feel your resentment growing around me, thick and red and suffocating. Like mine is suffocating you.

I'll take one of the dusty suitcases from under the bed. Half the money from the savings account. My wedding jewelry. My car. That would keep me for a few months. There

Affair

were cheap motels in the little towns on the peninsula, Redwood City, San Mateo. Rooming houses. And even in the city, in the not-so-good areas. Some of them run by Indians. I'd seen them on a news show a while back. Maybe someone would let me stay for a lower rate if I did some work. Filing, accounts, even cleaning rooms.

We're spiraling toward hate. And hopelessness. That's not what I want for the rest of my life. Or yours.

I'll go to that Mughal restaurant. Offer to cook for free for a few days. Surely when the owner saw how good I was he'd give me the job.

Sitting on the guest bed now in a house that had never, for all its comforts, been my home, I closed my eyes and tried to see my new life—not as I wanted but as it really would be. Struggling to maneuver enormous skillets and saucepans and tandoor ovens in a vast, dark kitchen with the smell of old grease heavying the air, amid the heat and the sweat and the curse words of the rushing waiters. Living in a one-room apartment above some garage where on my off-days I heated soup over a burner. Scrubbing the buckling linoleum in a motel toilet off of Highway 101.

It's better this way, each of us freeing the other before it's too late . . .

Yes, I believe it—I have to believe it. In spite of my beautiful, calm kitchen which I must leave behind. In spite of the pity in the eyes of the Indian women when they hear. The gossip in India. My parents' anger. Family dishonor. In spite of Ashok, the empty ache when I remember—as I know I will —the feel of his body next to me in bed, his hair smelling of mint leaves and dried rain.

. . . so we can start learning, once more, to live.

And Srikant—no, I won't think about him now. There'll be time enough for that later on, when I've begun to pull the unraveled edges of my existence into a new design, one I cannot guess at yet.

I tore a sheet out of the notebook.

Dear Ashok, I began.

MEETING
MRINAL

I WAS TAKING A MR. P'S PEPPERONI PIZZA OUT OF THE freezer when I heard the front door slam. A moment later Dean, as my teenage son Dinesh prefers to be addressed, sauntered into the kitchen.

"Hi, Mom!" he said, running his hands through his hair which, since his latest visit to the barber, stands up like the bristles of a scrubbing brush.

The last of the sun glinted on his stud earring, making me blink. He was wearing his favorite T-shirt, black, with MEGADETH slashed across it in bloodred letters. I tried not to sigh. At least he wasn't wearing his other favorite, in purple and neon pink, bearing the legend *Suicidal Tendencies*.

"Gourmet pizza again, I see." Now the sun glinted on his teeth as well.

I didn't know exactly how to read that smile—so many things were different about Dinesh in the last eleven months, since his father left. "Is that OK with you?" I asked, feeling a little guilty. "Shall I fix you something else?"

"Nah, don't bother, pizza's fine with me." He shrugged, beginning to turn away.

"Dinesh . . ." I started, then broke off. I wanted to run my hand along the roughness of his cheek, to ask him, like I used to, to tell me all about his day. But the old words and gestures seemed somehow inadequate.

He gave me a quick, inquiring look over his shoulder. But when I said nothing more, he loped off down the corridor to the master bedroom where he now slept, calling, *See you in a bit.* In a few minutes, through the closed door, the cacophonous pounding of hard rock filled the house.

Dinesh had moved into the master bedroom a few days after the divorce papers were served. In a way, I'd been happy that he wanted to. I'd hoped it meant that he was beginning to accept the situation. The room had been lying empty, and it gave him a place to set up his musical equipment. At times I wonder, though, what he does in there when he's not playing his CDs or practicing his electric guitar, when I don't hear the rise and fall of his voice on the phone, the short, self-conscious laugh that means (I think) that a girl is at the other end. The nights when sleep eludes me, I sometimes stand in the passage and watch the thin strip of light that shows from under the door he always locks religiously behind him. I picture him lying awake on the big queen bed that used to belong to his father and me, and I want so badly to knock that my arm aches all the way from my fingertips to my shoulder.

I put the pizza in the oven and began rummaging for salad material in the refrigerator, where several plastic-wrapped vegetables displayed various stages of fungal growth. After a search, I managed to come up with a quarter of a tired-looking lettuce, some radishes shriveled to half their size, a passable cucumber, and a couple of tomatoes that slid around only a little inside their skins.

That wasn't bad at all. Since Mahesh left, I hardly cook anymore, specially Indian food. I've decided that too much of my life has already been wasted mincing and simmering and grinding spices. I'm taking classes instead at the local college, not something fluffy like Quiltmaking or Fulfillment Through Transpersonal Communication but Library Science, which will (I hope) eventually get me a full-time job at the Sunnyvale Public Library where I now work afternoons.

The last two quarters I've been taking a fitness class as well. I'd like to believe this has nothing to do with Mahesh leaving. I enjoy the class. At first I'd been out of breath all the time, my body a mass of clumsy, aching muscles. But now I can do them all, the high kicks, the jumping jacks, the more elaborate routines. At night in bed I run my fingers with bitter satisfaction over the trim new lines of calf and thigh, my flat, hard stomach. A pleasant tiredness tingles in my palms, the soles of my feet. It helps me sleep, most nights. If sometimes I miss those hours in the kitchen, the late afternoon light lying golden and heavy over the aroma of garlic and fried mustard seed, I would never admit it to anyone.

I wonder if Dinesh, too, misses the curries and *dals* flavored with cumin and cilantro and green chilies, the *puris* and *parathas* rolled out and fried, puffing up golden brown. Nowadays he mostly eats at Burger King, where he has taken a job. Perhaps he just has more important things to miss. I don't know. We don't talk that much since his father moved to San Francisco, to his new life in an apartment overlooking the Bay, where he lives with Jessica, his red-haired ex-secretary.

Recently when I think of Dinesh I have a sinking feeling inside me. I tell myself that I shouldn't be too concerned about his clothing or hairstyle, or even the long hours when he shuts himself up in his room and listens to music that sounds furious. That they're just signs of teenage growing pains made worse by his father's absence. But sometimes I call his name and he looks up from whatever he's doing—not with the irritated *what, Mom,* that I'm used to, but with a polite, closed stranger's face. That's when I'm struck by fear. I realize that Dinesh is drifting from me, swept along on the current of *his* new life which is limpid on the surface but with a dark undertow that I, standing helplessly on some left-behind shore, can only guess at. That's when I fix salads, lots of salads, as though the cucumbers and celery and alfalfa could protect him from failing grades, drugs, street gangs, AIDS. As though the translucent rings of onions and the long curls of carrots could forge a chain that would hold him to me, close, safe forever.

When the phone rang, I didn't bother to stop slicing. I knew Dinesh would pick it up. All the calls are for him anyway. But then I heard him open his door and yell, above the din of the stereo, "It's for you, Mom."

"Ask who it is," I shouted back without interest. I've cut myself off from most of the friends of our married days. At first I tried attending a few affairs, dinners and *pujas* and graduation parties for children going on to Stanford or Harvard. But I'd be the only woman in the room without a husband, and the other wives, even those too well bred to whisper, would look at me with pity, as though at something maimed, an animal with a limb chopped off. Behind the pity would be a flicker of gratitude that it hadn't happened to *them*, or a gleam of suspicion because now I was unattached and therefore dangerous.

It's probably another real estate agent, I said to myself as I started chopping the rusty edges off the lettuce, asking if we wanted to sell the house. They must subscribe to some kind of a divorce gazette, the way they'd descended on me in droves even before the legal settlements were complete, all of them speaking in exactly the same pinched-polite voice that makes me tense up even now. Those first couple of months, after the third or fourth call of the day, I'd be in tears. Remembering, I brought the knife down hard on the lettuce and watched with satisfaction as brown pieces flew out.

Eventually, of course, I will have to let the house go. The alimony payments from Mahesh are fair, and there's my part-time job, but the money's still not enough and every month I have to dip into my savings. "Why don't you move to an apartment, Asha," my supervisor keeps telling me. "It'd be a lot cheaper and you wouldn't have to fight the memories." She's right. But Dinesh has lived in this house all his life. I feel that if I can hold on to it until he graduates, a year longer (eleven more payments, to be exact), I will have made up to him partly for my failure to hold on to his father. But perhaps once again I am mistaken in thinking that this matters to him.

"It's someone called Marina-something. You going to pick it up or what?" Dinesh sounded irritated. He dislikes

277

anyone disturbing him when he's listening to his music. "Says she's calling from England."

I didn't know a Marina. I didn't know anyone, in fact, who lived in England. But I hurried to the phone guiltily, the way I always do when I know it's long distance.

"Asha!" The woman at the other end sounded tantalizingly familiar. She spoke with the clipped British accent of affluent Indians educated at convent schools run by foreign nuns. "It's Mrinalini!" She paused, confident of being recognized. *Who . . . ?* Then it struck me. How could I have not known, even for a moment, even though I hadn't heard her voice in years? Because it was Mrinalini Ghose, who had been my classmate and best friend and confidante and competitor all through my growing-up years.

"Mrinal!" I whispered into the phone, and a mix of happiness and sorrow swept over me, making me dizzy. "How are you? What are you doing in England?" I spoke in Bengali, stumbling a little over the intimate *tui* I hadn't used for so long. Were scenes flashing through her head, the way they were through mine? Our secret visits to the Maidan fair where we'd gorge ourselves on the fried onion *pakoras* that I could smell even now. All those nights I'd slept over at her house, in the big mahogany four-poster bed with the curved lion paws, both of us whispering and giggling for hours after the *ayah* turned the lights off. (About what? I couldn't remember. It seemed unbelievable that once I'd stayed up half the night just to talk.) Every year before our final exams, we'd meet at her house—which was larger and quieter than mine—to study. We'd recite the names of the major rulers of the Mughal dynasty to each other, or list the metaphors in Ham-

278

let's *To be or not to be* speech, while the cook brought up yet another pot of ginger tea which she had brewed specially for us because it was supposed to clear the brain. "I can't read another line," I'd tell her when I left. "I'm going to get a good night's sleep." But once home, I'd force myself to stay awake and study some more because I wanted so much to beat her. Most times, though, she ended up with the higher rank. Maybe she was just smarter. Or maybe she too stayed up and studied after I left.

She had been sent by her computer firm in Bombay, Mrinal said, to attend a technology transfer conference in London. She was coming to another one in San Francisco next week. That's why she was calling.

"We've got to get together, Asha! I haven't seen you in *ages*. I'm dying to meet Mahesh, too—the time I saw him at your wedding was so brief, it doesn't really count. And your son—so handsome, just like his father. Of course, I've seen so many photos over the years I feel I know them already. . . ."

I closed my eyes and leaned my forehead against the cold white of the wall. The traditional Indian words of hospitality crowded my mouth. *It'll be so wonderful to see you after all these years. You must stay with us, of course.* I knew they were what Mrinal expected. But I couldn't say them.

The day my marriage had been arranged, halfway through my second year of college, I'd called Mrinal. I remembered it perfectly, a dim monsoon afternoon with gray-bellied clouds grazing the tops of the tall office buildings in the distance, and a salty, sulphur smell in the air, like lightning. Excited, I'd stumbled over the words as I told her how handsome my husband-to-be was, what a good job he had, how I would be moving to California to live with film stars. Under the excitement had been a secret triumph that *I'd* been the one to be chosen first, that I, who everyone said wasn't as pretty, was going to be married before Mrinal.

Mrinal had listened in silence for a while. Then in a quiet voice she asked, "Is this what you really want, Asha? It's a big decision. You don't even know him—you've only met him once."

"What's all this westernized nonsense about *only meeting him once?*" I snapped. Part of my anger came from disappointment. I had wanted so much to impress her with my news. "This is how it's always been done, especially in traditional families like ours." My voice sounded prim and pinched and terribly old-fashioned. I knew Mrinal was thinking of all our rebellious conversations about love and romance and choosing our life partners. But they'd only been foolish adolescent fancies, with no connection to our real lives. "Your mother got married this way, and so did mine. And they're perfectly happy."

"Yes, but our mothers didn't even complete high school. Times have changed, and so have we." Mrinal spoke in a maddeningly equable voice. "I wouldn't be in such a hurry if I were you."

"Oh, really?" my growing temper made me sarcastic. "And what would madam do?"

"I'd wait awhile, finish college, get a job maybe. Don't you remember how we always used to talk about the importance of women being financially independent?"

"No, I don't," I lied.

"Ashoo!" Mrinal said reproachfully. Then she added, "And you write so well, too. Professor Sharma always says how you have the makings of a novelist."

"And besides," I said, choosing to ignore her last comment, "who says I can't be financially independent after marriage?"

"All I'm saying is, I'd learn a bit more about the world and what I wanted out of it before I tied myself down. . . ." The pleading note in her voice frightened me. I didn't want to hear any more.

"Well, I'm not you, thank God," I'd shouted and slammed down the phone.

We'd made up of course, and Mrinal had helped with all the wedding preparations—buying saris, making invitation lists, choosing luggage for the journey. On the morning of the wedding, she'd done my hair over and over while I wailed that each style made me look uglier. When it was time for me to leave with my new husband, we'd clung to each other, promising to be friends forever. But throughout—even as, exchanging the fragrant red-and-white wedding garlands, Mahesh's hand had brushed my throat, sending a shiver through me—I was wondering whether I'd been too hasty, whether I'd made the wrong decision. Whether Mrinal had won again after all.

Now, with the phone pressing its coldness against my ear, I heard Mrinal's voice, tiny, metallic, a little disappointed, asking if I was still there, if I was all right.

"Of course I am," I said, forcing a laugh and switching to English, which seemed a more appropriate language for lying. "I was just checking the calendar. It's really hectic for us all next week. Mahesh's going to be out of town till Friday. They're sending him to Philadelphia to straighten out some R and D projects. Dinesh is busy Mondays and Wednesdays with his karate, Tuesday he has Toastmasters," (I was improvising wildly by now) "he's the youngest member, you know, Thursday . . ."

Out of the corner of my eye I saw a movement in the kitchen. It was Dinesh, checking on the pizza. He glared at me. My voice faltered, but I couldn't stop now. "I can't quite read what he's written here—maybe volunteer work at El Camino Hospital. I'm pretty tied up, too. . . . What a pity, if only you'd let me know earlier. . . ."

"Ashoo, don't tell me you're too busy to see me!" said Mrinal, calling me by my special name that only she used. I could hear the hurt in her voice. "I found out about the U.S. conference just before I left India. I was so busy running around trying to get a visa that I didn't have a chance to call. But I've been thinking about you all the way to London."

Something twisted inside me then, like it was breaking, and I knew I'd have to meet her. The knowledge filled me with excitement and dread. "I'll cancel something," I said. "Where are you staying?"

"What's all this shit about me and karate?" Dinesh burst out even before I'd replaced the receiver. "And Toastmasters— *Toastmasters*, give me a break!" I could see an artery pulsing in his temple. He's inherited that from Mahesh. "I'm not good enough for your friend just the way I am, is that it? And why'd you have to lie to her about *him*"—he wouldn't use his father's name—"being out of town on business." He imitated my Indian accent, thickening it in exaggeration. "Why couldn't you just tell her the fucking truth—that he got tired of you and left you for another woman."

That's when I slapped him. It shocked us both, the action, the way it happened, involuntarily almost, while a part of me was still trying to fathom the depths of hurt and rage from which his words had erupted. I'd rarely hit Dinesh when he was growing up, he'd always been such an obedient boy. What frightened me now was that I'd *wanted* to hurt him, that I'd put all the strength in me behind that swing of the arm. We stood there facing each other, my palm ringing with the impact, a splotch of red spreading over his cheek. I wanted to throw my arms around him and cry for what I'd just done, but all I could say, even though I knew it was totally wrong, was "never use that word in front of me again."

Dinesh's hands curled into fists like he wanted to hit me back, and I wondered wildly what I would do if he did, but all he said in a cold voice that went through me like a knife was "you make me sick."

"You make me sick, too," I heard myself yell as he slammed the bedroom door. "Just remember, I'm not the only one your father left when he moved out. I didn't hear him asking *you* along, Mr. Smart-ass!"

And then I was so ashamed that I *did* feel sick. I went into the bathroom and tried to throw up, but nothing happened and I felt worse. I sat on the toilet seat for a while, trying to figure out how my life, which had seemed perfect a year ago, had turned into such a mess. When I came out, the smell reminded me of the pizza in the oven, by now a charred black mass. I threw it into the garbage and went to bed.

Dinesh was avoiding me. He left the house early each day— even on the weekend—and came back late, when he was sure I'd be asleep. In the mornings I'd go to the kitchen and find the dinners I fixed for him the night before still sitting on the stove top, untouched. When I lifted the lid, the congealed food would give out the faintly sweet odor of rot.

One Friday night, determined to talk to him, I waited up. I wasn't sure what I was going to say—something to explain my long and complicated relationship with Mrinal, maybe something to assure him I loved him just as he was. It had been a humid afternoon, the still, sticky air hard to breathe. I hurried home from work and then spent the rest of the day in the kitchen making *kachuris*, which have always been Dinesh's favorite dish. For hours I stuffed the dough with the spicy crushed peas, rolling out the perfect circles, sliding them into the hot oil, and lifting them out when they were just the right golden color. Once in a while I would brush a floury hand across my sweating forehead, wondering if I was going about it all wrong.

In the evening, unexpectedly, it rained. I opened all the windows and the cool smell of wet earth filtered into the house. I felt a sudden happiness—though surely I had no reason for it—a sudden hope that things might turn out all right. I lay down on the sofa in the dark to wait for Dinesh, and when I fell asleep I had a dream. In the dream his face

came to me. Not as it is now, with his earring and his muti-
lated hair and the anger wrenching at the sides of his mouth,
but his baby face with its silky unlined glow. The way he slept
on his side, his plaid blanket clutched in his fist, his pursed
mouth making little sucking movements. The way his eyes
would dart under his thin lids when he was dreaming. It was
such a clear image that I could smell the milk-smell of him,
and the side of my neck tingled where he always rubbed his
face after I had nursed him.

The slamming of the door woke me. Then I heard his
footsteps receding down the darkened passage toward his
room.

"Dinesh," I called.

He didn't reply, but the footsteps stopped.

I hurried to the passage, groping for the light switch.
"Dinesh, I made some *kachuris*. I thought we could have
dinner together." Where *was* that switch?

"I ate out. . . ." Already his shadowy silhouette was
turning away.

"Dinoo," I called desperately, using his baby name
though I knew it was the wrong thing to do. "Dinoo, I'm sorry
for what happened." You shouldn't have to apologize, a voice
inside my head scolded. You're the parent. And besides, he
started it. I ignored the voice. "I want . . ."

"Spare me!" Dinesh said, holding up his hand, just as I
finally found the switch. In the sudden flood of harsh yellow
light, his expression was so forbiddingly adult, so like his father's, that it hit me harder than any physical blow. I stood in
silence and watched my son walk away from me until the
bedroom door shut behind him with a final, decisive click.

Rummaging through my closet, I tried to figure out what to wear. In two hours I was supposed to meet Mrinal for dinner on the top floor of the Hyatt in San Francisco, ("my treat," she had insisted, fortunately) and nothing I owned seemed right. In the afternoon sun that slatted through the blinds, the silk saris seemed either garish or old-fashioned. The *kurtas* looked drab. I didn't have any fancy western clothes because Mahesh had never liked how they looked on me. I wished I could ask Dinesh for advice, but since the night of the *kachuris* we hadn't spoken to each other.

It had been a summer day just like this one when Mahesh told me he was leaving. I'd been sifting through clothes, trying to decide what to wear to the Kapoors' twenty-fifth anniversary celebration that night, while he sat on the bed, looking out the window.

"Which do you like better?" I'd asked, holding up a cream-and-orange sari and a blue *kurta* with silver flowers. Mahesh liked to choose my outfits when we went out. He knew exactly what made me look my best.

But on this day he kept staring at the lawn as though he hadn't heard me. He'd been this way a lot lately, preoccupied. Worrying about work, I thought. But when I'd ask him if everything was OK at the office, he always said yes.

I asked him again which outfit he wanted me to wear.

"I don't care," he replied in a voice that didn't sound like his. "I can't take this anymore, Asha."

All his life, he told me then, he'd been doing what other people wanted, being a dutiful son, then a responsible husband and father. Now he'd finally found someone who made him feel alive, happy. He wanted the chance to really *live* his life before it was too late.

I remembered how calm I'd felt as I listened to him. Calm and mildly curious. Because of course this wasn't really happening to me. Besides, I had a host of pictures inside my head to prove him wrong—Mahesh smiling into my eyes on our honeymoon in Kashmir, the night water shimmering beyond our houseboat on Dal Lake; Mahesh and I looking down at the tiny scrunched-up face of our new baby, then catching each other's eye and breaking into the tremulous laughter of disbelief; all of us crowded into our bed Saturday morning, watching Bugs Bunny. And just the other day we had gone to buy a brand-new red Mazda Miata, father and son assuring me that a two-seater was not impractical, Dinesh excited, laughing, asking, *Can I drive this as soon as I get my license?*

"Haven't you been happy with us, ever?" I'd asked, my voice even.

"I thought I had," Mahesh had said. "I hadn't known what real happiness was then."

Now, as I noted how the dust motes hung in the sunlit air exactly like on that day, how the jasmines outside smelled the same, I feared that Mrinal would be wearing the latest fashions. Even when we'd been dependent on the meager pocket money our parents doled out, she'd had a flair for colors and styles. She'd go down to Maidan market and buy remnants from the wholesalers that sat outside with their bales of tie-dye cottons and silks, and then she'd create the most clever designs around the scraps she'd bought. And now that she was a top-level executive, she took good care of herself, as I could tell from the photos she sent me infrequently but regularly along with hastily scribbled notes that said she was thinking of me. The photos were of vacations in choice spots such as the Ooty hills or the beach at Kanyakumari where the three oceans meet. They hinted at glamour and allurement. In the latest one, sent a year ago, Mrinal was wearing a midnight-blue silk *kameez* with a daring scooped neck and golden *chappals* on her feet. She was leaning lightly against a good-looking man. The marble domes of the Taj Mahal shimmered in the background.

Sometimes, privately, I wondered how Mrinal felt about not being married. Surely she experienced some regret at family gatherings when sisters and cousins paraded their offspring and boasted about their husbands? But when I reexamined the photos where she posed against a fresco in the Ajanta caves or waved elegantly from the deck of a cruise ship with her direct, open smile, my doubts faded. *She has the perfect existence—money, freedom, admiration,* I would say to myself enviously, suddenly wanting it for myself, *and she doesn't have to worry about pleasing anyone.* Underneath my envy, though, I was happy for her. Whenever my own life depressed me with its clutter and its ordinariness, I took a strange solace in thinking of Mrinal's, which seemed to me to be fashioned with the same clean, confident strokes with which she had once designed her clothes.

I'd been hard put to match Mrinal's photos, but I'd done my best with pictures of the Yosemite falls and the Golden Gate Bridge. I, too, accompanied my photos with hastily scribbled notes, though I could easily have found the time to write a letter. But somehow that would have been like admitting that my life, less busy than hers, was also less successful. After I received the Taj Mahal picture, I'd asked a friend to come over and take a picture of the three of us in our new Mazda. I still had a copy of that photo, Mahesh and myself sitting in front with the top down while Dinesh leaned against a car door, elegant as any model. I remember looking at the photo and thinking how much I loved father and son. How they seemed as much a part of me as my own body, so that I couldn't imagine a life, ever, without either of them. *Wish you could come see us,* I had written gaily, unthinkingly, across the back of the copy I'd had enlarged for Mrinal before I slipped it into the envelope.

I'd fought the divorce every way I knew—reasoned, pleaded, tried the silent treatment, cooked Mahesh's favorite meals. I'd even bought myself a gauzy black negligee from Victoria's Secret. I'd taken a long time in the bathroom that night, brushing my hair till it shone down my back, rubbing lavender oil on my wrists and throat, trying different lipsticks. When I stepped out, Mahesh had looked up from the journal he'd been reading in bed. He'd taken off his glasses and rubbed tiredly at the corners of his eyes.

"Don't do this to yourself, Asha," he had said. The sadness in his voice had been worse than anger, or even contempt.

That was the night he had moved out.

Now, as I dressed myself slowly in a raw-silk *salwaar-kameez* that I hoped looked smart without being gaudy, I tried to figure out what I was going to tell Mrinal tonight. But all I could think about were the dark circles under my eyes that my makeup didn't quite hide, the telltale streaks of recent gray in my hair.

"This way, please."

The maître d', a tall man in an intimidating black-and-white tuxedo, wove his way smoothly through the crowded restaurant. My legs trembled a little as I followed him. I was still tense from the drive. I wasn't used to negotiating city traffic, and the ten-year-old Chevy that I drove (Mahesh had taken the Miata when he left) hadn't helped matters. The plush burgundy carpet into which my feet sank, the tinkle of silverware and sophisticated laughter, the flash of a bracelet or a discreet tie pin, the gleam of a bare shoulder, of a wineglass held up to the light—all increased my discomfort. My experience with restaurants was limited to infrequent visits, when Dinesh was little, to Chuck E. Cheese, where we shouted out our orders to the sweaty, aproned pizza chef over the excited shrieks of children and the clang of pinball machines. Or, as he grew older, to the neighborhood Shanghai Eat-Here-or-Take-Out, where the sticky odor of chili-sesame oil hovered over orange Formica tables. As I awkwardly followed the maître d' I knew I didn't belong here, and that every person in the room, without needing to look at me, knew it too.

Then I saw her. She was sitting at a window table, facing away from me. I stopped, in spite of the maître d's questioning look. I wanted a moment to compose myself, to observe her before she knew I was there. Perhaps I was hoping to learn, from her unguarded posture, something that would give

me an advantage in our coming meeting. Outside, the Bay
Bridge strung itself over the water, a glimmering necklace of
light. The evening was so clear that one could see all the way
across to where the bell tower of Berkeley pierced the dark
like an illuminated needle. But Mrinal wasn't looking at the
view. Instead she stared down at her hands. I tried to read the
slope of her shoulders, the curve of her cheek. I wanted—I
admit it—to discover a secret sorrow, perhaps a weariness
with life. But all I could see was the easy grace with which she
held her body, like always.

She must have sensed my presence, because she turned.
When she saw me, a smile of such pleasure crossed her face
that I felt ashamed of having spied on her.

"Ashoo dear, how lovely you look!" She rose and hugged
me tight to her. "You're a lot slimmer than in the photo you
sent me last year!" I could smell her perfume, something
musky and expensive. Behind her shoulder the sparkling skyline of the city changed slowly as the restaurant revolved.
Mrinal's face sparkled too. She had on a glittery foundation
and just the right amount of mascara, and she looked a lot
younger than her age, which, like mine, was thirty-eight. She
was wearing a maroon off-the-shoulder tunic with narrow
churidar pants, a chic blend of East and West. It was perfect
for her.

"I can't *tell* you how much I've looked forward to this!"
Mrinal laughed out loud. It was a glad, full-throated sound,
uncaring of being overheard, just the way I remembered it.
"How many years has it been? Almost twenty? There's so
much you can't write, that you have to share face-to-
face. . . ." She held my hands in hers and, looking down, I

saw the polished ovals of nails the exact maroon of her outfit. A diamond glittered on her ring finger.

"You look lovely, too," I said, making an effort to smile back. There was a heaviness in my chest. I couldn't tell if it was dejection or envy. "Yes! There's tons of news to catch up on! But first, tell me about that divine ring! Could it be an engagement? Is there a lucky man waiting somewhere?" My voice sounded coy and false even to my ears.

"No," said Mrinal. A shadow seemed to flit across her face, but perhaps I was only seeing what I wanted to see. "Do you like it? I bought it in London this time. A sort of be-good-to-myself gift."

I was impressed, more than if a man *had* given her the ring. Mrinal and I had both been brought up by mothers who believed that women should be happy with whatever their men decided they ought to have. A woman who grasped things for herself, we had heard over and over, was greedy. Selfish. The most expensive thing I'd bought for myself in my entire life had been a bottle of Chantilly perfume, $19.99, at Ross's Dress for Less. It had taken me twenty minutes of feeling guilty in front of the fragrance counter before I paid for it, and then I'd justified it by reminding myself that Mahesh's company's Christmas party, which I was expected to attend, was coming up. I wanted to tell Mrinal that it was great that she had been able to overcome our childhood conditioning, but the waitress was asking us what we would like to drink.

"How about two vodka martinis, shaken not stirred?" Mrinal smiled. "Remember?"

I nodded. We'd been avid James Bond fans all through high school, fascinated by his violent, magical world—so different from ours—of golden guns and intricate machines and bikini-clad beauties. If we ever escaped our conservative, teetotaler parents, we had vowed, if we ever made it to the promised land, England maybe, or America, we would celebrate by drinking Bond's special drink.

"Do you know, I never did try one all these years," I said. "Mahesh"—it was not impossible to say his name, after all—"only likes wines."

The waitress was putting our drinks on the table. She wore a short black skirt and a sequined halter top. Her red hair fell in flipped layers to her shoulders. I tried not to think of Jessica.

"Oh yes," Mrinal was saying as she raised her drink to her lips. "Mahesh. Tell me all about the mysterious and romantic Mahesh!" She drank deftly, tilting the glass as though the gesture was an old, accustomed one. "I can't tell you how sorry I am at not meeting him. And your charming son, too."

The floor tilted and spun. Maybe it was the martini, bitter and burning on my tongue, making me cough. Another disappointment. I took a deep breath and opened my mouth. The words poured out, all the right ones. It wasn't difficult at all.

"You're so lucky," Mrinal said when I finished talking. She was pleating and unpleating the edge of her napkin, and this time there really was a shadow in her gaze. It spilled into the hollows underneath her eyes. "You don't know *how* lucky you are, Ashoo, to have such a loving, considerate husband, such a good, responsible son."

"But you're lucky, too," I said, a little surprised at her vehemence. "You're doing so well in your career, traveling whenever you want, moving up in the company, never having to worry about money. You're so much prettier than me, there must be *dozens* of men dying to marry you. Sometimes I wish I could change places . . ." I stopped, unwilling to divulge my fantasies.

Mrinal sat silent for a moment, looking down at her ring, twisting the diamond around to catch the light. Then she said, "You're right. There's a lot in my life that I'm proud of. The freedom. The power. Walking into a room full of men knowing none of them can push me around. Seeing the reluctant admiration in their eyes when I close a tough deal." She spoke slowly, consideringly. "It's what I always wanted. I'd never give it up to dwindle into a wife, like that woman—what was her name—said in that play we studied in Lit class."

Dwindle. I tried not to flinch at the word. I remembered the woman who said that, Miramante in Congreve's *Way of the World*. We had studied her speech together after class, Mrinal and I, sitting in the back of the college library, underlining our favorite lines and repeating them to each other. Her words had seemed so spirited and clever in that musty hall hung with dim oil paintings of old dead men, founders and principals, who stared down disapprovingly at our excited, laughing faces.

"The truth is not as simple as we thought then," I said, sighing.

Meeting Mrinal

"I know." Mrinal sighed too. "Some mornings when I wake up I don't want to open my eyes. I know exactly how everything will be—the color-coordinated bedspread and carpet and curtains and cushions. . . ."

"Mrinal, please," I interrupted urgently. Somehow it was very important that she not say any more.

But she went on, inexorable. ". . . the four-foot-high TV, the stereo speakers in the corners, the hanging plants placed just right, the bright light falling on it all . . ."

She ground her knuckles into her eyes and when she brought them away her mascara was smudged. I stared at her. It was the first time I'd seen Mrinal cry.

"I was going to pretend everything was fine," she said. "I wanted you to admire me, envy me. That old competition thing. But when I heard you talking about your husband and your son"—her voice faltered on the word—"when I saw the love shining in your face, I couldn't keep it up."

The tears made black streaks down her cheeks. She wept like she laughed, unashamedly, without reserve. I wanted to go around to her side of the table and hold her. I wanted to weep like that too, to confess. But it was as though I were trapped deep inside something, a tunnel perhaps, or a well, with all that dark, cold water pressing down on me. So I sat there, silent, while Mrinal wiped her eyes and apologized for creating a scene, saying she didn't know what got into her. And then it was too late.

"I'm happy for you, Ashoo, I really am," she said when we kissed each other goodbye. "Take good care of those two wonderful guys that God has given you."

When I pull into the garage late in the night, I use the remote to shut the garage door behind me as I always do, but I don't switch the engine off right away. I sit with the window open in the old brown Chevy, picking at the cracked vinyl of the dashboard, listening to the familiar, comforting thrum. The events of the evening replay themselves in my head, over and over. In the back of my mind a small, seductive thought swims in and out of focus: how easy it would be to just sit here until the fumes fill my lungs. I close my eyes and see the gray, gauze-like smoke drifting gently into the cavities inside me, taking over.

I'm not sure how long I've been sitting in the garage. There's a sweet, heavy smell in the car now. It laps at me, rises past my hips and breasts and mouth to my eyes. And I'm crying—all those tears I didn't shed when Mahesh left, and when Dinesh turned away from me down that harshly lit night corridor. I'm crying for Mrinal in her spacious bed in her luxury apartment, lying alone for the rest of her life, and for myself, who will probably do the same. But most of all I'm crying because I feel like a child who picks up a fairy doll she's always admired from afar and discovers that all its magic glitter is really painted clay. Somehow believing in Mrinal's happiness, thinking that unregretful lives like hers were possible, had made it easier to bear my individual sorrows. What would I live on, now that I knew perfection was only a mirage?

The smell is heavier now. I can feel it in my pores. It begins to layer itself over my skin, thick and glistening as oil.

It's getting harder to think. I need to wait only a little longer for it to cover me completely.

But I know that's not the answer. Not that I'm sure of what the answer is, of even if there is one. I just know I must turn off the engine before I'm no longer able to. I reach for the key, but I can't see it. I grope in the dark, viscous swirl that has opened up around the steering wheel, and for a panicked moment I think I'll never find it. But then it presses its metallic coolness into my palm, precise and reassuringly solid in a world of amorphous shapes. I twist it sharply and stumble from the car toward the switch that will open the garage door. In the new silence my coughs are a sharp, tearing sound, loud enough, I think, to wake the neighbors. When the garage door rumbles open, I am almost surprised to find no one waiting outside, robed and belligerent, armed with questions.

"Mom."

The voice from behind startles me. I swing around to face it and am struck by a sudden dizziness. The floor beneath my feet is rippling treacherously, preparing to dissolve.

"Do you feel OK?" Dinesh's hands grip my upper arms. His fingers are strong and confident with youth. "Mom, are you *drunk?*"

I can't focus too well on his face, but I hear the shock in his voice and beneath it a surprisingly prim note of disapproval. It makes him sound almost . . . *motherly*. I want to laugh. But then he sniffs, and his face changes, its features wavering as though seen through water. "What's with all the fumes in the garage? Mom, what were you *doing?*"

His voice shakes a little on the last word. I notice with

297

surprise that he's wearing a blue pajama outfit that I bought him sometime back. Along with his tousled hair, it makes him look unexpectedly young. Afraid of what I might say.

I want to respond with something positive and significant, perhaps something about how I love him too much to abandon him no matter how enticing suicide might seem. I want to hold him tight like I used to when he was little and there had been a thunderstorm. But all I can manage is to whisper, "I think I'm going to throw up."

"Whoa, wait till I get you to the bathroom," Dinesh says. He wedges a shoulder into my armpit and half drags, half carries me to the sink—so dexterously that I wonder if he's done it before, and for whom. He holds my head while I bend over the sink, retching, and when I'm done, he wipes my face carefully with a wet towel. Even after he finishes, I keep my eyes tightly shut.

"Be back in a minute," he says. He shuts the bathroom door—an act of kindness, I think—behind him.

In the mirror my face is blotched, my eyes swollen. I stare into them, feeling like a complete failure. I've lost my husband and betrayed my friend, and now to top it all I've vomited all over the sink in my son's presence. I think of how hard I always tried to be the perfect wife and mother, like the heroines of mythology I grew up on—patient, faithful Sita, selfless Kunti. For the first time it strikes me that perhaps Mahesh had a similar image in his head. Perhaps he fled from us because he wanted a last chance to be the virile Arjun, the mighty Bhim. And for a moment I feel a sadness for him, because he's going to realize it too, soon enough—perhaps one morning when he wakes up in bed next to Jessica, or as he throws her a sidelong glance while maneuvering the Mazda into a parking spot—that the perfect life is only an illusion.

Dinesh is back, with a red plastic tumbler which he fills with water. "Drink this," he says in a tone I myself might have used when he was a sick child. I raise the tumbler obediently to my mouth. The water is warm and tastes of toothpaste. Even without looking at him, I can feel him watching me, waiting for some kind of explanation. I can feel, too, the fear still rising from him, can almost see it, like the waves of heat that shimmer off summer pavements at noon. But I can't think of a single thing to say. So I stand there under the loud, accusing whirr of the bathroom fan, staring at the worry line gouging Dinesh's brow (he's got that from me), running my finger along the edge of the empty plastic tumbler.

Slowly an image takes shape somewhere behind the stinging in my eyes. It is so disconnected from what's going on that I think I'm hallucinating from all the carbon monoxide. It's a fired clay bowl, of all things, simple and unadorned, its glaze the muted brown of fallen leaves. For a moment I'm confused, then I recall that I saw a slide of it in my spring Art Appreciation class. I've forgotten the time period and the potter's name, though I know he was someone old and famous. I turn the bowl around and around in my mind till I come upon what I'm looking for, a small snag on the paper-thin lip, and I hear again the teacher's nasal New York accent telling us that this was the master potter's signature, a flaw he left in all his later works, believing that it made them more human and therefore more precious.

"Mom!" Dinesh's voice breaks through my thoughts. There's an anxious edge to his voice. I realize he's been asking me something for a while.

"Sorry," I say.

"I said, how did your evening go?"

I pause for a moment, tempted. Then I say, grimacing, "I made a mess of things." I'm surprised by the lightness the admission brings. In the rush of it, I daringly add, "I'll tell you about it if you want. I could make us some hot *pista* milk. . . ." I reach out to draw him to me, a little afraid that he will pull away, will say, *Nah, Mom, I got stuff to do.* But he lowers his head so that his bristly hair tickles my cheek and gives me a quick, awkward hug.

"Sounds OK to me." He is smiling now, just a little. "Hey, Mom, you haven't made *pista* milk in a long time."

Later I stand over the stove, stirring the blended pistachios into the simmering milk, watching with wonder as it thickens beautifully. I know there will be other fights, other hurtful words we'll fling at each other, perhaps even tonight. Other times when I sit in the car, listening to the engine's seductive purr. Still, I take from the living-room cabinet two of the Rosenthal crystal glasses Mahesh gave me for our tenth anniversary, and when the creamy milk cools, pour it into them.

Tomorrow I'll start a letter to Mrinal.

The glasses glitter like hope. We raise them to each other solemnly, my son and I, and drink to our precious, imperfect lives.

 300

GLOSSARY

The words below are from different Indian languages (mostly Bengali and Hindi). Some words, such as "bearer-boy" are Indianized British expressions from colonial times.

adivasi	member of indigenous tribe (the word itself means original people)
almirah	large closet
alu	potato
amchur	powdery mix made from ground mangoes, black salt, and other spices
amreekan	American
apsara	celestial nymph (from Indian mythology)
arre bhai	hey brother, a customary expression among men
ata	custard apple
ayah	nanny
babu	master, gentleman; common appellation for Bengali men
baisakhi	violent April thunderstorm
banja	barren

Glossary

bearer-boy	young servant employed for running errands
bhadralok	people of good family
bhai	brother, a term often used between male friends
bhaiya	brother, a more informal term
bharta	spicy dish made from roasted eggplant
bhaviji	sister-in-law; *ji* at the end of a word indicates respect
bindi	dot worn on forehead by many Indian women; a red one usually signifies that the woman is married
biriyani	fried rice dish seasoned with onions, raisins, and spices; can be prepared with vegetables, meat, or chicken
boudi	older brother's wife
bride-viewing	the process, involving a meeting of the potential bride and groom in the bride's home, by which marriages are arranged
brinjal	eggplant
bustee	slums
chachaji	uncle (father's brother)
chai	tea
champa	sweet-smelling gold-colored flower
chand-ke-tukde	epithet of admiration, literally, piece of moon
chapatis	Indian wheat bread similar to tortillas
chappals	sandals
charak	a fair held at a particular time of year

Glossary

choli	close-fitting blouse worn with sari
chula	wood- or coal-burning stove
churidar	narrow pants worn by women (and sometimes men) under a long tunic (*kurta*)
dacoit	bandit
dain	mythical witch who devours human flesh
dal	lentil soup
darwan	gatekeeper
desh	country, a term often used by expatriate Indians in referring to India
dhakai	fine handloomed sari made in Bangladesh
dhania	coriander
dhoti	piece of cloth tied around the waist and reaching to ground; worn by men
didi	older sister
dupatta	long scarf worn with tunic (*kameez* or *kurta*)
filmi	pertaining to films
firingi	foreigner, westerner
genji	man's undershirt
ghazal	poetic song (from the Muslim tradition)
ghu-ghu	brown bird, similar to dove
girgiti	lizard
gulabjamun	dessert of fried dough balls soaked in syrup

Glossary

hasnahana	sweet-smelling flower
hing	asafetida
jadu	magic
jhi-jhi	cricket-like insect that makes a buzzing noise
kachuri	stuffed balls of dough, spicy, rolled out and deep-fried
kadam	tree with fragrant ball-like blossoms that flower during the monsoons
kajal	black paste used as eyeliner
kala admi	dark-skinned man
kalia	spicy curry dish (usually fish) particular to Bengal
kameez	close-fitting tunic worn over pants by women
karela	bitter melon
kaun hai	who's there
kheer	dessert made of thickened milk
khush-khush	fragrant grass out of which thick window-coverings are made. These are sprayed with water in summer to keep out the heat
kokil	black songbird
kul	sour fruit used for making pickles
kulfi	ice cream
kumkum	red paste or powder used for a dot on a woman's forehead
kurta	long loose tunic worn over pants by both men and women

Glossary

lauki	large green squash
lichu	litchi
mali	gardener
maharajah	king
malmal	soft cotton fabric
mandi	bazaar
mashi	aunt (mother's sister)
memsaab	lady of the house, a respectful term used mostly by servants
michil	procession
momphali	peanuts
neem	tree with bitter medicinal leaves
nimbu-pani	lemonade
paan	betel leaf
pakora	spicy snack made of vegetables dipped in batter and deep-fried
palloo	the end of the sari that falls over the shoulder, sometimes spelled *pallav*
panipuri	popular roadside snack made of crisp deep-fried puffs filled with potatoes and a spicy sauce
papad	crisp lentil wafers
paratha	Indian wheat bread rolled out and panfried
patisapta	complicated dessert of stuffed lentil crepes in syrup
peepul	large tree with heart-shaped leaves
phul gobi	cauliflower
pista	pistachios

Glossary

pista kulfi	pistachio ice cream
prasad	food offered as part of a prayer ceremony
puja	prayer ceremony
pulao	Indian fried rice, generally vegetarian
puri	Indian wheat bread, rolled out and deep-fried
qurma	highly spiced dish made with vegetables or meat
raga	Indian melody
rajah	king
rasogollah	dessert made of curdled milk balls cooked in sugar syrup
rogan josh	spicy lamb curry
sahibi	westernized
salwaar-kameez	set of long tunic and loose pants worn by Indian women
samosa	a snack made from wheat dough, rolled out, stuffed, and deep-fried
sandesh	dessert made from sugar and curdled milk
sari	long piece of fabric worn by Indian women
shapla	water plant
shiuli	small white flower that gows in Bengal in the winter
shona	term of endearment used for children, literally, gold
singara	same as *samosa*

Glossary

sitar	Indian stringed musical instrument similar to guitar
surma	eyeliner
tabla	classical Indian drums
tulsi	basil plant, considered sacred in India
veranda	balcony
wallah	a suffix denoting possession or belonging; e.g., union-*wallahs:* men belonging to a union
yaksha	mythical demon, male, guardian of household or treasure
yakshini	female of *yaksha*
zamindar	landowner
zari	gold thread